FALLING HARD

A COLORADO HIGH COUNTRY NOVEL

USA *Today* BESTSELLING AUTHOR

PAMELA CLARE

FALLING HARD

A Colorado High Country Novel

Published by Pamela Clare, 2017

Cover Design by © Carrie Divine/Seductive Designs
Image: MRBIG_PHOTOGRAPHY/iStock

Copyright © 2017 by Pamela Clare

ISBN-10: 0-9987491-0-9

ISBN-13: 978-0-9987491-0-5

Dedication

This book is dedicated to our nation's Gold Star families.

Consider donating to http://www.goldstarwives.org to show your support for those who've sacrificed their dearest blood in service to our country.

Acknowledgements

Many thanks to Michelle White, Jackie Turner, Shell Ryan, Pat Egan Fordyce, and Benjamin Alexander for their support while I wrote this book and for helping me to proofread.

Thanks to Benjamin Collins for answering some physics questions. You've answered my questions on so many subjects. You're kind of a big deal that way.

Special thanks to Jessica Scott—author, PhD, US Army captain, and general badass—for answering questions related to the U.S. Army and for helping me in so many ways since the nightmare that was 2014. I am deeply grateful.

Many thanks to the members of the Scarlet Springs Readers Group on Facebook, whose enthusiasm for this series inspires me.

Chapter One

January 5

Ellie Meeks hurried across the grocery store parking lot, walking as fast as she could with a toddler in each arm and a fever of one hundred two. She kept her head bowed, an icy wind driving snowflakes into her face and making her shiver. The last thing she'd needed was to get sick and miss work again.

Damned streptococcus microbes.

She didn't have to be an RN to know that's what it was. Daisy had come down with strep three days ago, and now she and Daniel both had fevers and sore throats. She'd had to leave her shift at the hospital early and hadn't even made it to her car before her mother had called to say Daniel was running a fever, too.

The store's automatic doors opened for her, a blast of warm air hitting her in the face. She carried the kids to a double-seated shopping cart, set them in their seats one at a time, and buckled their safety belts.

She swallowed—*ow!*—and tried to put on a cheerful smile. "Who wants macaroni and cheese for supper?"

Neither Daniel nor Daisy showed any sign they'd heard her, tears on Daniel's flushed cheeks, Daisy sucking her thumb. That was all right. Ellie didn't have the energy for anything else, so Kraft Dinner it was.

She moved through the aisles, trying to remember everything on the list she'd left at home. Eggs. Milk. Orange juice. Butter. Oatmeal. Bananas. Hot dogs. Two boxes of macaroni and cheese. Laundry detergent. Fabric softener. TP. A few cans of chicken noodle soup and peach slices just to be safe. More children's Tylenol. A new menstrual cup because she'd lost the other down the toilet in an act of sheer brilliance.

Every woman needs strep and her period at the same time.

She turned toward the pharmacy window to pick up the prescriptions for amoxicillin that her father had called in for them—and almost ran into Mrs. Beech, her old high school English teacher. "Oh! I'm sorry, Mrs. Beech. Excuse me."

She would have walked on, but Mrs. Beech came to a full stop in front of her cart, her gaze fixed on the twins. "Are these your little ones?"

No, they're just some random kids I grabbed in the parking lot.

Ellie bit back that grumpy response. That was her fever talking. "Yes. They've been sick with strep throat, so you might not want to get too close."

"How old are they?"

"They'll be three in April."

"Aw." Mrs. Beech beamed at Daniel. "You look just like your daddy. He was a student of mine a long time ago. God rest his soul."

A shard of pain lanced through Ellie's chest. Not that Mrs. Beech had said anything Ellie hadn't said herself. Daniel had his father's dark hair, his blue eyes, his nose, even his smile. Still, it hurt to hear Mrs. Beech talk about Dan in the past tense.

"You must thank God every day that these two little ones came into your life. It's a way of reminding you of Dan, keeping a piece of him with you."

Ellie didn't need anything to *remind* her of Dan. He'd been her husband, for God's sake, the love of her life. She had to grit her teeth. "Yes."

Daniel rested his head on his sister's shoulder, whimpered.

Ellie couldn't blame him. If his throat hurt as much as hers did …

She touched her hand to Daniel's forehead. "He's burning up with fever. I need to get them home."

"I hope he feels better soon."

"Thanks." Ellie pushed the cart down the aisle, fuming.

God, she *hated* it when people said that—as if giving birth to twins six months after her husband's death somehow made losing him easier to bear. Yes, she was grateful for her children and loved them with her heart and soul.

But two new lives couldn't erase the pain of another that was lost. Why was that so hard for people to understand?

She reached the pharmacy window and found herself blinking back tears.

"Hey, Ellie." Herb Bosworth, who'd been the town's pharmacist for the past forty years, met her at the window, carrying two small white paper bags. "You look awful. I'm sorry you and Daniel caught this, too. It's going around."

"Thanks." She took the prescriptions and set them in the cart.

"Feel better soon."

"Thanks. I'm sure we will."

Daniel started crying in the checkout lane, and nothing Ellie could say or do comforted him. Daisy, who adored her brother and was an empathetic little girl, started to cry, too. Ellie was tempted to join them. She debated opening the acetaminophen and giving Daniel a dose right here in the store but decided against it. Daniel didn't like taking medicine, and fighting with him in public would only upset him more.

"He's sick," Ellie explained to the woman in line ahead of her who turned and frowned at the kids.

The woman—a stranger—looked away without a word.

Five minutes later, Ellie pushed the cart out the front door and back into the snow, wind biting into her skin, fat flakes blowing almost horizontally. She pushed the cart through a couple of inches of accumulation to the car and got the kids buckled into their car seats. "We're going to be home soon, and I'll give you some medicine to make you feel better. Okay, Daniel, sweetie?"

She wrapped his favorite blanket—a blue baby blanket—around him, then put the groceries in the trunk. She would have to scrape off the windshield, but she wanted to start the car first and get the heater going. She opened the driver's side door, got into the front seat, turned the key in the ignition and…

Nothing.

She tried again, but the engine didn't make a sound. "Damn it!"

She closed her eyes, fought an impulse to cry.

You can't cry. You're the adult, remember?

She had jumper cables in the back. If she popped the hood and took out her cables, someone would see and offer to give her a jump. This was Scarlet Springs, after all. People helped each other here.

She pulled on the hood release, opened the door, and stepped out into the cold, fighting a wave of dizziness that had her leaning against the vehicle. Slowly, she made her way to the trunk and retrieved her jumper cables.

"Need a hand, ma'am?"

She turned and found herself looking at a dark parka, the man who wore it towering over her. She looked up, recognized him. He was one of the volunteers with the Rocky Mountain Search & Rescue Team. Someone had told her that he'd served as an Army Ranger. She'd seen him around town a few times. She hadn't been able to help but notice him—especially that time she'd seen him standing shirtless on the pier at the reservoir.

Pecs. An *eight*-pack. Obliques.

Hey, she could still tell a hot guy when she saw one.

"Thank you so much. My car won't start. I've got my twins in the backseat. One of them is sick."

He took the jumper cables from her. "Get back in the car where it's warmer. I'll give you a jump."

Relief and gratitude washed through her. "Thank you."

She sat in the driver's seat and shut the door, looking over her shoulder at the kids, both of whom were quiet now. "We'll be home soon. This nice man is going to help us get our car started."

She watched as he strode through the snow to a dark SUV and climbed inside. He drove toward her and parked his vehicle nose-to-nose with hers. Then he climbed out again, raised her hood, and got to work connecting the cables.

When they were in place, he walked over and bent down next to her window, snowflakes on long eyelashes. "Try starting it now."

He had a touch of a southern accent, though she couldn't place it.

"Okay." She turned the key.

Nothing.

How could that be?

The man fiddled with the jumper cables, then motioned for her to try again.

Still, the car wouldn't start.

Ellie closed her eyes, fighting despair. She didn't need an expensive car repair on top of everything else right now.

When she opened her eyes again, he was standing beside her window. "It's not your battery, ma'am. If it weren't dark, I'd poke around and try to figure out what's wrong, but I can't see much, especially not with snow falling like this. Why don't I drive you and your kids home? You can worry about the car later."

She shook her head, reaching into her handbag for her cell phone. "I'll call my dad. He can be here in twenty minutes."

"I'll have you home in ten. You can take a photo of my license plate number and send it to your father if that makes you feel safer."

"Oh, no. It's not that." She wasn't afraid of him. He was on the Team, after all. He'd probably been through a dozen background checks. "My little boy and I are sick with strep throat, and I don't want to get you sick, too."

"All the more reason to get you home, ma'am." He grinned, his teeth white in the darkness. "Besides, I have a monster immune system. I don't get sick."

Jesse Moretti stowed away the jumper cables and transferred the woman's groceries from her trunk to the cargo hold of his Jeep, while she got both kids buckled into their car seats in the back. He climbed into the driver's seat and turned up the heater, looking at the children in his rearview mirror.

He hadn't had little kids in his vehicle since, well … ever.

The little boy whimpered. His sister sucked her thumb.

"We'll get you home. Okay?" His gaze settled for a moment on the children's mother. Beneath the fatigue and fever, she had a pretty face, with high cheekbones, a little upturned nose, and a full mouth. There was snow in her dark blond hair, which was pulled back in a ponytail. It was too dark to see the color of her eyes. "I'm Jesse Moretti."

"Thanks for the help, Jesse." She gave a forced smile, clearly feeling like shit. "I'm Ellie Meeks. That's Daniel and Daisy in the back."

Daniel and Daisy.

Cute.

He shifted his vehicle into drive, pulled out of the parking lot, and turned left onto the highway, rush hour and snow bringing traffic to a crawl through the center of town.

"I live on Snow Creek Road just beyond mile marker—"

"I know where you live."

That didn't sound creepy at all, dumbass.

Did he want her to think he was some kind of stalker?

He tried again. "We're neighbors. We share a property line. I've seen you playing out back with your kids."

The first time he'd seen her, he'd been standing on his back deck with his real estate agent just before buying the property. She'd been sitting on a blanket, playing with two babies too little to sit up or crawl. His realtor had told him her husband had been killed fighting in Iraq.

That was a story Jesse knew only too well.

Since then, he'd done what he could to support her, shoveling her walk early in the morning on his way to work, moving her trash bin onto the curb when she'd forgotten trash day, and keeping an eye on the house, especially during the summer when tourist season made the crime rate spike.

"You bought the old cabin?" Her face lit up with a genuine smile this time. "And you never came down to introduce yourself?"

"I guess I never got time."

Bullshit. He had avoided it.

He'd spent ten years of his life in sustained combat operations with Alpha Company, 3rd Battalion, 75th Ranger Regiment in Iraq and Afghanistan, and had seen his share of death and slaughter. He had his own emotional shit to deal with. He couldn't take on anyone else's.

"You're with the Team, aren't you?"

"Yeah. I'm a primary member." He didn't want to brag, but he'd worked his ass off to make the cut, spending every free moment learning to climb, honing his skills on tough technical routes, even getting certified as an EMT.

"What's it like?"

He got that question a lot but never had a real answer. How could he explain what being on the Team meant to him? "It's busy."

"I bet—especially in the summer."

"Yeah." But this past summer hadn't been busy—not for him.

After a rescue he'd led had gone terribly wrong, Megs, director of the Team and a real hardass, had benched him, refusing to let him go out on operations until Esri, the trauma therapist who gave free counseling sessions to Team members, evaluated him. At first, he'd refused. The last thing he'd wanted was someone digging around in his head. Besides, Megs had been overreacting.

Sure, he'd been shaken up. Who wouldn't have been? He'd watched a little girl drown and hadn't been able to do a damned thing for her. But benching him hadn't made things better. Far from it.

Megs didn't understand how important working with the Team was for Jesse, how it held his world together. He'd had no choice in the end but to do what she'd demanded and meet with the therapist. It hadn't been as bad as he'd feared. In fact, Jesse kind of liked Esri, though he'd stopped going to sessions once Megs let him go active again.

"The Team is all volunteer, right?"

"Yeah. No one who works for the Team gets paid, but being able to wear the yellow Team T-shirt feels like a badge of honor for most of us." Jesse was almost as proud of it as he was of his Ranger tab.

"If it takes up so much time, how do you make a living?"

"I work for Scarlet Mountain Resort—ski patrol in the winter, trails crew in the summer. I handle explosives for avalanche control. My boss likes having a Team member on staff, says it makes him feel safer. He lets me take time off for rescues."

Scarlet Springs was one of the few towns in the world that owned its own ski area—Scarlet Mountain Resort. With some first-class terrain and slopes that were only an hour-and-a-half drive from Denver, it was a favorite of locals. Let the tourists battle their way up I-70 to the big resorts. Skiers from Colorado's Front Range came to Scarlet.

"Do you like your job?"

"It pays the bills, and I like staying active, working outdoors." The more exhausted his body was, the less likely he was to think too much. "My dad wanted me to come back to Louisiana and work at a refinery. But I knew from the moment I set eyes on these mountains that I was here to stay."

Why had he told her that?

"Is that where you're from—Louisiana?"

"Born and raised." Jesse stopped at the crosswalk as a big, shaggy figure stepped into the street, head down, walking into the wind.

It was Bear. Big like his namesake but with the mind of a child, he made his home somewhere in the mountains west of town, living off the land and the kindness of those who bought him meals or gave him change in exchange for a blessing or Bible verse. No one seemed to know where he'd come from or how he'd ended up the way he was. For decades, the residents of Scarlet had accepted and watched over him.

"I wonder how far he has to go to get home," Ellie said. "It's so cold."

"Bear knows more about surviving in the mountains than the rest of us combined." In the two and a half years that Jesse had lived in Scarlet, he'd never known Bear to ask for anything more than spare change or a warm meal.

Jesse accelerated, felt the Jeep's rear tires slip just a little, and shifted into four-wheel drive. The snow was coming down hard now, fat flakes clinging to his windshield wipers. "How about you? Where are you from?"

"I grew up here. I moved to Kentucky to be with my husband. He grew up in Scarlet, too, but was stationed at Fort Campbell. I moved back after … He was killed while serving in Iraq. I was four months pregnant."

Jesse tried to ignore the way her words pierced that dark place inside him. "I'm sorry. It must be hard to raise twins by yourself."

"Especially on nights like tonight." She turned her face away from him, looked out the window. "My parents have been a big help. My mom watches the twins when I work. My dad is a pediatrician, so I get free doctor's visits and house calls. People in Scarlet set up a scholarship fund for the kids for college. My neighbors have been great, too. They shovel my walk, move my trash can, help with yard work. I don't even have to ask. They just do it."

He suppressed a smile. "That's good. When someone lays down his life for his country, people ought to do more for his family than just offer condolences."

He glanced over at her, found her looking at him.

"Yes—and thanks."

They made the rest of the short drive without talking, Daniel's whimpers and the squeak of the wiper blades breaking the silence.

Jesse pulled into her driveway and parked. "You take care of the kids. I'll get the groceries."

"Okay. Thanks."

He climbed out into the wind and made his way to the back of his vehicle, icy flakes biting his cheeks. He retrieved her groceries and started toward the house, only to find her sitting, half in and half out of the vehicle, clinging to the door.

"I'm just … dizzy."

It was time to get tactical.

Arms full of groceries, he walked over to her. "Do you have your house keys? I'll carry the groceries in, then come back for you and the kids. You shouldn't be carrying them if you're dizzy."

She fumbled in her pocket, pulled out the keys and handed them to him.

Jesse trudged through the snow to the front door, stomped the snow off his boots, then unlocked the door and stepped inside, flicking a light switch. He carried the groceries to the kitchen, then strode back outside to his vehicle.

She was right where he'd left her.

"Can you make it inside on your own?" He didn't want to leave such small children alone in his vehicle or the house.

She nodded. "I think so."

He steadied her while she got to her feet, then watched as she walked inside. When she was safely through the door, he opened the passenger side door to discover that the twins had unbuckled themselves. "Hey, Daniel and Daisy. I'm Jesse. I'm going to carry you inside."

Jesus, Moretti. That's the best you can do?

Really, it was.

He reached for them, half expecting them to back away from him in horror. Instead, they came easily into his arms, Daniel with his blanket, Daisy with her thumb in her mouth, their trust strangely touching. He lifted them out of the Jeep, kicked the door shut, and carried them inside to where their mother stood, still in her parka, waiting, her pretty face white as a sheet.

He set the children down at her feet. Daisy toddled off in tiny snow boots, while Daniel leaned against his mother's leg, blue blanket clutched in a little fist.

"You should sit down and…" His gaze met Ellie's, and his brain went blank for a moment, his breath catching.

Green.

Her eyes were green.

She shook her head. "I need to put this stuff away and make dinner."

Trying to act like the earth hadn't just shifted beneath his feet, Jesse stepped back and looked around him. Her home was warm and cozy, toys scattered across a braided area rug in front of the sofa, wood stacked next to a fireplace with a wood stove insert. On the mantel sat a display case holding a folded American flag—the flag from her husband's funeral—along with several service medals and ...

Adrenaline hit his bloodstream.

A USASOAC patch.

Son of a bitch.

Her husband had been a pilot with the 160th SOAR—the Special Operations Aviation Regiment.

Well, shit.

"I'll go get the car seats." He walked back outside, fighting an impulse to run, torn between getting the *hell* out of here and wanting to do more to help her.

What the hell is wrong with you?

He clamped down on his emotions and retrieved the car seats from his vehicle. Back inside, he found her on her knees, wrestling the kids out of snow boots, mittens, hats, and coats.

He set the car seats down on the polished wood floor. "I'd be happy to look at the car tomorrow when I get off work. I'm good with engines."

She got unsteadily to her feet. "That's kind of you, but I'll just have it towed to the garage."

He reached into his jeans pocket, pulled out his wallet, and took out a business card. "Here's my phone number. I'm only a minute away if you need anything."

She accepted the card, a blond eyebrow arching, a smile tugging at her lips. "*Boat* repairs? Do you get much business in Scarlet?"

He understood her amusement. Colorado was a landlocked and arid state with few bodies of water big enough to accommodate boating. "I grew up on the Gulf Coast and love the water. I've got a speedboat that I take out on the reservoir every summer. I'll have to take you all out sometime."

What had he just said?

She smiled. "Thanks again, Jesse."

He gave her a nod. "You're welcome, ma'am."

"I just hope we don't repay you by getting you sick. Be sure to wash your hands."

"Don't worry about me. Like I said, I don't get sick."

"These are pediatric germs—kid germs, the worst."

"Get some rest and feel better soon." He stepped out into the wind and walked through falling flakes back to the car, grateful for the cold.

Jesus.

Ellie was a SOAR widow.

Now that he thought about it, Jesse was pretty sure he'd known her husband.

Chapter Two

Ellie woke to the sound of Daniel crying and glanced at her clock. It was just before five in the morning—past time for their next dose of acetaminophen. Struggling against dizziness, she got out of bed and pulled on her bathrobe. "I'll be right there, sweetie. Hang on."

She walked to the kitchen, where she swallowed two Tylenol and poured apple juice into a sippy cup for Daniel. When that was ready, she measured out a dose of acetaminophen into a medicine spoon and carried it, together with the juice, to his room. She found him sitting up in bed, his beloved blankie clutched to his cheek. She sat down beside him and pressed her wrist to his forehead.

He was hot—at least a hundred and two, she guessed.

She really ought to take his temperature, but the thermometer was back in the kitchen, and she was too damned tired. "I know you feel icky, sweetheart. It's time for more medicine."

He opened his little mouth and took the medicine without a fight, then buried his head against her chest.

"I brought you some apple juice." She wanted to keep him hydrated and knew from experience that apple juice was her best bet at getting him to drink. "Can you take a few sips for me? I know it hurts to swallow, but your body needs lots of good juice to fight the bad germs."

He took a swallow, then another, then turned his head away.

"Good job." She set the juice on his bedside table, wrapped him in his blanket, and held him, stroking his back, her cheek resting against his dark, downy hair. "I'm so sorry you're sick. You'll start feeling better soon. I promise."

"Soon" was a relative term. To an almost-three-year-old, Ellie supposed the word meant "right away." In reality, they'd gotten their first doses of antibiotics about ten hours ago, so they had about fourteen hours to go before the medicine kicked in.

Exhausted and certain that Daniel wouldn't want her to go, she made him an offer. "Do you want to sleep with mommy?"

He nodded.

She scooped her son up and carried him down the hallway toward her room. She had just tucked him into her bed when she noticed a scraping sound coming from outside. She peeked out her window to see a man shoveling what had to be more than two feet of snow from her sidewalk. She didn't have to see his face to know who it was.

Jesse Moretti.

She recognized his parka, his big build, and the Jeep idling at the curb.

He'd done so much to help her. She needed to make sure she thanked him properly with a card or a phone call or something.

She had turned back toward her bed when the thought struck her. Maybe *he* was the person responsible for shoveling her walk these past two years. When had he moved into the neighborhood?

No. It couldn't have been him alone. Could it?

She slipped out of her bathrobe, crawled back into bed, and wrapped an arm around Daniel, fatigue and illness quickly dragging her under.

Jesse stowed the snow shovel in the back of his Jeep then climbed into the driver's seat, glancing at Ellie's dark windows as he headed up the highway toward work. He hoped she and her little guy were feeling better.

Jesus.

What a small fucking world it was. Jesse had come to Colorado to get Iraq and Afghanistan out of his mind, and he'd ended up buying a cabin behind Crash's widow. What were the odds?

Dan Meeks. Crashhawk, or Crash for short.

Jesse was so used to thinking of Dan by his nickname that it hadn't clicked for him until he'd seen the SOAR patch and had thought for a moment about Ellie's last name. Crash had been one of the best damned

Black Hawk pilots Jesse had ever known. There'd been a good half dozen times when he and his crew had appeared from the sky like avenging angels, raining hellfire down on the enemy and getting Jesse and his element to safety.

Jesse parked in the staff parking lot of Scarlet Mountain Resort and trudged uphill through the dark in almost three feet of fresh powder to the chalet-style building that served both as Ski Patrol HQ and the First Aid Center. Plow crews were busy clearing snow from the sidewalks around the lodge and the massive guest parking lots, sunrise still a good hour and a half away.

Jesse stomped the snow from his boots and stepped through the door. "Mornin'."

"Hey, Moretti." Matt Mayes, ski patrol supervisor, sat at the dispatch desk, his avalanche rescue dog Boomer dozing near his feet. A former champion alpine skier, Matt still ripped up the slopes at age fifty-nine. "Coffee's fresh if you want some."

Jesse walked into the kitchen and poured himself a cup, calling to Matt over his shoulder. "What's the forecast?"

"At the moment, it's minus ten on top with a wind chill of minus twenty-five. They're calling for clearing skies with a high of about thirty."

That would mean busy slopes. There was nothing like blue skies after a big snowfall to drive the state's hardcore powder hounds into the mountains. It didn't matter how cold it was. Of course, the weather in the Rockies could change without warning. That's why the dispatch desk watched the forecast throughout the day.

Jesse took a sip of his coffee. It was thick and black and bitter—exactly the way he liked it. If this shit didn't wake you up, you were probably dead. "Hey, do you know anyone who rides horses?"

Matt looked confused. "You want to go riding?"

Jesse shook his head. "SnowFest is coming up in a month or so, and I want to sign up for the skijoring race."

Forget paragliding, BASE jumping, and slacklining. Skijoring was the most insane sport Jesse had seen in his time in Colorado. Skiers made their way down a snowy street in the middle of town, skiing over big ramps and collecting rings along the way—all while being towed behind a galloping horse.

Yeah. You couldn't make this shit up.

Most people would have told Jesse he was insane, but Matt just nodded. "I have a few ideas. I'll ask around."

"Thanks, man. I really appreciate it."

Other patrollers began to arrive—Travis, Ben, Christa, Kevin, Amanda, Doug, Steve. They shuffled in, poured themselves coffee, and gathered at the dispatch desk.

Matt glanced down at his clipboard, where he'd written the day's schedule in chicken scratch, assigning each patroller to one or more trails. "We got almost thirty-six inches of new snowfall. We've had the snowcats running on the greens and blues. Christa and Travis, I'd like the two of you to hit Little Bear Mountain and mark any hazards."

"Little Bear again?" Travis muttered.

Little Bear was home to most of the greens and blues—beginner and intermediate trails. Travis had a thing for the expert-only stuff, the black diamond and double-black diamond runs.

Matt ignored Travis. "Doug, you've got the blues on Bella Vista. Amanda, work with the grooming crew on the terrain park."

The freestyle terrain park was the newest addition to the resort and featured jumps, rails, and a 20-foot-long half-pipe. It was a hit with snowboarders.

"Jesse, Ben, and Kevin, head up to Eagle Ridge, throw some bombs, and check out the double-blacks and the glades. We've got dry powder on top of hardpack, so the risk of avalanche is sky high. Roger is already up on the mountain, making sure all the patrol huts are shoveled and toasty warm for you. We've got miles of terrain to open and not a lot of time. Let's get to it."

Matt had trusted Jesse with explosives from the moment he'd joined ski patrol because of his military experience. Jesse had to admit that he much preferred blowing up snow to blowing up people.

Kevin walked over to him. "Get geared up and pack the fuses and charges. Try to steal a thermos of coffee if there's any left. I'm going to get the sled."

Ben stepped out of the kitchen, his gaze met Jesse's. "What a dick. He always drives, and we always ride."

"It's called seniority." Jesse couldn't help but grin. "But, hey, we get to blow shit up and ski glades on a fresh powder day. I'm not complaining."

Skiing through glades—stands of trees—was one of the most dangerous things a skier could do and Jesse's new favorite winter pastime.

Ben acknowledged the truth of what Jesse had said with a nod and a greedy grin. "The stoke meter is on high today."

Jesse grabbed a radio and hand mic out of the charger, then went to the locker room for his gear. He traded his blue parka for his red ski patrol parka with its yellow cross, then grabbed his skis, boots, and his helmet. Five minutes later, he and Ben were skiing to the locked facility where they kept the explosives. Kevin was already there, sitting pretty on the blue Sherpa, his skis in the rack. The snowmobile had been custom-built so that it could carry a team of four patrollers, together with gear, skis, and a patient on a litter.

"Did you bring coffee?" Kevin called out.

"There wasn't any left," Ben shouted.

"Fuck!"

Jesse stepped out of his skis and propped them against the building, then swiped his ID, opened the door, and flipped on the light. It took him and Ben all of five minutes to gather what they needed—a dozen charges, and double that number of fuses and pull-tab igniters. They packed the igniters and fuses separately from the charges and piled all of it onto the back of the Sherpa. Then they stowed their poles and skis in the rack and climbed aboard the snowmobile.

Jesse called up to Kevin. "We're good to go."

The Sherpa's engine roared as they headed up the mountain.

J esse watched while Kevin studied the terrain. The man was an expert at knowing when to call a slope safe. It was one of the most important jobs at the resort. If he fucked up, people could die.

Jesse was learning to read the landscape, but it would take years before he'd have anything approaching Kevin's skill. Still, some things were obvious even to him. That big cornice hanging from the cliff at the top of the ridge would have to be blasted into oblivion. That would dump more snow onto the slope below, which would have to be bombed, too.

Yeah, they had their work cut out for them.

Kevin pointed. "Let's take down that cornice. Two charges—one high, one low."

The goal was to trigger a series of small avalanches so that the shifting layers of snow would be settled before skiers hit the slopes.

Jesse prepared the charges. Not much bigger than cans of soup, each held two pounds of pentolite—a chalky mix of trinitrotoluene, aka TNT, and pentaerythritol tetranitrate, or PETN. A single charge could easily blow the three of them to shit if mishandled.

Ben bent down to watch. "Did you work with pentolite as a Ranger?"

Jesse chuckled at the idea of Rangers throwing soup cans. "Uncle Sam had more powerful shit for us to play with." He inserted the fuses, then attached the igniters. He held out one charge for Ben, kept the other for himself. "You ready?"

Ben nodded. "Let's do this."

They got into position, then synced their movements, igniting the fuses at the same time. They had 90 seconds to throw and take cover before the charges exploded.

Kevin watched from behind. "Jesse, you throw high. Ben, go low."

"Got it. On three," Jesse said. "One, two, three."

He threw his charge, aiming for the top of the cornice. "Fire in the hole!"

They skied away, taking cover behind a large boulder, the seconds ticking by.

BAM!

A cloud of snow fell around them, bits of rock striking the boulder.

They skied out from behind their cover to find the cornice gone, its weight of snow scattered on the slope below them.

Kevin opened his mouth to say something but was cut off.

WHOOMP!

A deep rumble filled the air as the snow on the slope below them shifted.

Kevin grinned. "This slope is primed to slide."

"So … more charges then?" asked Ben.

"Yep."

Jesse got to work building more bombs.

By late afternoon, Ellie's sore throat and fever were gone. Daniel was feeling better, too, judging from the way he bounded around the house in his Superman pajamas, little cape fluttering behind him.

Thank God for antibiotics.

Certain they all needed something healthful and restoring for supper, she decided to make chicken soup from scratch using some frozen chicken stock she'd made during the holidays. Her vision of how the evening would go— the kids playing peacefully in the playroom while she cooked and listened to NPR in the kitchen—was not at all how things turned out.

She'd just begun sautéing an onion when she heard Daisy wail. She wiped her hands on a towel and hurried to the playroom to find her little girl in tears.

"Danny fwoo a bock," she sobbed, holding her right cheek.

"Let me see." Ellie kissed her. "You're going to be okay."

Then she turned to Daniel, who stood there looking like he might cry, too. "Did you throw a block at your sister?"

Daniel wasn't yet as verbal as Daisy, which left him at a distinct disadvantage when it came to these situations. "Day boke it."

"She broke something you built?"

He nodded, despair and tears filling his blue eyes, his lower lip quivering.

"That's not a reason to hit your sister. You hurt her. See?" She touched her finger to the red mark on Daisy's cheek.

This was too much for Daniel, who probably hadn't meant to hurt his sister. He began to cry, too.

Ellie resisted the urge to hug them both and stayed focused on the lesson. "Tell Daisy you're sorry."

He managed to get the words out amid his tears. "Sowwy, Day."

Ellie looked at her daughter. "You upset Daniel when you knocked over his blocks. That wasn't a nice thing to do."

Daisy's lower lip quivered. "It was too taw."

"Too tall?" Ellie had to bite back a smile. "Daniel can build whatever he wants to build. You don't get to decide what's too tall. That's not your choice to make. Now, what do you say to your brother?"

"Sowwy, Danny."

And peace was restored.

Unfortunately, she'd left the stove on, and the onion was burned, leaving her to start over.

Ten minutes later, Daniel tripped and bumped his head on the floor. Then Daisy shut her finger in the toy box. No real damage was done in either case—except to Ellie's nerves. In the end, she did what she swore she'd never do. She popped in a DVD and left Elmo to babysit the kids while she made dinner.

Life as a single mother was anything but graceful.

J esse dropped down the ridge into Snow in Summer, a dense glade that cut from Eagle Ridge toward the double-blacks below. His skis surfed through the powder, sent it billowing into his face, a cloud of cold white. Face shots and fresh powder. Did winter get any better than this?

Of course, he wasn't up here to have fun. It was closing time after a long and busy day. His job now was to sweep the double-blacks and glades to make sure no guests were left behind when the slopes closed. He'd already caught a pair of losers trying to make their way uphill outside the resort boundary for one last run. They hadn't liked him much when he'd revoked their season passes for two weeks.

"You want to break the rules? You gotta pay."

But now the slopes were empty, not a soul in sight.

Jesse let skis and snow carry him, the day's tension melting away.

A glimpse of red.

Jesse stopped, then skied off into the trees for a closer look. Someone had probably lost a glove or something.

No, not a glove. It was a boot—and the boot was attached to a leg.

Adrenaline shot through Jesse's veins. "Son of a bitch."

He bent down, moved snow away with his hands, and found a young man upside down in a tree well, dried blood on his forehead. He reached down and felt for a pulse, certain the kid was dead.

The lucky bastard was still alive.

Jesse reached for his hand mic. "Forty-two to dispatch."

Matt's voice came back to him. "Go ahead."

"Code 3, Snow in Summer. I've got an unconscious man, probably mid-twenties, upside down in a tree well. It looks like he hit the tree with his head as he fell headfirst into the well. No helmet. Suspected head injury, possible internal injuries and spinal cord trauma. We're going to need a chopper."

"Copy that. Patrollers are being dispatched via snowmobile to help prepare for chopper transport. Hang tight. Do what you can."

"Forty-two out." Jesse shucked off his pack, reached inside, and pulled out the emergency blanket. He didn't dare move the kid by himself. All he could do until other patrollers arrived was try to keep him warm and monitor his pulse. He wrapped the blanket around him as best he could and listened for the sound of the approaching snowmobile.

B y the time Ellie got the kids fed and bathed, read them bedtime stories, and got them to sleep, she was exhausted, the lingering effects of illness leaving her sapped.

She was about to retreat to the sanctity of sleep when the phone rang. It was Claire, her younger sister. A massage therapist, Claire lived in Boulder with her husband, Cedar, a computer engineer.

"Hey, sis. Mom says you're having one hell of a weekend. What's going on?"

Ellie told Claire the whole story—how Daisy had caught strep and passed it on, how the car had died in the middle of the snowstorm, how Jesse Moretti had given her a ride, how Dad had gotten the car towed to the garage and arranged for a rental. "He was out there at five this morning, shoveling my walk."

"Dad needs to watch it. At his age—"

"Not Dad. Jesse Moretti. I heard a scraping sound and looked out to find him shoveling my walk."

"Oh. Oh! I want to hear more about this guy."

Ellie knew what her sister was thinking. "It's not like that. Jesse is just my neighbor."

A tall, good-looking, thoughtful neighbor, but Claire didn't need to know that.

"Oh, well." The disappointment in her sister's voice almost made Ellie laugh. There was a moment of silence. "But is he single?"

Hope sprang eternal with Claire where Ellie's love life was concerned.

"Yes—at least I think so." He hadn't mentioned a wife, and there'd been no ring on his finger. Yes, Ellie had looked. "He's with the Team and works as a ski patroller. I heard he used to be an Army Ranger."

He had that military bearing—an intensity, that constant awareness, a hint of aggression. She had noticed that despite being sick.

"So he's brave, ripped, and super athletic, but broke. Hmm."

"Claire, he's my *neighbor.*"

"So much the better. He won't have far to go when you hook up."

"We're *not* going to hook up." Even as she said the words, Ellie's pulse skipped, an image of Jesse standing shirtless at the reservoir flashing through her mind.

The man *was* blazing hot.

"It's been almost four years, sis. Four *years.*"

Ellie tried not to get irritated with Claire. Her sister had been her rock after Dan's death, flying to Kentucky, staying with her for six weeks. She'd helped Ellie make the funeral arrangements and held her hand through the service when Ellie had been broken with grief. She'd helped Ellie put her house on the market. Once the house had sold, it was Claire who'd dealt with the movers.

"You don't think I know that? But *if* I were going to get involved with someone, it wouldn't be a man who does risky things for a living. I lost one husband. I couldn't survive losing another."

"We all lose the ones we love, and they lose us. If you stop caring about people, you'll miss out on happiness. If you could go back in time, would you avoid getting together with Dan?"

"No, of course not! What a stupid question."

"I know you miss Dan, and I know you love those kids, but you need some adult time—if you know what I mean, and I think you do."

Oh, yes, she did.

Sex.

She hadn't been with a man since the night before Dan deployed that last time in 2013. His death, her pregnancy, and the birth of the twins had made sex the farthest thing from her mind. But lately…

Still, the idea of getting naked with some random guy held no emotional appeal. Dan had been the love of her life. When she imagined having sex with another man, it only made her miss him more. She wasn't even sure she'd be able to enjoy it. Her heart just wasn't in it. Apart from sexual frustration and the love she felt for the twins, she had long since gone numb.

"Maybe you should invite Jesse over for dinner—you know, just to thank him."

Yeah … no. That wasn't going to happen.

But she did need to call him or send a thank-you card.

"On that note…" Ellie got up from the sofa and started toward her bedroom. "I need to get some sleep."

She thanked her sister for checking on her and ended the call, then brushed her teeth, tears filling her eyes when she met her own gaze in the mirror.

Almost four years. It felt like an eternity.

Oh, Dan.

Chapter Three

The next day turned out to be the strangest in Jesse's short career as a patroller. It started out normal enough. He responded to a few injury calls—two skiers with knee injuries and a snowboarder with a dislocated shoulder.

Nothing strange about that.

Then, shortly after noon, he helped evacuate a teenager who had wiped out getting off the ski lift and couldn't get back on his feet. It took Jesse all of two seconds to realize that the kid wasn't injured. He was stupid drunk.

From there, the day took a dive off the deep end.

Jesse was patrolling Aspen Glow, one of the double-black diamond trails, when a man ran out from the cover of the trees, barefoot and buck naked, flapping his arms and making weird bird-like noises.

What the fuck?

Jesse called it in, then did his best to restrain the guy, who was at risk for hypothermia and even frostbite, but the man fought like a wildcat, seemingly impervious to the cold. By the time Jesse managed to subdue the man, he was winded, his face inches from the guy's junk. It took him a moment to realize what he was hearing.

Cheers.

Jesse looked up to find people on the lift applauding, some even filming him or taking photos with their smartphones.

Shit.

He focused on his job. "Don't fight me, buddy. I'm not trying to hurt you. Let's get you warm."

Whether the man understood him, Jesse couldn't say, but the fight seemed to leave him. Jesse wrapped him in an emergency blanket and waited for what felt like an eternity for a rescue team to show up with a toboggan. A crowd gathered on the slope around him.

"Don't block the slope. The show's over, folks. Move along."

But the show *wasn't* over. When the team arrived, the man started to fight again, yapping and howling like a wounded animal. It took four men to move him to the toboggan and strap him down.

While the others gathered up the man's clothes and gear, which lay in a pile among the trees, Jesse was given the honor of skiing down with the toboggan, its passenger yipping and whooping all the way back to the lodge and the waiting ambulance.

"Psilocybin mushrooms," one of the EMTs said. "We see this shit a lot."

Jesse shook his head. "Why the hell would anyone want to take a drug that makes them stupid?"

"No clue." The EMT closed the ambulance doors. "Thanks for bringing him safely down."

"Just doing my job."

By the time Jesse finished his last sweep that evening and headed back to the locker room, he was bone tired. Most of the patrollers were already there, sitting around, unopened beers in hand, their parkas and boots still on. No one took off their gear or cracked open a beer until all the patrollers were safely down for the night.

"Hey, Jesse." Ben grinned. "I heard you got into an MMA match with a naked dude on Aspen Glow."

This made everyone laugh, except Amanda, who had apparently missed the call.

"What?" Amanda stared at him. "Seriously?"

Jesse ought to have known he'd be ribbed about this. "The guy ran at me from the trees, whooping and flapping his arms. The EMTs said he was tripping on mushrooms."

Amanda shook her head. "Just when you think you've seen everything…"

"There's a video on Facebook," Steve held up his smartphone. "Check it out."

Jesse went to sit near his locker, shaking his head at the sight of his fellow patrollers bending over a cell phone to watch him wrestle a naked guy.

"Full-frontal male nudity, and I missed it," Amanda said.

Travis laughed. "I guess that's one way to freeze your balls off."

"Whoa!" Doug glanced over at Jesse as the video came to an end. "You trying to sixty-nine him, Moretti?"

Jesse flipped him the bird.

Then Kevin stepped inside, snow on his boots, cheeks red from the cold, his appearance initiating the *pop* of a half dozen beer tabs and bringing the day to an end.

Matt got to his feet. "Thanks for your work today, people. And, hey, Jesse, the parents of the kid you found yesterday called. They wanted to thank you and to let us know that it looks like he's going to make it."

A warm rush of satisfaction cut through Jesse's fatigue. "That's good news."

Every time he helped save a life, he felt an indescribable sense of relief, as if all were right with the world—at least for a few minutes. Esri, the Team therapist, had wanted to explore this with him, but Jesse thought she was being ridiculous. Didn't everyone who did rescue work feel that way after a good call? She was making an issue out of nothing.

Travis called over to him, shouting to be heard over so many voices and the clunking and slamming of gear and locker doors. "We're heading to Knockers. Want to join us?"

Named after the legendary Tommyknockers that supposedly dwelled in the mines above town, Knockers was Scarlet Springs' answer to the brewpub craze, but with a twist. It had a climbing wall—and the best damned pizza in the state.

Jesse wasn't hungry—and he had plans. "I've got to get to a Team meeting."

He packed away his gear, clocked out, and headed to his Jeep.

He drove down the mountain and straight to The Cave—Team headquarters—where the parking lot was filled to overflowing. This wasn't just a meeting for primary members. Megs had also called in secondary Team members—those who provided support services—as well as provisional members who hoped to become primary members one day.

Jesse stepped inside and walked toward the operations room, the day's tension slipping away as he crossed the large bay that held the Team's two rescue vehicles and all of its climbing and rescue gear. As much as he enjoyed his job as a ski patroller, *this* was his home away from home.

In the ops room, Megs had already started roll call, her shoulder-length gray hair tied back in a ponytail, bright red reading glasses perched on her nose. "Nice of you to join us, Moretti. Heard you had an exciting day."

Jesse stopped and stared at her. "Not you, too."

"It's all over the Internet, man." Creed Herrera held up his smartphone, a shit-eating grin on his face. "You took down that skinny naked guy like a boss."

Laughter.

"That skinny naked guy was tripping and a lot stronger than you'd think." Jesse got himself a cup of coffee then sat between Eric Hawke, the town's fire chief and one of the Team's best climbers, and Herrera, who until this moment had been Jesse's best bud. He started to remove his parka, but felt strangely cold and so left it on.

Megs continued her way down the list, using full names despite the fact that they'd worked together for years and probably knew each other better than they knew their families. "Malachi O'Brien. Isaac Rogers. Gabe Rossiter … is excused. Jack Sullivan."

That was the thing about Megs. She was a perfectionist who never cut corners. That quality had helped her become a legend back in the days when rock climbing was a fringe sport dominated by men. Sometimes her nitpicking got on Jesse's nerves, but that attention to detail and refusal to take shortcuts had given the Team its reputation as the best search and rescue team in the nation. Jesse could respect that.

"Nicole Turner. Austin Taylor. Lexi Taylor … who is looking very pregnant."

Lexi, the Team's accountant and wife of Austin Taylor, the Team's best lead climber, ran a hand over her rounded belly, a smile on her pretty face. "Only ten weeks till my due date."

Roll call completed, Megs set her clipboard aside and pulled her glasses off her nose. "Okay. Glad to see all of you here. We've got a few pieces of business tonight, and then you can go waste time staring at your TVs or your phones or do whatever it is you do. The first item on the agenda is SnowFest."

"It's that time of year again," said Chaska Belcourt, who was as good a climber as he was a mechanical engineer. The son of a Lakota Sun Dance chief, he'd come to Colorado to study engineering and had stayed for the climbing. His sister Winona, a vet who ran a rehab clinic for wildlife, had joined him.

Megs went on. "I don't need to remind you—or maybe I do—that the Team gets about fifteen percent of its annual operating budget from SnowFest proceeds. We've been asked to volunteer again this year, and I expect each and every one of you to sign up. Hawke is the only person who gets a pass because he has to play fire chief all weekend."

All eyes turned to Hawke, who nodded. "It makes up a chunk of the fire department's budget, too."

Megs held up a printout. "We've got the usual events—ice climbing, the polar bear plunge, a snowman competition for kids, the snow sculpture contest for adults. Knockers is sponsoring a new shotski event—"

"A ... *what?*" asked Sasha Dillon.

Petite, blond and only twenty-three, Sasha was the country's top-ranked female sports climber and lived off professional sponsorships.

Talk about a dream life.

Megs explained. "A shotski is where shot glasses are fixed to the back of old skis, and four people as a team drink a shot at once, trying not to spill a drop. The winning team gets some kind of prize."

"A hangover," said Harrison Conrad, the Team's mad dog alpinist. As big as an ox, he had climbed Everest twice now and had his sights set on K2 next year.

Megs went on. "It seems you're right, Conrad. The morning after the shotski, Knockers is hosting the 'Hair of the Dog Breakfast.'"

Laughter.

"There will be bonfires at night, food vendors all day, bands playing at the main event tent, lots of drinking, and, of course, skijoring. The organizers are seeking volunteers to work each of these events. They would also like help at the first-aid tent. The official sign-up is online. It's first come, first choice. Those of you who wait will have to take what's left."

After that, Megs gave them a quick budget update then asked for someone to fill in for her on the dispatch desk for two weeks in March when she and Mitch Ahearn, her partner and also a primary Team member, were heading to Alaska for serious skiing. And then the meeting was over.

Jesse got to his feet, feeling dizzy.

"Want to head out for a brew?" Herrera slapped him on the shoulder, then frowned. "Hey, you okay? You don't look so good, man."

"Today kicked my ass. I'm heading home."

Twenty minutes later, he fell into bed, chilled to the bone.

Ellie bundled up Daniel and Daisy at six Monday morning, piled them and their car seats in her rental car, and drove them to her parents' house, where her mother met her at the door, still wearing pajamas. Ellie set the kids and the diaper bag down on the sofa. She reached into the bag and pulled out two bottles of amoxicillin. "Here are their antibiotics. Daniel still fights me about it sometimes."

Her mother took the medicine. "You won't give Grandma a hard time, will you, Daniel?"

Daniel didn't answer, but curled up on the sofa with his blanket, still sleepy.

Ellie gave her mother a hug and a kiss on the cheek. "Thanks, Mom."

It would be so much harder to leave the kids if she'd had to put them into daycare. It wasn't about saving money. It was about knowing that the children were in the safest, most loving hands while she was at work.

Her mom smiled. "Have a good day. Daisy, come help your old granny make coffee. Can you say 'caffeine'?"

Ellie hurried back to her car and drove to Mountain Memorial, Scarlet's little hospital, which sat a few blocks from the center of town. She was on call every other Monday, and today she'd been called in. Apart from days like today, she worked only three days a week. With the DIC payments she got from the VA and the small amount of Social Security she received for the kids, she didn't need to work full-time. It was important to her as the twins' only parent to spend most of her time with them.

She arrived to find that they'd put her on Labor & Delivery for the day. She had four years of surgical nursing experience, but she'd taken a position as a float nurse working Fridays and weekends. Floating required her to move from unit to unit depending on patient load. A lot of nurses hated floating, but Ellie wanted to avoid the unit politics that had made her last nursing job in Kentucky so stressful. Besides, no two days as a float nurse were alike, and working across so many specialties kept her nursing skills sharp.

Ellie spent the morning with an older couple that had opted for a C-section for the delivery of their in-vitro twins, their nervousness and excitement reminding her of how she'd felt when she'd found out that she was carrying two babies. She shared her C-section experience with them, hoping to reassure them.

Kelly, the mother-to-be, teased her husband about his nervousness, then looked over at Ellie. "How did your husband hold up?"

The question hit Ellie in the chest.

She fixed a smile on her face. "Your husband will do just fine. The only thing you have to worry about is how you're going to get sleep with two newborns at home."

She stayed with the couple in the operating room, her throat going tight when the new father wept at his first glimpse of their sons, both of whom announced their arrival by screaming their little heads off.

Grief blindsided her, surging cold from behind her breastbone.

Dan hadn't lived to see his babies.

Don't think about it. Don't think about it.

She reached over, stroked one baby's cheek with a gloved hand, willing herself to speak in a normal voice. "They're beautiful—just perfect. Congratulations."

Her patients in good hands, she fled the operating room, tore off her mask, hair net, and booties, and walked straight to the courtyard, where she stood in the cold and snow, drawing in deep breaths.

You're a professional. Get it together.

When her emotions were under control once more, she went back inside and had just started back to the L&D nurse's station when Pauline, the hospital's assistant director of nursing, came up behind her, heels clicking on the tile. "How are you feeling, Ellie?"

Ellie put on her game face. "Much better. Thanks."

"We still need someone to coordinate the first-aid tent for SnowFest, and no one has volunteered. I would like that person to be you this year."

Ellie had forgotten about SnowFest. "How many hours would that take?"

"I've done it a few times. I had a couple of organizational meetings and did my best to delegate to other volunteers. You'll work the event that weekend rather than your regular schedule here at the hospital. You'll be head nurse of the tent." Pauline said this as if it were an honor. "You can even take the twins."

Oh, glory. Because having two almost-three-year-olds running around a first-aid tent wouldn't distract anyone, least of all Ellie.

Ellie spent her afternoon with a young dreadlocked couple from Ward who wanted as natural a birth as possible—minimal monitoring, no pain meds, not even an IV. They'd brought a doula, who swept into the room all scarves and velvet skirts, her long silver hair smelling like patchouli.

"Rose? I didn't know you were a doula."

Rose owned Rose's New Age Emporium over on First Street and was known more for her tarot readings, astrological charts, and gossip than anything else.

Rose gave her a mysterious smile, as if she had a great secret to share. "Birth is all about energy, and I'm an energy worker."

Okay, so she *wasn't* a certified doula.

Ellie did her best to support the couple's birth plan, leaving most of the hands-on support—and one hundred percent of the chanting—to Rose. By the time Ellie's shift ended, the mother had only dilated to four.

Ellie stopped at Food Mart on her way to pick up the kids and got a call from Frank, who owned the local gas station and garage.

"The copper contacts on your starter are shot to hell. I can replace them for you for one-fifty parts and labor and have the car back to you late tomorrow," he said.

What choice did she have?

"Thanks, Frank."

She picked up the kids, drove home, and made spaghetti and salad for supper. After some play time, baths, and stories, she tucked them in bed. She had just poured herself a glass of wine and plopped herself in front of Netflix when she noticed it sitting on the coffee table.

Jesse Moretti's business card.

She still hadn't thanked him.

She picked up the card, held it for a moment, trying to decide whether to call or just send a card. It would be less personal to send a card. There would be no chance of the conversation drifting or getting awkward. She could write a few words and be done with it. Then an image flashed into her mind of Jesse stepping through her door, six-foot-plus of man holding Daniel and Daisy in his arms, concern on his rugged face.

She found her cell phone and dialed his number, her pulse spiking when it rang.

"Moretti."

His voice was rough, as if he'd been asleep.

"It's Ellie Meeks. I hope I didn't wake you."

"Yeah. Well… No worries."

She *had* woken him. "I just called to thank you for everything you did to help us the other night. You made a big difference for us. I know you shoveled my sidewalk, too, so, yeah, thanks for that also."

Good grief, girl!

She was babbling.

"You're welcome." His voice was rough, almost as if …

"Are you ill?" That's the last thing Ellie had wanted to happen. "Oh, God. You caught it, didn't you?"

"I don't know. Maybe. I've got a wicked sore throat and a fever, I think."

"Have you taken your temperature or seen a doctor?"

"No, ma'am."

She made a guess. "You don't have a doctor, do you?"

Or a thermometer either.

"No."

That meant he had no choice but to go to the emergency room for treatment, where he'd wait for hours. Unless …

"My father is a doctor. I'm sure he'd be willing to come check on you and bring you a prescription for antibiotics."

"I'll be fine. I don't want you to go out of your way."

"Like you did for me?" He was stubborn. Fine. So was she. "Strep isn't like a cold. It can permanently damage your heart if it goes untreated."

"Seriously?" He sounded like he didn't believe her.

"Hey, I'm a registered nurse, remember? I'll call my dad and let you know when we're on our way."

Chapter Four

"Thanks for doing this, Dad."

Ellie's father nodded. "You're welcome. He helped you out. I think he's the same fellow who fought like hell to save the poor Fisher girl last summer. Seems to me he deserves a break."

Ellie's father turned into the gravel driveway, his headlights illuminating Jesse's A-frame cabin. Its steep, overhanging roof covered a wide porch in front and was extended horizontally on the east side to serve as a carport, sheltering Jesse's SUV and a covered boat. All the windows were dark.

"Are you sure he knows we're coming?"

She nodded. "Maybe he fell asleep."

Ellie had called her father the moment she'd gotten off the phone with Jesse. She'd told him about the situation and asked him to help. He'd agreed when he'd heard who the patient was. Her parents had driven to her house straight away, her mother staying with the kids, who were asleep, so that Ellie could accompany her father.

Her father parked behind Jesse's SUV, and they climbed out, Ellie grabbing his medical bag from the backseat. No path had been shoveled to the front door, so they walked to a side door beneath the carport.

Ellie knocked, her gaze traveling over a pile of neatly stacked firewood, the polished planks of the heavy wooden door, the skis leaning against the wall. A minute crept by with no answer. She was about to knock again, when she heard the sound of a deadbolt turning.

Jesse opened the door, wearing a red and black flannel shirt, which he'd left unbuttoned, and a pair of faded jeans. He flicked on a light and stood back to let them enter. "Sorry. I drifted off."

His face was pale, dark circles beneath his blue eyes, his short, dark hair rumpled.

"I'm sorry you caught this. After everything you did to help us…"

Dark brows drew together. "It's not your fault."

Ellie's father stuck out his hand. "I'm Dr. Rouse, but you can call me Troy. Thanks for watching out for my daughter and grandkids. Let's see if we can get you feeling better. Why don't you have a seat somewhere, son?"

The cabin's main room had wood floors and was divided between a kitchen, a living area with a leather sofa and a big television, and a dining area with a rectangular wooden dining set. A wood stove stood on a raised platform of brick in the center of the space, giving heat to the entire cabin, firewood piled beside it. There were two doors in the far wall, no doubt leading to his bedroom and the bathroom. It was cozy and clean, if a bit Spartan. The log walls were almost bare—no artwork or photographs, no shelves with books or keepsakes, nothing but a calendar hanging by the phone and a large, plastic fish mounted as a fake trophy in the kitchen.

Jesse led them to the table, drew out a chair, and sat, his shirt opening to reveal firm muscles and a trail of dark curls that disappeared into his jeans.

He's sick, for God's sake.

Ellie shifted her gaze to her father, watching while he took Jesse's temperature with an ear thermometer, chatting him up.

"I heard you served with the Army Rangers."

"Yes, sir."

"And now you're with the Team."

"Yes."

"Two upstanding institutions. I thank you for your service to both. My son-in-law, Dan, served as a special operations pilot flying Black Hawks. He was killed in Iraq."

Ellie wished her father wouldn't bring this up with people, but she knew he'd loved Dan like a son. She wasn't the only person who was still grieving.

"That's what Ellie told me. I'm sorry."

Her father read the digital temperature display. "You've got a fever of one-oh-three-point-eight. I bet you feel like hell."

Jesse nodded and raised a hand to his throat. "I've got a sore throat and a bad headache. I keep getting chills."

Poor guy! He wouldn't be sick if he hadn't stopped to help her.

"That's the fever. Let's take a look at your throat."

Ellie took the ear thermometer from her father and handed him his pocket scope and a tongue blade.

"My daughter's a registered nurse. I trained her so she could help me when I make house calls. It's hard to get good help these days."

Jesse nodded, as if seeing the wisdom of this.

Ellie couldn't help but laugh. "Don't listen to him. He told me *not* to be a nurse."

"Someone with her brains ought to be a doctor."

Ellie shook her head. "I *wanted* to be a nurse, Dad."

It was an old argument.

Her father flicked on the scope's light, held the tongue blade ready. "Open wide."

Jesse did as her father asked.

It only took her father a glance.

He removed the tongue blade and flicked off the scope. "Your throat looks like shit. I won't bother with a throat culture. You've got strep."

Jesse looked up at Ellie, a lopsided grin on his face that made Ellie's pulse skitter. "Kid germs, huh?"

She nodded. "The worst."

trep throat.

So much for your monster immune system, buddy.

"Ellie said something about this damaging the heart."

"If it goes untreated for a long time, you can get rheumatic fever. Trust me—you don't want that."

Hell, no, he didn't—whatever that was.

The doc packed his things away in his bag. "Are you allergic to any drugs?"

Jesse shook his head. "No, sir."

"Well, then, you've got a couple of options. I can write you a prescription for ten days' worth of antibiotics that you can take to the pharmacy tomorrow morning when it opens, or I can give you an injection of penicillin now. Either way, you'll start to feel better about twenty-four hours after your first dose."

Jesse thought he understood what the doc was saying. "So, it's either a shot now and done, or start pills tomorrow?"

The doc nodded. "That's right."

Jesse would rather be well sooner than later. "I'll take that shot."

The doc watched him through heavily lidded eyes that were green like his daughter's. "Just so you know, the injection is given in a large muscle. Generally speaking, that means your glute."

Did the doc think getting a shot in the ass was a deal breaker?

Jesse found himself grinning. "In the army, they give you vaccines for diseases that haven't been invented yet. I've gotten more shots in my behind than I can remember."

"Okay then." The doc reached into his bag, took out a small vial of medication, along with a syringe and a needle, both of which were encased in packaging. "What's your weight?"

"I'm two-twenty." Jesse got to his feet, turned his back to Ellie and her father, and started to unzip his jeans.

A cough. "I'll ... uh ... step into the kitchen, give you some privacy."

Jesse glanced over his shoulder, saw pink in Ellie's cheeks. He hadn't thought this would embarrass her. She was a nurse, after all. She probably saw bare butts every day—and more. Why should seeing his ass make her blush?

The answer shot through the fevered haze in his brain.

She's attracted to you.

Nah. He was probably out of his mind. Fever. Germs.

He would have offered to move this show to his bedroom, but she was already walking away, her back turned toward him. He unzipped his jeans and pushed them just low enough in back to bare the muscle the doctor needed.

The doc rubbed a cold alcohol wipe over the skin high on his right buttock. "Now you'll feel a stick and some pressure as the penicillin goes in."

Son of a ...!

It hurt more than Jesse had expected.

"Done."

Jesse tugged up his jeans, zipped his fly. "Thanks."

"We'll need to hang around for about fifteen minutes to make sure you don't have an allergic reaction." The doc dropped the syringe into a small biohazard container. "Let me know if you start itching or feeling short of breath."

Jesse glanced around the room, wondering where he'd left his wallet. "How much do I owe you?"

"Owe me?" The doc frowned. "Not a red cent. You helped my daughter, and I'm returning that kindness. We take care of our own in Scarlet."

Uneasiness and warmth warred with each other for space behind Jesse's sternum. He wasn't used to needing help. At the same time, he'd lived as an outsider in this town for most of three years now. It was nice to hear that someone felt he belonged. "Thanks."

Dizziness forced him to sit, his head throbbing, his body aching with fever. He wished he could lie down again, but his mama had beat good manners into him with a wooden spoon. Besides, it was probably time to stoke the fire. While he was at it, he should carry in more firewood, too.

Ellie turned to face him, still in her self-imposed exile in the kitchen. "Can I make you a cup of tea with honey? It will help your throat."

He felt embarrassed and gratified at the same time. When was the last time a woman had done something like that for him? "There's no need to go to any trouble."

"It's no trouble." She set about making him a cup of tea, opening cupboards till she found what she wanted and putting a mug of water into his microwave.

"While I'm here, I might as well stoke that fire." The doc got up, walked to the wood stove, and opened the cast iron door. "You could use some firewood, too."

Ten minutes later, Jesse found himself sipping a cup of hot tea with honey across the table from Ellie and her father, a fire blazing in the wood stove and enough wood piled by the hearth to last until morning.

The doc gave him one last quick check. "You look good to me. Take Tylenol for your fever and your throat, and drink lots of fluids. You'll feel much better by this time tomorrow."

"Thank you, sir. Thanks to both of you."

Ellie reached across the table, gave his hand a squeeze, her cool touch sending a shiver up his arm. "Thank *you.*"

He looked into her eyes, felt his fever rise. "What are neighbors for?"

J esse plugged his iPod into his stereo, started his hard-rock playlist, and cranked the volume. Electric guitar blasted through the cabin. He pulled on latex gloves and stood in his boxer briefs in the center of the living room, surveying the battlefield that was his home. Germs had gotten the better of him. Now they would die.

Operation Annihilate was about to begin.

As far as Jesse was concerned, antibiotics were a fucking miracle drug. Almost exactly 24 hours after Doc Rouse had given him that shot, he'd begun to feel better. He'd woken up this morning planning to make up lost hours by working on his regular day off, but Matt didn't want him anywhere near the other patrollers until his fever had been gone for a full 24 hours.

"Keep the plague to yourself."

Patrollers didn't get paid sick days—a reality Jesse had never had to face before—so this was going to be hell on his next paycheck.

Note to self: Stay far away from children, even cute ones.

What about their mother?

He brushed the question aside. It was time for full-scale germ warfare.

He started in the bedroom, stripping his bed and throwing his sheets and blanket in the washing machine on hot. He disinfected his alarm clock, the doorknobs, and light switches with bleach wipes, then moved on to the bathroom. He scrubbed the sink, the toilet, and the tub, then cleaned all of the surfaces—the doorknob, the light switch, the soap bottle, the handles on his medicine cabinet.

He caught sight of his reflection in the mirror, saw the stupid smile on his face.

Knock it off, dumbshit.

He'd been thinking about *her* again.

So Ellie was attracted to him. So what? She wasn't his type.

Okay, so he didn't really have a "type." He didn't care whether a woman was blond or brunette. He didn't care how big her breasts were, didn't care if she was short or tall, skinny or curvy. He just liked women.

When it came to relationships, however, he avoided all but the uncomplicated kind. Getting involved with Ellie would be anything *but* uncomplicated.

For starters, she was a mother—of twins no less—and children had never been a part of Jesse's plan. Hell, no. He'd rather cut off his nuts with a dull razor blade than fuck up some poor kid's life the way his father had fucked up his.

But more than that, Ellie was Crash's widow. Getting it on with the widow of a brother-in-arms was deep in the no-go zone, a serious violation of the code. It didn't matter how pretty she was or how long it had been since Jesse had gotten laid. It was his duty to have her back, not get her onto her back.

That thought wiped the smile off his face.

He finished the bathroom, moved on to the kitchen and then the living room, finally sweeping and mopping his wood floors. When he had finished, he carried the bucket of water toward the side door. He would toss the water outside into the snow, where the sun and cold could kill any remaining germs.

He opened the door—and gave a shriek. "What the … ?"

Ellie stood frozen in place, her fist raised as if about to knock, her mouth open in surprise. Her gaze moved over him, head to toe, her cheeks slowly turning red.

It was then that he remembered he was wearing only a pair of boxer briefs and yellow Playtex gloves.

Son of a bitch.

"I'm so, so sorry to startle you. I … um…" Her gaze snapped up to meet his. "I came to check on you, to make sure you were… uh … feeling better."

"I'm fine. I'm good. Thanks." *Pull it together, idiot!* "No worries. I'm just cleaning. I didn't realize you were here."

Had he just screamed?

Jesus.

She nodded, hugged her arms to her chest as if she were cold. "I'm glad you're better. I'll let you get back to it. I need to pick up the kids."

With that, she turned and hurried down his driveway toward her car.

He watched her leave, then stepped outside and tossed the contents of the bucket onto the snow, feeling like an idiot.

Way to go, buddy.

"He answered the door wearing only underwear and rubber gloves—and you walked away?"

Ellie sank back into the sofa cushions, rolling her eyes so hard she thought her sister must have heard it over the phone. The kids were asleep, and it was her time to relax. Not that this particular conversation was relaxing. "He didn't answer the door. I never got to knock. I startled him. He had no idea I was standing there."

It had surprised Ellie, too, but not nearly so much as the sight of him in those snug black boxer briefs. The man was well endowed.

"Details, details. That does nothing to change the fact that the man was cleaning—*in his underwear!*" Claire all but shouted those last words. "A sight like that would have made most hetero women seriously horny. Tell me you at least enjoyed checking him out."

"I didn't check him out." Oh, yes, she had—from head to toe and back again. "Okay, so maybe I did—a little."

And Jesse had noticed. Ellie had seen it in his eyes.

"I bet he was ripped. Climbers usually are."

"Yes, he was." Ellie took a sip of her wine and closed her eyes, remembering all that beautiful, masculine terrain. Broad, powerful shoulders. Scars from combat. Biceps encircled with tribal tattoos. Rounded pecs scattered with dark curls. That eight-pack. Those obliques.

"Could you see a bulge?"

Ellie's face flamed. "What kind of question is that?"

Okay, she *had* seen that bulge—seen it and felt a jolt of lust in response.

"Oh, come on! Since when did you become a prude? When you and Dan slept together, you told me everything. You even told me how big his—"

"Good God! Would you knock it off?" Ellie had been fresh out of college then, silly and naïve. She'd had no idea how unpredictable or painful life could be, how everything she loved could be torn from her in an instant. "Well, I haven't slept with Jesse yet, have I?"

There was a moment of silence.

"Not *yet*, huh?" Claire sounded satisfied. "Was that a Freudian slip?"

"You've got me flustered. I'm not going to sleep with him at all. I'm not—"

"You're not ready. So you've said." Claire let it go, changed the subject. "Hey, you still have Mondays through Thursdays off, right?"

"I'm on call every other Monday."

"I bought tickets for you and me for Scarlet Mountain Resort's next Women's Day on Tuesday. I haven't been on the slopes yet this season, and neither have you."

"Well, I'd have to find—"

"I've already asked Mom if she would watch the kids, and she said yes. You need to get out and have a little fun. I'll even buy lunch."

What could Ellie say? A day skiing with her sister? "Wow. Okay. Thanks."

They talked about other things after that. How Cedar was hoping for a raise at work. How much Claire loved her new office. How she and Cedar wanted to get a puppy so that they could practice being parents.

"You can practice with Daisy and Daniel any time you like," Ellie offered.

"I knew you would say that. I thought we'd start with something easier and work our way up to human children."

Ellie wasn't sure a puppy was that much easier to manage than a toddler, but she held her tongue. As they ended the conversation, she found herself wondering whether Jesse would be on duty next Tuesday.

Chapter Five

Jesse was sitting in the lodge eating lunch, when his Team pager went off. He pulled it out of his pocket and scrolled through the message.

AVALANCHE. UTE RIDGE TRAIL. ONE SKIER MISSING.

Shit.

He slid the pager into his pocket and reached for his mic. "Forty-two to dispatch."

Matt answered. "We heard the call go out on the radio. You're cleared to go."

Jesse shoved the rest of his lunch back into the bag, retrieved his skis from the rack outside, and skied the short distance to the Ski Patrol chalet. He was in and out of the locker room in under two minutes.

"Hope you find him!" Matt's words followed him out the door.

There wasn't much chance of that, but Jesse didn't have the heart to say it. He had responded to four avalanche calls in his time with the Team. Not once had they recovered a live person. When he'd asked Megs about this, she'd told him it was the norm in Colorado. Most avalanches happened in the backcountry, far from towns and cities. If the victim's buddies couldn't find him, there was almost no chance that he would still be alive by the time rescuers arrived on the scene.

"There is always hope, and so we try," she'd said.

Driven by that hope, Jesse ran to his vehicle, stowed his skis and boots in the back, then climbed into the driver's seat and set out for Ute Ridge Trail, a good ten minutes away. Knowing that every one of those ten minutes could make a difference between life and death, he pushed on the gas, driving as fast as he could.

Megs' voice came over his police radio. "The missing skier is a male, aged twenty-two. The victim's friends say he was wearing a beacon."

That was good news.

"The sheriff's department is loaning us its chopper. A K9 unit will arrive via helicopter."

More good news. A well-trained avy dog could find a victim in a fraction of the time it took human rescuers.

Eight minutes later, Jesse reached the Ute Ridge parking area. As the first person on the scene, he now became Incident Command. He grabbed the radio from its charger and clipped the mic to his parka. "Sixteen-ninety-four, arrival on scene. I'm heading up to the slide area as Ute Ridge Command."

Megs replied. "Copy, Ute Ridge Command."

The passing seconds weighed on Jesse as he climbed out of his vehicle, strapped on his snowshoes, and took his avalanche beacon out of his backpack. Full of rescue gear that changed with the seasons, the pack stayed in his vehicle at all times.

In the distance, he could hear the thrum of an approaching chopper.

He turned on the beacon's transceiver, then shouldered his pack and set out up the trail at a run—or as much of a run as he could manage in snowshoes. He'd gone about a hundred yards when the trees gave way to a broad expanse of snow. In the summertime, this was a meadow, but winter revealed what it truly was—the debris field of an avalanche track. Bits of trees and rocks lay jumbled in the snow, torn from the mountainside.

Higher on the slope, he saw two men moving in disorganized circles. They were shouting something—a name.

"Jason!"

Why the hell weren't they using their damned transceivers?

One of them spotted him and waved his arms.

Jesse waved back to let them know he'd seen them.

The thrum of the chopper's rotors grew louder as it buzzed overhead, the pilot surveying the scene, looking for a safe place to land.

Jesse worked his way uphill, pushing himself to go faster.

Beep.

He'd gotten a ping.

"Ute Ridge Command, I've got a signal. Following it to the source."

He held up his transceiver, saw that it was directing him to a point about eighty yards uphill—about fifty yards lower on the mountainside than the victim's two friends had been searching. He moved as quickly as he could, sucking in lungfuls of air, his heart thrumming, his gaze on the display.

Sixty yards. Fifty. Forty-five. Forty.

Thirty yards.

Jesse was winded now, his thighs aching, his lungs straining for breath, but he didn't stop. He couldn't stop.

Twenty yards.

From somewhere behind him came the sound of slowing rotors. The chopper had landed. The others were here.

Ten.

Jesse slowed, checked the display.

According to the transceiver, the victim should be right … *there.*

He reached for his mic. "I've located the source of the signal."

"Copy. The rest of the Team is headed your way."

Down at the base of the slope, Conrad, Ahearn, Taylor, Hawke, and Kenzie were already on their way up the mountainside, a golden ball of fur bounding through the snow ahead of them.

The victim's friends saw that Jesse had stopped. They must have guessed that he had picked up the signal. They headed straight for him.

Jesse pulled his shovel out of his backpack, extended the telescoping handle, and started to dig, chopping at the hard-packed snow and pushing it downhill.

"Did you find him?" one of the young men shouted.

"Stop!" Jesse held up a hand. "Don't compact the snow on top of him. Get downhill from me, and start digging."

They looked guiltily at each other.

"We don't have shovels."

You're fucking kidding me!

Jesse didn't waste breath telling them they were idiots but kept digging.

From somewhere nearby, he heard a bark.

Charlie, the golden retriever, had picked up the scent and was running his way. In the time it took Jesse to move another shovelful of snow, Charlie was there, digging, his claws as effective as steel.

Jesse helped the dog, moving the snow, digging with him.

Conrad's booming voice came from behind him. He shouted at the victim's buddies. "If you're not going to help, get the hell out of the way!"

Then Conrad was digging, too.

Charlie barked again.

A glimpse of blue.

Now Hawke, Taylor, and Ahearn were there, all of them shifting snow as fast as they could.

A leg.

Movement.

Jesus!

He was alive.

J esse walked into Knockers with Herrera, craving pizza and beer, the sound of bluegrass rising above the hum of voices. They'd held a debriefing at The Cave for the Team members who had participated in the rescue, and now everyone was starving.

Rain, who'd worked at Knockers for as long as Jesse had lived in Scarlet Springs, met them just inside the door, a smile on her face, her long blond hair piled on top of her head. "I heard you brought down an avalanche victim alive today, Moretti. Way to go."

Jesse couldn't help but grin, still on a post-rescue high. "I didn't do it alone."

Rain was gorgeous in her own way—sexy rose tattoos on her arms, little nose ring, long hair, curves. She pointed. "Megs and the others are already here."

Ahearn, Conrad, Hawke, Kenzie, Megs, Belcourt, and Sasha were seated around the big table closest to the climbing wall. Megs was filling Sasha in.

"One of his buddies had a transceiver, but it wasn't working because Mr. Freaking Genius hadn't changed the batteries."

Sasha stared at Megs in disbelief. "You're kidding me."

"Backcountry skiing one-oh-one—check the batteries in your transceiver." Hawke dragged a corn chip through salsa. "There's no cure for stupid."

Jesse reached for the beer menu. "They didn't have shovels either."

"What kind of idiot goes skiing in the backcountry without a shovel?" Ahearn shook his head. "They're damned lucky it wasn't one of them who got buried. We'd have had a lot less to go on."

Kenzie smiled, reached under the table. "Charlie would have found them. Wouldn't you, boy?"

Jesse looked under the table to find Charlie curled up at her feet, napping. "Hey, buddy. Good job today."

Charlie opened his eyes and wagged his tail, but the rest of him lay still. The poor pooch had worn himself out.

"So the victim's going to be okay?" Belcourt asked.

Jesse nodded. "He had a fractured tibia and clavicle, and he was pretty shaken up. Apart from that, he's okay."

"I bet he'll never go skiing with those two ass clowns again." Conrad took a swig of his beer. "If it had been left to them, he'd be dead tonight."

"On that happy note, have all of you signed up for SnowFest?" Megs looked straight at Jesse. "Before you say a word, you should know that I already know the answer to that question."

Shit.

Jesse had forgotten about that. "I'll get on it."

"Did someone order the large Classic?" Victoria, Hawke's wife, appeared at the table wearing a big smile and a white chef's coat and carrying a large pie in a steel pan.

Hawke grinned, raised his hand. "I did. How else could I see my wife? Why don't you sit right next to me and help me eat it, darlin'?"

Victoria laughed. "And leave Rico to handle all the pizza orders? He'd never forgive me. Besides, you have Jesse. He can have my half."

"Fine—but he's nowhere near as good-looking as you are."

"No argument from me," Jesse said.

A transplant from Chicago, Victoria had given up a fast-paced career at some big PR firm to be with Hawke. The two were crazy in love. The way Jesse saw it, Scarlet Springs had gotten the better part of the deal because Victoria had brought real Chicago-style deep-dish pizza to Knockers, saving the town from culinary boredom.

She set the dish down in the center of the table, the scents of garlic, sausage, and tomato sauce making Jesse's mouth water. "Enjoy."

Jesse didn't mind if he did.

W hen he got home, Jesse logged on to the SnowFest website, clicked the link for volunteers, and looked over the schedule. There weren't many slots left.

The shotski was covered. So was the polar bear plunge, the ice climbing competition, and the snow sculpture contest. The skijoring event had a few slots, but Jesse was hoping to compete, so that wasn't an option. That left the kids' snowman competition or the first-aid tent.

He clicked on the first-aid tent, his gaze falling on the name of the organizer.

Ellen Meeks.

Hmmm.

This whole thing had just become much more appealing.

E llie dropped the kids off at her mother's place Monday morning after a busy weekend working in the emergency room. "I'm sorry, Mom, but I just don't see how I'm supposed to run a meeting with two toddlers running around."

"You don't have to apologize, honey. Believe me, I understand." Her mother gave her a hug and a kiss on the cheek. "Just remember I've got that eye appointment at one."

Her mother needed surgery for cataracts and had been putting it off for months.

"I'm not letting you wiggle out of that. I'll be back long before then." Ellie bent down and kissed the twins. "Be good for Grandma, okay?"

Feeling irritated at being forced to give up part of her day off, she drove to the library, where she'd reserved a conference room. She reminded herself that SnowFest accounted for some portion of the hospital's annual operational budget. Still, there were people on staff who attended the event and didn't have kids. Couldn't Pauline have drafted one of them to organize the first-aid tent?

Ellie had spent a few hours last night looking through the folders Pauline had given her. Organizing this whole thing was a bigger responsibility than she'd been led to believe. She'd already put in an order for a long list of supplies with Central Supply at the hospital. She still had liability insurance requirements to manage and about thirty-six hours to fill with qualified volunteers. She hoped she had enough people to staff the tent throughout the three-day event. She would be there eight hours each day starting at seven, but the tent was open until nine at night.

She grabbed the expandable file organizer that held the folders and all of the paperwork for volunteers, climbed out of the car, and walked inside to the reference desk. "Ellie Meeks. I reserved a conference room for ten a.m."

A young woman she didn't know set a clipboard on the counter in front of her. "You're in the Summit Room. I'll need you to sign for the key."

Ellie signed her name, put the date and the time, then took the key and made her way upstairs. She found a handful of people waiting outside the locked door, most of them nurses she knew from the hospital. "Good morning."

Lolly Cortez, an older RN who worked in the ER, gave her a sympathetic smile. "I was wondering who Pauline had roped into doing this."

Ellie tried to act less irritated than she felt. "I guess it was my turn."

She unlocked the door, stepped inside, and flicked on the light, then went about setting out the paperwork volunteers would need to fill out, along with copies of the schedule. People shuffled into the room through the open door behind her, taking their seats.

She looked up—and froze.

Jesse.

He moved toward a vacant chair—all six-feet and four-inches of him. He looked wind-blown, as if he'd just come off the slopes, his hair rumpled, his cheeks red from cold. His lips curved into a smile. "Hey."

"Hey."

There was something in that smile, something in his eyes, too, that made her heart beat faster—and left her feeling uneasy. Was he interested in her?

Oh, no. No. Ellie didn't want that. Did she?

She searched for something to say. "Are you … uh … off today?"

He shook his head. "My boss gives me time off for Team stuff."

"Oh. Yeah. Right." He'd told her that already.

She willed herself to break eye contact and greet the others in the room. Most were nurses from the hospital, but there were a few paramedics from the fire department as well. "Thanks for being here this morning, and thanks for signing up to help staff the first-aid tent. I'm going to pass around the volunteer forms. If you could each take one and fill it out, we'll get started."

She moved point by point through the basics—how many hours each of them would need to volunteer to fill the schedule, what supplies the hospital would be donating, what she expected of them during their time on duty. Then she ran through the check-in procedure.

"What kinds of patient visits can we expect?" Lolly asked.

"Good question." Ellie pulled out the report from last year's festival. "Last year, we had fifteen cases of hypothermia, one person with chest pain, a bloody nose, six people with altitude sickness, a twisted ankle, an ice climber with abrasions and lacerations, two severe hangovers…"

That brought laughter.

"… and two hospital transfers from the skijoring event—a dislocated shoulder and suspected concussion, and a broken wrist."

She could feel the heat of Jesse's gaze on her as she spoke, his attention making it hard to think. She avoided looking his way, willed herself to focus on the job.

"Part of our agreement with the town of Scarlet Springs is that we'll have at least one person certified in CPR and AED use in the tent at all times. That means I'll need a copy of your current certifications. If you didn't bring them with you, that's fine. You can scan them and email them to me. I'll need to have them on file before the festival opens. Are there any other questions?"

A few hands went up.

Ellie did her best to answer.

Yes, the fire department would once again have an ambulance on site. Yes, the tent would have heat and electricity. Yes, there would be a warm-up room for anyone suspected of having hypothermia. Yes, they would have oxygen and AEDs. No, she didn't care whether a person did all six of their volunteer hours in a single day or spread them out over three days, as long as the tent had full coverage. Yes, she would need as much help as she could get unpacking the supplies and setting up. No, they wouldn't need to set up the actual tent itself.

Jesse held up his hand. "How do you plan to handle it if someone needs help but is unable to get to the first-aid tent? The festival takes up most of downtown and stretches all the way to the reservoir. That's a big area to cover."

She hadn't thought about that. Nothing in Pauline's file addressed this issue. "I imagine we'd try to bring aid to them or ask the fire department to respond."

Jesse seemed to consider this. "I could ask the Team to lend us one of its utility task vehicles. A UTV would make getting from one side of the event to the other a lot faster. It can handle snow and ice, and it can maneuver between booths—something an ambulance can't do. Also, there's room on the back to carry a litter should anyone need to be transported."

Ellie could only see one problem with that. "Most of us don't know how to drive one of those things."

He laughed, his face lighting up with a grin that she felt all the way to her toes. "You drive it like a car—automatic transmission, steering wheel, brakes."

"Oh. Okay." She cleared her throat. "Thanks. Let me know what Megs decides."

Relieved to have the initial meeting behind her, Ellie returned the key to the reference desk and walked outside—only to find Jesse leaning against her car, arms crossed over his chest, mirrored sunglasses hiding his eyes. She did her best to keep things professional. "Can I help you with something?"

"Help?" He grinned, looking sexier than any man should. "No. I wondered if you would like to join me for lunch."

So she hadn't been reading him wrong. He *was* interested in her.

Shit. Shit. Shit.

She fumbled for her keys, her mind racing for a way out of this, an excuse. Then she remembered. "I need to pick up the kids. My mom has an appointment at one."

He glanced at his watch. "A cup of coffee then?"

Damn.

She hated to hurt his feelings, but she needed to make herself clear.

"Jesse, I …" Why did these things have to be so difficult? "I'm grateful for everything you've done for the kids and me, and I appreciate your volunteering for the first-aid tent. But I know what you're trying to do. I'm just not ready to date yet."

One dark brow arched. "You think I signed up to volunteer for the first-aid tent to get closer to you?"

The way he said it made it sound like the most absurd conclusion possible.

"I signed up for this because I was sick over the weekend and all the other events had filled up. Megs would bust my ass if I didn't volunteer for something. I asked you to lunch because we're neighbors."

Oh. God!

She stared up at him, her cheeks burning, the sharp edge of guilt pressing into her. She was such an *idiot!* "I guess I misunderstood. I just thought … I'm sorry."

But she'd seen interest in that smile, in those eyes.

His forehead relaxed. "Don't worry about it. I'm sure I'll see you around."

He turned and walked away, leaving Ellie to stare after him.

Chapter Six

"Okay, what's eating you?" Claire glanced over at Ellie, her hands on the steering wheel of her Subaru Outback as they made their way up the mountain toward the ski resort. "You might fool Mom and Dad, but you can't fool me."

Ellie looked out the passenger side window at the snowy landscape. "I hurt his feelings."

"Whose feelings?"

"Jesse's." Ellie told Claire about the meeting and the conversation in the parking lot. "I thought he was trying to start something, but he was just being friendly. I know I hurt his feelings. I feel so bad about that, so embarrassed."

"Oh, Ellie, honey. You really are hopeless at this stuff, aren't you? He was totally asking you out. The guy is into you. Why you didn't just say 'yes' is beyond me. Could it hurt to have lunch with him?"

Ellie's head snapped around. "Why do you say that?"

"Well, he's hot. You've said so yourself. And if—"

"No, I mean why do you say he's into me? He said—"

"I know what he said, but he was just protecting his ego."

"How can you know that for certain?"

"Oh, come on! Isn't it obvious?"

Ellie looked out the window again. "I just hope we don't run into him today."

"I was kind of hoping we would. I want to check him out for myself."

Ellie could only imagine how that conversation would go. "If I see him, I'm going to ski away as fast as I can."

Claire changed the subject. "It looks like we're going to have perfect weather."

It was only a thirty-minute drive to the ski area. Claire parked. They got their lift tickets, then put on their boots and skis and skied to the lift line. The line wasn't as long as it typically was on the weekends, though a busload of middle school kids from Boulder were ahead of them, probably here for ski lessons as part of a PE class.

Ellie glanced over at the Ski Patrol chalet, her pulse taking off when the door opened, and a man in a red parka stepped out.

It wasn't him.

She wasn't sure whether she felt relieved or disappointed.

Stop doing this to yourself.

She couldn't let her confused feelings about Jesse ruin this day. She was here to spend one-on-one time with her sister, not to waste energy worrying about what he thought of her now. She'd been honest with him.

But had he been honest with her?

She set that thought aside, looked up at the cloudless blue expanse of the sky, inhaled the scent of pine and snow, and willed herself to relax. They'd almost reached the front of the lift line, so she shifted both poles into her right hand.

Claire turned to the lift operator. "You've got a great job."

He grinned, dimples in his tanned cheeks. "Fresh air, sunshine, lots of skiing. There's no better job in the universe."

It was Ellie and Claire's turn now. They skied into place.

"Do you know Jesse Moretti?" Claire asked the lift operator.

Ellie gaped at her sister. "What—?"

"Moretti?" The lift operator nodded. "Sure. You a friend?"

Ellie answered. "No, just a neigh—"

Claire cut her off. "Tell him Ellie Meeks is here."

"Will do."

Ellie didn't have a chance to respond or protest because in that instant the chair scooped her and her sister up and carried them up the hillside.

"Why did you do that? You know I don't want to see him! Now he's going to think I wanted him to find me."

Claire surveyed the scenery, a satisfied smile on her face. "Lighten up. You have physical and emotional needs. You need adult companionship. What would it hurt if you got together with this Jesse guy for a while? You don't have to marry him. If he's into you, then why not go for it?"

"You don't understand."

It wasn't as simple as Claire made it sound.

Since Dan died, nothing had been simple.

"Ellie Meeks wanted me to tell you she's here," Kenny said over the radio. "She was headed up the Little Bear lift with another woman."

"Copy that. Thanks." Jesse started back down the slope, patrolling Silver Bullet, one of the resort's double-blacks.

He would never understand women, even if he lived to be a hundred. Yesterday, Ellie had made it clear that they were nothing but neighbors. Today, she'd had one of the lift operators flag him as if she wanted to see him. It made no sense.

What made even less sense was the fact that Jesse was happy about this.

No, he wasn't going to ask her out again. He'd gotten the message. He wanted to see her because he needed to apologize.

When she'd turned him down and then suggested that he'd volunteered for the first-aid tent just to get closer to her, he'd let himself get butthurt. He'd acted like she'd read him wrong, let her believe she was out of line.

Way to be an asshole, buddy.

He was a better man than that. He could take "no" for an answer.

Okay, so maybe she hadn't been entirely right. He'd had to choose between the kids' snowman contest and the first-aid tent. That had been a no-brainer. But he *had* been looking forward to spending time with her.

Of course, there was no chance of him running into Ellie. They were on different mountains on opposite sides of the resort.

He was wondering whether he might be able to find her on his lunch break when a skier in a lime-green jacket and red hat flew past him, bombing his way down the run, almost colliding with other skiers and breaking a half dozen safety rules as he went.

There was no way Jesse could catch him, not without putting other skiers on the slope at risk. He reached for his mic. "Forty-two to dispatch."

Matt replied. "Forty-two, go ahead."

"I need a couple of patrollers at the base of Silver Bullet. We've got an out-of-control skier. He's wearing a lime-green jacket and a red hat."

"Copy, forty-two."

Jesse skied to the bottom of the run, expecting to find the kid in the green jacket spending some quality time with a few patrollers. Instead, he found Amanda and Steve standing empty-handed.

"Sorry, Jesse," said Amanda. "I guess we missed him."

"Shit."

Jesse went on a few more patrol runs, stopping to aid a skier who was having an asthma attack. When the skier had been evacuated via snowmobile, he headed down to the lodge for lunch. He'd just taken a seat when Kenny walked by, headed for the grill.

Kenny saw him, waved. "Sorry about your friend, man."

Jesse had no idea what Kenny meant. "My friend?"

"Yeah, you know. The woman who wanted to see you. They brought her down in a toboggan about ten minutes ago—knee injury or something."

"Jesus." Jesse had heard that call, but he'd had no idea it involved Ellie.

He shoved his lunch back into the bag and got to his feet, then headed over to the First Aid Center. A knee injury was the last damned thing Ellie needed. How was she going to keep up with the twins? How would she work? If it was a break or a torn ligament, she might even need surgery.

Damn it.

He stepped inside.

Ellie stood in the middle of the room, talking on her cell phone and walking back and forth, still in her ski boots. She wasn't limping. She didn't look injured at all.

She ended the call and walked over to him. "Hey."

"I heard you'd been hurt."

"Oh, that was my sister." She pointed to a dark-haired version of herself that was lying in one of the beds, her leg elevated and splinted. "Jesse, meet Claire."

Ellie pushed Claire's wheelchair out to the parking lot. "I called the ER and checked her in. We shouldn't have to wait too long."

Jesse walked beside them, carrying their skis and boots. "Smart."

Ellie couldn't help but feel drawn to him. It wasn't just that he looked like every Colorado girl's vision of heaven in that Ski Patrol parka. It was the fact that he cared about her. She'd seen the worry on his face when he'd burst through the door at the First Aid Center. He'd thought she was hurt, and once again he'd come to help her.

"I don't need to go to the ER," Claire protested.

"Stop being stubborn. I'm the registered nurse, so I get to make these decisions. Besides, Cedar is meeting us there."

Claire looked up at Jesse. "Do you see how she bullies me?"

Jesse didn't seem to know that Claire was joking. He kept his silence, the wariness on his face telling Ellie that he felt it unwise to wade into an argument between sisters.

"We both rebelled against my father. I became a nurse instead of a doctor, and Claire went into woo-woo and became a massage therapist."

"Massage is *not* woo-woo."

Jesse glanced over at Ellie, caught the smile on her face, and the confusion on his faded. "Do you always tease each other like this?"

"Yes," they answered in unison.

"What's the point of having a *much* older sister if you can't tease her once in a while?" Claire asked.

"What?" Ellie feigned outrage. "I'm only eighteen months older."

They reached Claire's SUV.

"Now what?" Ellie unlocked the doors with the fob.

Jesse opened the rear passenger side door. "Claire, it would be better if you rode in the back instead of up front. That way, you can keep your leg elevated."

Ellie nodded in agreement. "Good idea."

"Oookay." Claire looked confused.

"Why don't you stand on your left leg? I'll climb in from the other side, lift you onto the seat, and help you scoot backward. You can use the other door as a backrest. Ellie, can you support her injured leg?"

"Absolutely."

With Ellie to steady her, Claire got to her feet—or her foot. "Now what?"

"Stand with your back to the seat." Ellie helped her get turned around.

Meanwhile, Jesse climbed in from the other side and crawled across the bench seat toward them. "You ready?"

"What am I doing?"

"You're not doing anything. I'm going to lift you into the vehicle." Jesse caught her just beneath her breasts and lifted her backward onto the seat.

The look on Claire's face as he picked her up almost made Ellie laugh. And for a moment Ellie wished *she* were the one with the injured knee.

"Got her leg, Ellie?"

"Yep."

Jesse helped Claire scoot backward across the seat, then climbed out and shut the rear driver's side door, giving Claire something to lean against.

"Are you comfortable?" Ellie asked her sister.

Claire mouthed, "Oh, my God! He's got muscles!" Then she spoke aloud. "Yes."

Ellie turned to find herself looking into Jesse's blue eyes, warmth skittering through her. "Well, that worked."

Damn, he was distracting.

His lips quirked in a lopsided grin. "Sad to say, but I have a lot of experience putting injured people into vehicles."

Ellie was certain that was true. "Thanks so much for your help. You seem to be in the habit of rescuing my family members and me."

"Hey, don't mention it. Can we, um, talk for a minute?"

Ellie opened her mouth to answer, but Claire beat her to it.

"Yes! Sure. Fine with me. The two of you need to talk."

Ellie glared at her sister and slammed the back car door shut. "Sure. What is it?"

His brow furrowed, his expression going serious. "I was telling the truth when I said that I didn't sign up for the first-aid tent to get closer to you. It *was* pretty much my only option, and Megs *would* have kicked my ass if I hadn't signed up for something."

So he wanted to make her feel like an idiot again?

She started to push past him.

He caught her shoulders. "Would you let me finish?"

She stepped back, arms crossed over her chest. "We need to get to the ER."

He drew a breath, then went on. "I asked you to lunch because I want to get to know you better. And, yes, when I saw that you were running the first-aid tent, I felt a hell of a lot better about signing on. I'm attracted to you, Ellie, and I think you're attracted to me, too. Look at me and tell me that's not true."

She stared up at him, stunned. "I ... I ..."

When nothing else came out of her mouth, he lowered his head—and kissed her. It was just a fleeting kiss, the slightest brush of his lips over hers, but it robbed her lungs of breath and left her lips tingling.

He stepped back, his pupils dark. "Call me."

Ellie watched him walk away, then climbed into the driver's seat.

"Well, well," said Claire. "I'm almost glad I fell."

Jesse walked back to his locker, sat, and removed his ski boots, sure he'd lost his fucking mind.

He had kissed Ellie.

He hadn't planned it. She'd stood there, looking up at him through panicked green eyes, and he hadn't been able to stop himself. As kisses go, it had been tame—no tongue, no fingers in the hair, no breasts pressed against his chest. But *damn* ...

He'd kissed his share of women, but that little peck had rocked his world.

In that moment, he'd forgotten the long list of reasons why he didn't want to get involved with her—the twins, the fact that he'd known her husband, the baggage he'd brought back from the war.

Okay, so that was only three reasons. But they were three very *good* reasons. He ought to write them down and memorize them because right now they didn't seem nearly as important as kissing her again.

Jesus! That *right there* proved it. He *was* losing his mind.

And yet even as he yelled at himself, he couldn't get truly angry. For the first time in what seemed a very long time, he was looking forward to something that wasn't climbing or skiing. Of course, there was always the chance that she wouldn't call.

He shoved his boots in his locker, took off his parka, and hung it on its hook.

Matt walked up behind him, a piece of paper in his hand. "Hey, Jesse, I made a few calls. Nate West, son of the owner of the Cimarron Ranch, says he'd be happy to team up for the skijoring event. He and his dad breed quarter horses. Here's his number."

"I've heard of the Cimarron." Jesse had been invited there for a trail ride once but hadn't been able to make it. He took the number, tucked it in his pocket. "Thanks."

Ben sat down across from him. "I saw you kiss that hot little number in the parking lot. Who was she?"

"Hot little number?" Jesse didn't like hearing any man call Ellie that, but he didn't get the chance to say so.

Matt glared at him. "Hey, we've got rules about getting it on with guests."

"Wear protection!" shouted several patrollers in unison.

"Damned straight." Matt walked back to the dispatch desk, chuckling.

"Who was she?" Ben wasn't giving up.

Jesse was torn between irritation and laughing at the kid's persistence. Had he been this annoying in his early twenties? "That was my neighbor. Her sister fell and injured her knee. I was helping out."

"Interesting 'helping' technique."

Jesse shut his locker, slapped Ben on the shoulder. "Watch and learn, grasshopper. Watch and learn."

A s it turned out, Claire had torn her anterior cruciate ligament and her meniscus. Based on the MRI results, Dr. Southcott recommended surgery. He discharged her from the ER with crutches, pain killers, and instructions to elevate and ice her knee until she could see a surgeon.

Cedar drove Claire home in his vehicle, while Ellie drove Claire's Outback down the canyon to their home in Boulder. When Claire was inside, Cedar left Ellie to watch over her while he took off to get some Thai takeout.

Ellie did her best to get Claire comfortable, helping her take a shower and put on her PJs, giving her a dose of pain meds, and settling her on the sofa in front of the TV with an ice bag and a cup of tea.

"I'm so sorry, sis." Ellie could see behind Claire's cheery façade and knew she was in pain. "The codeine ought to kick in soon."

"I'll be okay. My big sister's a nurse. She'll make sure of it."

"You bet I will." Ellie sat in the armchair beside the sofa. "Do you want to watch something on TV? I could put in a DVD or—"

"He kissed you."

A thrill shivered through her. "I'm trying not to think about that."

In truth, Ellie was finding it hard to think about anything *but* that kiss. Remembering it brought the sensation back—the softness of his lips, their heat, the nearness of his body.

What would it be like to be kissed for real by him?

"I could feel his muscles when he lifted me into my car. Good grief, girl! I can only imagine what he looks like naked. But then you got a glimpse."

"Yes! Yes, I did. And he was ripped, okay? He was gorgeous. Part of me wanted to run my hands over his chest just to enjoy the feel of him."

"So call him. You've got his number, right?"

"I'm not sure I can."

"You're not sure you can call him? Did you forget how to use a phone?"

"No! I'm not sure I can sleep with him. What if we're in bed together and all I can think about is Dan?"

"Did you think about Dan when he kissed you?"

The answer to that question hit her squarely in the forehead. "No."

"Call him, Ellie. Give him a chance. How many more years are you planning to live this sexless existence? You deserve happiness. Dan didn't want you to be lonely. He wanted you to have a full life. You know that."

Dan had told her more than once that she was to live her life to the fullest should anything happen to him. She'd promised to do just that. But she'd never imagined how hard it would be to live with that promise.

Ellie nodded, her throat tight.

"So you'll call him?"

"I'll think about it."

Ellie was still thinking about it when her father came to pick her up and to check on his younger daughter. She thought about it all the way up the canyon. She thought about it when she gave the kids their bath, read them stories, and put them to bed.

She walked into the kitchen to pour herself some wine. But rather than getting a glass out of the cupboard, she walked to the rear window and looked across her backyard and up the mountainside toward his cabin. There, among the trees, she caught a glimpse of golden light spilling from his kitchen window.

She picked up Jesse's business card, which still sat on the kitchen counter, then reached for the phone.

Chapter Seven

Jesse had turned off the water in the shower when his cell phone rang. He reached for a towel, strode naked into the living room, and grabbed the phone off the coffee table. His heart gave a hard knock when he saw the name on the display.

Ellie.

He answered. "Moretti."

There was a moment of silence.

"Hi, Jesse. It's Ellie. I hope I didn't wake you."

"It's not quite my bedtime yet." Tomorrow was his day off.

"I wanted to thank you for helping my sister this afternoon." The nervousness in her voice told him this was *not* why she'd called.

"I was happy to do it."

"Also, I appreciated your honesty. I know it's not easy sometimes—you know, communication and relationships. Not that you and I are in a relationship or anything. I didn't mean to suggest that."

Okay, this was funny. "I got what you meant."

"Anyway, I'm grateful we had a chance to talk today."

"Yeah. Me, too."

Another pause.

"I wondered whether you'd like to come over for a glass of wine. The kids are asleep. I have scotch if you don't like wine. I could make tea or coffee if you don't drink alcohol. I just thought maybe we could ... get to know each other. You know, talk. And, just to be clear, I'm not suggesting anything else."

So fucking was probably out. "Got it."

"Would you like to come over?"

Hell, yes, he would. "Give me ten minutes to get dressed, and I'll walk down. You caught me getting out of the shower."

"Oh! Oh. Okay." She cleared her throat. "See you in ten minutes."

He ended the call and walked back to the bathroom, feeling a foot taller and energized. He towel-dried his hair, then slathered his face with shaving cream, and shaved away two days' growth of beard.

Was it the kiss that had gotten to her? Had she been thinking about it all day the way he had?

You'd like to think so, wouldn't you, dumbshit?

Forget kissing anyway. Ellie had said just talking.

Yeah, okay. Jesse could respect that.

He finished shaving, rinsed his face, and walked off to his bedroom to get dressed. He stared into his closet at the broad assortment of battered blue jeans, T-shirts, flannel shirts, sweaters, and climbing clothes he owned, and he found himself wondering what a classy woman like Ellie Meeks would like to see on a man.

She was married to an army pilot, remember?

Okay, right. She wouldn't be expecting a skinny tie or pleated slacks. Besides, Jesse didn't own anything like that anyway.

He pulled on a black T-shirt and slipped a gray flannel shirt on top of that. A clean pair of boxer briefs, some jeans without holes, and a pair of wool socks, and he was good to go. Just to be on the safe side, he tucked a condom into his pocket.

Yes, he'd heard what she'd said. Yes, he would respect her limits. But sometimes sex just happened. If it did, he wanted to be ready.

He put on his boots, slipped into his parka, then grabbed his keys and stepped out into the night.

O *h, God! Oh, God! Oh, God!*

Ellie stared at her reflection in horror. She had invited a man over to her house—and not just any man, but a sexy man who had kissed her today, her freaking neighbor!

What in God's name was she supposed to wear?

Unable to decide, she scurried from her bedroom to her bathroom, brushed her hair, washed her face, and put on mascara. She was ready from the neck up, at least.

She hurried back to her bedroom and stared into her closet. Casual. She should keep it casual. It was nine o'clock on a weeknight, and they were getting together in her living room. What could be more casual than that?

She put on a clean pair of panties and her sexiest, pushiest push-up bra, then yanked her skinny black jeans off their hanger, put on a white lace camisole, and pulled her heather blue V-neck cashmere sweater over her head. She'd just smoothed her hair back into place when a knock came at the back door.

Shit!

She gave herself a quick once-over in the mirror—and froze. Dan had given her this sweater for Christmas one year.

Panic shot through her.

She glanced at the wedding band on her finger. What the hell had she been thinking to invite Jesse over like this?

Another knock.

It was too late to change her clothes—too late to change what she'd set in motion.

She flicked off her bedroom light, hurried to the back door, and opened it. Every thought in her head vanished.

He smiled down at her, clean shaven and smelling of shampoo and fresh air, snow clinging to his jeans up to his knees. "Hey."

"Hey." She might have stood there staring at him if the air hadn't been freezing cold. She stepped aside to make room for him. "Please, come in."

He did his best to stomp the snow off his boots outside, then stepped inside onto the little doormat. "The snow was a deeper than I thought."

While he took off his boots, she grabbed a dish towel. "You can probably brush most of it off with this."

"Thanks." He set the dish towel on the table and slipped out of his parka, revealing a gray flannel shirt layered on top of a black T-shirt that stretched across the muscles of his chest.

You're staring.

She retrieved two red wine glasses from the cupboard, set them on the counter, and chose a bottle of shiraz from her wine rack, her mind racing for something conversational to say. "Did the rest of your day go well?"

She was amazed by how calm and collected she sounded. She hadn't felt this nervous with a man since ... well, she didn't know when.

She glanced over her shoulder, saw he was brushing snow off his jeans.

"A kid hit a tree."

What was he saying? Oh, yes. She'd asked him about his day.

"Ouch," she managed to say. "Was he okay?"

She reached into the drawer where she kept the wine opener.

"He had a head injury. We evacuated him via helicopter."

She turned, wine and corkscrew in hand, to find Jesse standing a few feet away, his gaze fixed on her. Her pulse skipped. "I forgot how big you are."

An image of the bulge in his boxer briefs flashed into her mind.

Her cheeks burned. "Tall ... I meant tall. You're very tall."

Without breaking eye contact, he took the wine bottle from her. "Let me."

"Why did you join the Rangers?"

Jesse sat on one side of the sofa, while Ellie sat on the other, looking good enough to eat, her jeans and that fuzzy sweater hugging sweet curves, pink polish on her toenails, her hair hanging thick and blond to her shoulders. Until tonight, he hadn't seen her up close without a bulky winter coat. He certainly wasn't disappointed.

Wine had taken the rough edges off her nerves. She'd been so tense when he'd arrived that he'd made extra sure to keep his distance. And so here they were, on opposite ends of the sofa, just talking.

Not that he was complaining.

"I grew up in a tiny town in Louisiana. My grandfather, my uncles, my dad— they either worked on fishing boats or in the refineries. I just couldn't do that. I wanted to get away, see the world, be a part of something bigger. I'd always been bigger and stronger than the other boys, so I figured I'd join the army, try for my Ranger tab, and kick some terrorist ass for Uncle Sam."

"How did your family take that?"

"My mom yelled and cried and threatened to shoot me in the knee cap. Her son was not going to go overseas and die in some stupid war. My father took it as a rejection. He and I have never been close." The truth was darker than that, but he didn't want to ruin the mood. "I haven't talked to him since my mother died. That was five years ago."

"I'm sorry. Why did your mom die? She can't have been that old."

"Heart attack. It runs in her family."

"Sorry." Then Ellie smiled and shook her head, giving a tipsy little giggle.

"What?"

"You wanted to escape from your small town—and you ended up in *Scarlet*." That made her laugh.

He could see the humor. "Except that Scarlet is the gateway to the mountains, and there's nothing small about them."

She took another sip of wine. "What brought you to Colorado in the first place?"

"After I left the Rangers, I went to New Orleans to live near my sister, but I had a hard time getting back into the swing of civilian life."

That was an understatement. He'd come back with a head full of death and rage and started drinking. He'd tried to get help from the VA, but the wait times had lasted longer than his sister's patience. She'd given up on him.

Well, they'd never been close anyway.

"I'd seen pictures of the Rockies and came out to Colorado to try to get Afghanistan and Iraq out of my head. I fell in love with the mountains at first sight."

He could still remember that moment when he'd caught his first glimpse of the high peaks with their glittering white summits. "I got my first climbing lesson a couple of days after seeing climbers in Eldorado Canyon State Park, and I was hooked."

Climbing cleared his mind, cut through the wall that seemed to have grown up around his emotions, made him feel whole and human again.

Ellie stared wide-eyed at him. "You've only been climbing for a couple of years—and you made the Team?"

He nodded. "It was hard work. I climbed every day, no matter the weather. When I realized I needed a job if I wanted to stay, I took a spot on the trails crew at Scarlet Mountain Resort and then learned to ski that fall, hoping to land a spot on ski patrol."

She was still staring. "You must be a natural athlete."

"I guess we all have to be good at something." Jesse was tired of talking about himself. "Why did you become a nurse?"

She shrugged. "Growing up with a father who was a doctor gave me an interest in the medical field. I wanted to be more directly involved with patient care, so I decided to be a nurse. I worked as a surgical nurse until ..."

A shadow passed over her face.

"It's okay, Ellie. You can talk about him."

"I was a surgical nurse until Dan was killed. I had just learned that I was carrying twins. He was so excited. I was happy and a little scared. We talked about names over Skype. He liked Otis Henry for a boy's name and Daisy Mae for a girl. I told him no way could I name a child Otis." She laughed at this. "The Internet connection was lousy, but he had to go anyway. And then a few days later ... he was gone."

Jesse knew the crushing weight of grief, knew how deeply it cut. Then he remembered that *this* was why he'd kept his distance from her all this time. He'd had his own grief to bear and had been certain he couldn't shoulder any part of hers.

But now, sitting close to her like this and seeing the pain on her sweet face, it seemed as simple as reaching out and taking her hand.

"It must have been hard." Jesse's voice was soothing, his thumb rubbing circles over the back of her hand. "What about Dan's parents? Did they help?"

Ellie shook her head. "They never liked me. They're still angry at me for following his wishes and not putting a cross on his headstone."

"They got angry at you for following his last wishes?"

She nodded. "They wanted me to bury him in Florida, where they live now, but I refused. I rarely hear from them."

"Lame."

Ellie twined her fingers with his and held on. "Claire came out to stay with me. If it hadn't been for her …"

She hadn't meant to talk about this. She didn't want to dump this on Jesse. But now that she had started, she couldn't stop. "I had him buried at Arlington. I felt he deserved that honor. My sister helped me sell our house and move back to Scarlet. I knew I would need help during my pregnancy and after the twins were born. But nothing felt real to me, not even my babies. I would go to my prenatal appointments, listen to their heartbeats, and it all felt…"

"Like it was happening to someone else," Jesse finished for her.

Her gaze snapped to his. "Exactly."

It was on the tip of her tongue to tell him that he was empathetic for a man, but even with the two glasses of wine she'd had, she knew that sounded patronizing.

"When I reached thirty-six weeks, I started having contractions. I chose a C-section. I was so afraid something might go wrong. I couldn't lose them, too. One minute I had a huge belly, and the next there were two crying babies. Daniel looked so much like his father. I wish Dan had lived to see them." Her throat went tight, and she blinked back tears. "Sorry. I didn't mean…"

Jesse leaned forward, wiped a tear from her cheek. "Hey, don't apologize."

She looked up, saw the concern in his eyes—and slid into his embrace.

For a time, he just held her, his strong body a refuge, one big hand caressing her hair. "It's going to be okay."

Maybe it was the wine. Maybe it was his scent. Maybe it was the feel of him. Ellie couldn't say. It had been so long since a man had held her like this, so long since she'd taken comfort from a man.

Slowly her grief faded, replaced by an altogether different emotion, her blood warming, awareness spreading through her body as she remembered the way he'd kissed her today and how it had felt. She sat back, looked up at him, ran her thumb over the fullness of his lower lip. From there it was so easy.

She leaned forward and lifted her lips to his.

He sucked in a quick breath, but he didn't pull away. "*Ellie.* You said talk only."

"I changed my mind. Kiss me."

He drew back, and for a moment she thought he was leaving. Instead, he took the wine glass from her hand and set it beside his on the coffee table. Then he was back, his eyes looking into hers, so serious. He cupped her cheek. "Are you sure?"

Hell, yes, she was sure. "Kiss me."

Before she could draw another breath, his lips claimed hers, the fingers of one big hand sliding into her hair, his other arm hauling her against his chest.

Oh. God!

At first contact, her senses reeled, arousal jolting through her. She was overwhelmed by Jesse—the burn of his lips on hers, the hard feel of his body, the spice of his skin. *This* is what it felt like to be held by a man.

It had been so long, so long.

He caught her lower lip between his, teased it with his tongue, then released it, his mouth covering hers again. When his tongue sought entry, she yielded, his tongue teasing hers with slick strokes she felt all the way to her womb. She stole control of the kiss from him, nipping first his upper and then his lower lip. He moaned, reclaiming his dominance, kissing her deeper and harder, the fingers in her hair clenching into a fist. Then, the kiss grew gentler, until he broke contact and pulled away.

She caught his face between her palms, her words a whispered plea. *"Please don't stop* ... unless... unless you want to."

"Are you kidding?" In a blink, he had her on her back, his weight pinning her to the sofa. "I could kiss you all night."

Jesse knew Ellie hadn't planned this, but damned if he could walk away.

Kissing Ellie was like nothing else. She kissed with her entire body, arching against him, her nails digging into his shoulders, her hips moving beneath him.

Jesus!

She turned her head to the side, exposing the delicate skin of her throat. He accepted her gift, licking and nipping the skin just beneath her ear, pressing his lips to the rapid thrum of her pulse. She moaned, the sound sending a jolt of lust straight to his erect cock, the heat between them driving him out of his mind.

One of her hands slid beneath his T-shirt. "I want to feel you."

He sat up, tore off his flannel shirt, and pulled his T-shirt over his head. Then he pressed her palms to his chest. "Be my guest."

He saw her pupils darken, felt her shiver, heard her little sigh of pleasure as she explored his pecs, teased his nipples with her thumbs, traced his scars and the tats on his arms with her fingers, then slid her hands over his abs. It turned him on to watch her enjoying the feel of him. Her hands spread sparks over his skin, making his muscles clench. But now it was his turn.

He stretched himself out above her once more, nuzzled her throat, kissing his way down the V-neck of her sweater to that sweet cleavage that had teased him all evening. "I want to touch you, too."

"*Yes.*" She wriggled beneath him, trying to get out of her sweater.

He took over, drawing it over her head and dropping it on the floor next to his T-shirt, only to find himself staring at a barrier of white lace that gave him glimpses of the soft, creamy flesh and silky, white bra beneath. Impatient now, he helped her peel off the camisole, but rather than rushing to take off her bra, he bent down and kissed the soft swells of her breasts, tasting her, teasing her, licking that line where soft skin met satin.

Her fingers slid into his hair, her breathing uneven. "*Jesse.*"

He slid a hand beneath her, found her bra clasp and undid it, then peeled the satin cups away. His cock jerked at the sight of her breasts—full and round with pale nipples that puckered under his gaze. He took each breast in his hand, squeezed lightly, teasing her areolas with his thumbs. "God, you're beautiful."

She shivered. "Do you think so?"

"God, yes." He lowered his mouth to one pebbled tip.

She gasped, then moaned as he sucked and licked first one nipple and then the other, teasing her with his tongue, tugging on her with his lips. "Oh, God, Jesse, you're driving me crazy!"

She was writhing beneath him now, her fingers fisting in his hair, the intensity of her response making him even hornier—if that was possible.

"*Fuck me, Jesse.* Please."

His heart slammed against his breastbone, lust thrumming through his veins. He felt one moment of pure elation—and then it vanished.

He couldn't do this. It didn't matter how much he wanted her. It didn't matter that the condom was burning a hole in his pocket. She'd had two glasses of wine, and she was still mourning her husband, Crash, a good man.

A man you knew. A man who probably saved your life.

She still wore his ring on her finger for God's sake.

"Ellie, I don't think we—"

Her fingers on his fly cut his words short as she made quick work of his zipper, pushed past the waistband of his underwear, and closed her hand around him, gripping him, stroking him.

Oh, hell, it felt good. *Damn.*

"I can't do this, Ellie." What *the hell* had he just said?

"Wh-what?" Green eyes went wide.

He ran his thumb over the curve of her cheek, tried to explain. "You didn't invite me over for sex, remember? I can't do this if it's going to end up hurting you. I don't want to be the thing you regret in the morning."

Chapter Eight

Ellie couldn't sleep, arousal buzzing through every fiber of her body, her mind filled with the taste, feel, and scent of Jesse. Every word he'd said, every touch, every kiss replayed through her mind again and again. Oh, he knew how to kiss, knew how to use his lips and tongue. And his hands…

He'd touched her, and she'd gone nuts. She'd run her hands over him, drinking in the feel of him, the sight of him—chest hair, muscles, tats, scars. She'd forgotten how wonderful it was to be strung out on desire, to burn for a man, to ache for him.

I could kiss you all night.

God, she wished he had! She'd wanted him so badly. Instead, he'd stopped.

I can't do this if it's going to end up hurting you.

He'd stopped for her sake. He'd stopped because he'd been afraid it wasn't what she truly wanted. He'd stopped despite the fact that he'd brought a condom. She'd seen the outline of it in the back pocket of his jeans not long after he'd arrived.

His thoughtfulness had left a warm glow inside her. A man who put a woman's well-being ahead of his penis—she liked that.

She liked even more what he'd said on his way out the door.

When you're ready, Ellie, I'll be here.

She drifted off at some point because when her eyes opened again, daylight was streaming through the cracks in the blinds. Daniel was sitting at the foot of her bed with his blanket playing with a handful of magnetic blocks, while Daisy lay beside her, sucking her thumb and cuddling her stuffed kitten.

Who needed an alarm clock when you had small children?

Rather than wishing the kids would just give her another hour of sleep as she did most mornings, she felt energized, awake, alive.

She sat up and drew them both to her, hugging them and kissing their chubby cheeks. "Good morning, my sweeties. Would you like waffles for breakfast?"

Daisy, as it turned out, had shed her overnight diaper and was running around half-naked, while Daniel was soaked. Ellie took off his diaper, put him in a pair of disposable training pants, and dressed him. Then she dressed Daisy, who was already potty trained for daytime, and put her hair into little pigtails.

"Okay, let's make waffles."

The kids stood together on a chair, "helping," while she made the batter from scratch and poured it into the waffle iron, their happy chatter making her smile. In the breaks between waffles, she scrambled some eggs and started a pot of coffee.

"Hot." Daniel pointed to the waffle iron.

"Yes, it's very hot. Don't touch it, or it will burn you."

Ellen scooped more batter—just as Daisy put her palm on the hot iron.

Daisy screamed.

Ellie dropped the batter back into the bowl, scooped her daughter up, and stuck her hand under a stream of cool water. "Daisy Mae! Why did you do that? I told you not to touch it. See? It *was* hot, wasn't it?"

Daisy nodded, crying her little heart out, while Daniel watched wide-eyed.

"Hot!" He pointed to the waffle iron again, looking like he might cry, too.

"Daisy is okay," Ellie reassured him. "You're okay, Daisy."

There were no blisters, just redness.

Thank God.

Ellie sat them in their booster seats at the table, then went back to making waffles without their help. When the waffles were done and the coffee brewed, she cut up a waffle for each of them and served them with real maple syrup, scrambled eggs, and a sippy cup of milk.

It was the perfect breakfast for a snowy winter morning. The kids ate contentedly, quiet now, their focus entirely on getting each piece of syrupy waffle into their mouths.

As Ellie ate, she glanced out the back window—and saw a trail in the snow leading from her back porch up the mountain to Jesse's cabin.

I don't want to be the thing you regret in the morning.

Would she have regretted it?

She looked down at the ring on her finger, twisted it. She couldn't be sure how she'd have felt because it hadn't happened. But wasn't that why he'd stopped? He'd wanted to give her time to think, to decide whether she truly wanted to have sex with him or whether last night was just about wine and loneliness.

And, God, she *was* lonely. She'd known that, but until he'd kissed her, she hadn't realized exactly how lonely she was.

She glanced up at the little photo of Dan she kept on the fridge. She hadn't thought of him once while she and Jesse had been kissing.

But Dan had wanted her to be happy. He'd made her promise—

It was Wednesday. Playgroup!

Damn! She was running late.

"Okay, kids, let's get you cleaned up. It's time to go play."

Jesse dragged his ass out of bed and shuffled into the bathroom to take a leak. His gaze fell on the clock. How could it be ten already?

Shit.

He hadn't meant to sleep that long. Then again, he hadn't slept much at all, sexual frustration keeping him awake, his mind filled with Ellie—the taste of her skin, the feel of her breasts in his hands, the soft sound of her sighs. He'd finally taken matters into his own hands, imagining that his fist was her sweet body. He'd come—hard. But that hadn't been enough to get her out of his mind.

It's your own fault, idiot.

Yes, okay, maybe it was. But whatever Jesse's faults—and his father had a list that was probably a mile long—he wasn't the kind of man who could take advantage of a woman's grief and loneliness just to scratch a sexual itch.

The last thing he wanted was to look into Ellie's eyes and see that he had added to her troubles.

She's not for you, anyway, remember?

Somehow, that didn't make him feel better.

He walked into the kitchen, grabbed the milk out of the fridge, and drank straight from the carton, leaning against the wall with one hand. That hand just happened to land on the button beneath the fucking fish Herrera had given him for his birthday.

Tinny music spilled out, making Jesse jump.

The fish's tail and mouth began to wiggle.

"Take me to the river/Wash me in the water."

Fuck this day anyway.

He put the milk away, took out a carton of eggs, and made himself an omelet with five egg whites, beating the eggs a bit too hard and tossing in whatever shit he could find—scallions, tomatoes, a leftover boiled potato, shredded Mexican cheese.

After he'd eaten, he left the dishes in the sink, dressed, and brushed his teeth. Then he grabbed his cell phone and gym bag and headed out the door. He needed to get vertical, work off this sexual frustration, clear his head.

He drove to the climbing gym, where he found Sasha already on the wall, her trainer on belay and shouting encouragement as she worked her way through a route with a steep overhang, her body almost parallel to the ground.

"Let your bones do the work. Your skeleton doesn't get tired. When you're not moving, let your muscles rest."

Jesse checked in with the front desk, then walked to one of the benches to put on his climbing shoes and harness. The rock gym, like The Cave, was a second home for him, the anticipation of challenging moves and burning muscles already clearing his thoughts. He'd just clipped into his harness when Herrera walked in, bag slung over his shoulder, mirrored sunglasses on his face, dark hair rumpled from the wind.

"Hey, man," he called when he saw Jesse. "You ready to kick your own ass?"

Jesse was more than ready.

They picked a 5-11c route next to Sasha.

"Mind if I go first?" Jesse asked.

Herrera's brown eyes narrowed. "Something eating you?"

"Don't ask." Jesse reached for the rope, looped it through his harness, and started tying his figure-eight retrace.

"It's too late for that."

"I didn't sleep last night." Jesse thought Herrera would let it drop.

He didn't. "You need a woman. Nothing makes for a good night's sleep like sex. You should get together with Rain."

"Rain?" Jesse drew the knot tight, double-checked his harness. "Why Rain?"

"I've seen the way she looks at you. She likes you, man."

"Rain is just being friendly. Besides, Joe will kick the ass of any guy who hits on her in his pub. You know that."

"So hit on her when she's not at work."

Chaska Belcourt walked by with his sister, Winona, both of them wearing harnesses. "How's eighth grade treating you boys?"

Jesse glared at Herrera. "Are you on belay or what?"

"On belay."

"Climbing."

"Climb on."

Jesse threw himself into the route, the toes of his left foot on a chip, his right hand on a small edge. He reached with his left hand, caught a crimper, and drew himself to the left, shifting his left foot onto a small edge and the toes of his right foot onto the chip. He stretched his right arm, caught an edge, and pushed upward with his left foot. Then he lunged upward toward a fat jug—and caught it.

As he climbed, his mind began to empty. He was barely aware of Herrera and Sasha's shouts of encouragement from below. By the time he'd climbed to the top of the wall, he was focused, in control of his emotions again.

Herrera lowered him to the mat. "Way to crush it."

Jesse was about to say that his practice on power moves was paying off when the sound of sirens came from nearby. One siren. Then another. And another.

He walked to the windows to see a fire rescue vehicle and two ambulances headed down the canyon. Hawke must be having a busy day.

"I wonder what happened." Jesse felt for his pager in his pocket, made sure it was on. "Did you get a page?"

Herrera shook his head. "Nothing.

Sasha held up her silent pager. "Me neither."

They walked back to the wall. It was Herrera's turn now. But no sooner had Herrera gotten tied into the rope than Jesse's cell phone rang.

He pulled it out of his pocket.

Ellie.

He was about to let the call go to voicemail—now was not the time to talk about last night—but something had him answering instead. "Moretti."

"Hi, Jesse. I'm really sorry to bother you, but there's been a multiple-casualty incident involving a school bus full of kids in the canyon."

Jesus. So that's what that was.

Ellie went on. "I've been called in to the ER to help, but my parents are in Denver with my sister seeing a surgeon about her knee. Most of my friends are nurses, and they've been called in too. I have no one to watch the kids."

Wait. What?

"You want me to watch your kids?" Even as he said the words, he knew she couldn't possibly have meant she wanted him to babysit.

"Yes—if you can. I'm really sorry to ask this of you, but I have no one else I can call who lives nearby."

"I don't know anything about kids." It was the truth.

"No, maybe not, but you have EMT training, and you were an NCO, right? How much harder could it be to watch over two toddlers compared to a camp full of soldiers?"

Okay, she had a point. "I'll be there as soon as I can."

He ended the call. "Sorry. There's been an accident with a school bus— multiple casualties. My neighbor is a nurse and needs me to watch her kids while she goes to help in the ER."

Herrera stared at him. "You—babysit?"

Yeah, he'd had that same thought. "I'm good with kids."

He hoped for everyone's sake that was true.

Ellie raced around trying to get herself ready for work and make sure Jesse
would have everything he needed. There was a box of Kraft Dinner and a
can of peaches on the counter top. The kids had already had their midday
dose of amoxicillin. The diapers and wipes were sitting on the coffee table,
next to a stack of DVDs that the kids liked—*Sesame Street, Thomas the Tank
Engine, Little Einsteins.*

"Daisy, do you have to go potty before I go?"

Daisy shook her head.

She checked Daniel's training pants one last time and was relieved to
find them poopy. That was one thing Jesse wouldn't have to deal with. She
quickly changed Daniel, took the dirty training pants out with the trash, and
washed her hands.

Her stethoscope. Where had she put it?

She found it on the kitchen counter and had just draped it around her
neck when she saw Jesse pull up in front of the house. She met him at the
door.

God, she felt guilty for asking him to do this.

"Hey, Daniel and Daisy, look who's here. It's Jesse. Do you remember
Jesse? He's the nice man who helped us when we were sick and our car
wouldn't start."

"Hey, guys." Jesse waved to the kids.

"Thanks so much, Jesse. I'm so sorry. I know this is your day off—"

"Hey, I'm doing my part. Those kids need your help, right?" His gaze
moved over her. "You look good in scrubs."

She looked down at herself. "You must be nuts."

He chuckled. "Okay, give me my mission parameters here."

"Just keep my kids safe and alive until I get home or until my parents get
here." She walked over to the table. "I've written everything down here—
when they need their next dose of medicine, the number for the hospital
switchboard, my parents' cell phone numbers, though they're not here and
can't really help. There's a box of Kraft Dinner on the counter if I'm not
home by suppertime. Daniel's wipes and training pants are on the coffee

table. He just had a BM, so I hope you won't have to deal with that. Daisy is potty trained, but she needs a little help wiping and such."

She saw the surprise on his face at this. "I'm so sorry. You've never changed a diaper, have you?"

He rested a big hand on her arm. "I've dealt with worse things than poop."

She supposed that was true.

"Thank you for doing this. I'll find a way to make it up to you." She stood on tiptoe and kissed him on the mouth, the contact like a jolt of caffeine.

Damn.

She popped a DVD into the player and turned on *Sesame Street*. "It's best if we don't make a big deal about my leaving."

But when she tried to sneak out, they saw her, and Daisy started to cry.

"It's okay, baby girl." Jesse scooped Daisy up. "Let's wave goodbye to your pretty mommy through the window."

"Thank you!" Ellie shut the door behind her and waved to Daisy as she climbed into her car.

She arrived at the hospital a few minutes later, clocked in, and went straight to the ER, where resources were stretched to their limit, a half dozen ambulances from three different organizations parked outside the emergency room and more coming up the street. Reporters roamed around the hallway, some with cameras, while parents and family members—people she knew—clustered together, waiting to hear if their sons and daughters were here.

"I need an MRI!" someone shouted.

"Get those fluids going. His blood pressure is dropping."

Ellie scrubbed up, put on a gown, grabbed a handful of gloves, and found Pauline. "Where?"

Pauline pointed toward the procedure room at the end of the hall. "Head injury. Life Flight is on its way. We need to stabilize him for transport."

Ellie hurried to the room, shouldered her way behind the curtain—and stopped. Lying on the gurney was Tyler Kirby, only six years old, with an open skull fracture.

God, no.

His face was bloody and lacerated—probably from glass. He was unconscious, and he'd been intubated, IVs in his little arms, a c-collar around his neck. His vitals did not look good, his BP and blood oxygen low, his little heart racing.

Doctor Warren, the hospital's trauma surgeon, looked up, her eyes telling Ellie everything she didn't want to know. "Start antibiotics running wide open and get a stat blood panel. And where the hell is the neuro consult?"

Ellie grabbed hold of the IV cart and went to work.

B abysitting toddlers was not for the weak.

Jesse discovered this during the ten minutes of constant wailing that had followed Ellie's leaving the house. Eventually he—with a little help from *Sesame Street*—managed to soothe Daisy and Daniel. Four hours had gone by, and so far, no one had been killed or injured. He considered that success.

But the evening wasn't over yet.

"Put on." Daisy held up a little plastic tiara with pink sparkles.

"You want me to put that on you? Are you a princess?" He started to put it on her little head, but she drew back.

She pointed to him. "Put on *you*."

She wanted him to put it on himself?

Uh. Really? Okay. He did as she asked. "Do I look pretty?"

She giggled.

Her laughter struck him right in the chest, melted his heart. The sound was pure, bright, innocent.

Daniel meanwhile was busy piling blocks in the back of a plastic dump truck and dumping them out again. That looked fairly straightforward, so Jesse helped, watching Daisy while she put every single stuffed animal she and her brother owned down for a nap on Daniel's blanket. Yeah, that wasn't going to end well.

Jesse's phone buzzed. He fished it out of his pocket to find a number he didn't recognize. "Moretti."

"This is Troy Rouse, Ellie's father. She gave me your number."

"Hey, doc." Jesse got to his feet.

"I'm sure you probably heard this, but the canyon is closed."

"No, I hadn't heard. It must've been a terrible accident."

"A drunk driver T-boned a bus full of school kids, causing other cars to hit the bus. They said the canyon is going to be closed for another hour or two at least while they finish the investigation and clean up. Meanwhile, we're stuck down in Boulder. How are my grandkids?"

"They're doing fine, sir."

"Good. I wish I were up there. Those kids on the bus—a lot of them are patients of mine. I wish I were at the hospital right now, helping out the way Ellie is."

"Are things going well there?"

"She says it was pretty rough going for a while. They lost one. That always shakes a person up."

Screams. Cold water. A pale, terrified face. Little hands reaching.

Jesse pushed the memory aside. "I'm really sorry to hear that."

"We'll let you know when the road opens. We're sitting in a parking lot at Sixth and Canyon, so we'll know as soon as traffic starts moving again."

"Don't worry about us. We're good." Jesse ended the call, a hollow feeling in the pit of his stomach.

The kids played in their playroom for a while longer. When that deteriorated into fighting—Daniel did not feel like sharing his blanket with the stuffed animals—Jesse managed to interest them in *Thomas the Tank Engine*. And then, like magic, they both fell asleep.

They were still asleep when Ellie pulled into the driveway a half hour later.

Thank God!

A sense of relief washed through Jesse. He had fulfilled his mission. He'd kept Ellie's kids alive until she'd returned.

He strode to the window, put a finger to his lips. "Shhh."

She entered quietly, her lips curving in a smile. "Are they asleep?"

"I guess I wore them out."

She set her handbag down and slid out of her coat. Her stethoscope was still around her neck, and there was dried blood on her scrubs and the tops of her white shoes—proof that her afternoon had been rough. "How did it go?"

"Fine. They weren't happy when you left. They bickered a few times, but I broke it up." What else should he tell her? "Daisy used her potty. I changed Daniel once."

Ellie was still smiling as if he'd said something funny. "You're a pro."

Jesse didn't want to brag, but he'd done pretty well. "How are things in the ER?"

She shook her head, let out a breath. "Everything is under control now. It was mayhem at first. We triaged thirty kids. We sent the most critical to Denver. Some went to Boulder. We lost one—a little boy who was only six. Open skull fracture. He had internal injuries, too. I was with him and his parents when he died. I know them."

God. How fucking awful.

"I'm sorry. That must have been hard."

"Yeah." She looked up at him, weariness and sadness disappearing, giving way to that same amused smile. She pointed to his head. "I like the tiara. The look suits you."

"What?" He reached up and felt Daisy's plastic tiara. He'd forgotten about it. He pulled it off. "Don't judge. We all need to experiment."

She laughed at this, then stepped out of her shoes, frowning when she saw the blood. "Would you mind watching them while I take a quick shower?"

He didn't need an explanation. "Go ahead."

"I'd love it if you would stay for dinner after that."

"Kraft Dinner? I'd love to."

Chapter Nine

Ellie stepped under the hot spray and let the tears come. Yes, they'd saved lives today, but they'd lost one. Losing any patient hurt, but a child...

She would never forget the agony on Carrie and Jim Kirby's faces as they ran through the ER to be with their little boy—or Carrie's heartbroken cry when all of their efforts to restart little Tyler's heart had failed.

Ellie sobbed out the despair she'd carried with her all afternoon. Then she remembered.

Jesse.

She couldn't leave him alone with the kids forever. He'd already gone above and beyond for her.

She swallowed her unspent emotion, washed away the sweat and blood and grief, shaved her legs, and dried off, taking the time to brush her hair and put on a little makeup. Then she slipped into a pair of old jeans and a gray Henley shirt, skipping the bra. She needed softness and comfort tonight, not underwire.

She caught her reflection in the mirror. She wouldn't impress Jesse tonight. Her eyes were red from crying, and there were dark circles beneath them from her night of horny non-sleeping.

Don't worry about it.

She walked out of her bedroom to find the kids sitting with Jesse on the couch watching *Sesame Street*. Daisy snuggled against his left side, sucking her thumb, while Daniel sat on his lap, holding his blanket.

Ellie's heart gave a little squish.

The twins' faces lit up when they saw her.

"Mama!"

They climbed down from the sofa and scampered to her, Daniel dragging his beloved blankie behind him.

She scooped them into her arms. God, it felt wonderful to hold them, to inhale their familiar scent, to know that they were safe. "Did you have fun with Jesse?"

Daisy said something about a bear on Daniel's blanket, and Daniel said something about his dump truck—or that's what it sounded like anyway.

She looked over at Jesse, found him watching her, his gaze warm, his lips curved in a half-smile. She put the kids down. "Is anyone hungry?"

"I have an idea about that." Jesse got to his feet. "Unless you really want that boxed stuff, I thought I could make my spaghetti. I know a few shortcuts. It wouldn't take long."

As much as the idea of not cooking appealed to her, Ellie doubted they had the ingredients on hand. "I don't feel up to running to the store."

"You don't have to do anything." He stepped into his boots, tied them, then grabbed his parka. "I'll just get what we need from my place. Be back in a few."

"Okay." Ellie turned off the TV and sank to the sofa, snuggling her kids close. "Can you tell me what you did today?"

As the twins shared their day with her, very little of it making sense, she did her best to let her stress fade away. It felt strange to let Jesse take over like this. It had been a long time since a man had made a meal for her.

He was back in a few minutes, a paper grocery bag under one arm.

She met him at the door, took the bag from him, and glanced inside. On top was a piece of paper—a copy of his EMT certification. "Oh, thanks for this."

While he slipped out of his boots and parka, she set the ingredients he'd brought on the kitchen counter—pasta, a gallon freezer bag filled with homemade pasta sauce, a package of sweet Italian sausage, a block of parmesan cheese, and salad fixings. "You make your own spaghetti sauce?"

"My Italian mother would roll over in her grave if I used sauce from a jar."

She laughed. "Just tell me what you need—"

He came up behind her, wrapped one arm around her waist, and kissed her cheek, his masculine scent spilling over her. "Unless you keep your pots and pans under your bed or something weird like that, I can handle this. You go chill."

J esse set the salad on the table. "Buon appetito."

Ellie slipped a bib over each twin's head. "You speak Italian?"

It took him a moment to answer. He had noticed that she wasn't wearing a bra the moment she'd stepped out of her bedroom, and some part of his mind was stuck on one thought: *boobs*. "Italian? Just a little, mostly cuss words."

Pull it together, idiot. You've already seen her boobs.

And touched them and kissed them and tasted them.

Damn.

She grabbed a few paper napkins. "Who taught you to cook? It's not a skill you picked up in the army. I know that much."

"My mother taught me." While Ellie served the kids, Jesse filled her plate and then his own. "I watched her cook. I like good food, so I paid attention."

Also, the closer he was to his mother, the less likely his father was to take a belt— or a fist—to him.

"Try to eat with your fork, Daisy." Ellie gave a helpless shrug as both kids began picking up pasta and bits of sausage with their fingers and shoving them into their little mouths. "How did you survive deployment? MREs aren't exactly gourmet."

"You can get used to almost anything, but if I never lay eyes on an MRE again, it will be too soon." He set a plate for Ellie and one for himself on the table and sat.

She closed her eyes and sniffed, her lips curving into a smile, her fingers curling around the handle of her fork. "This smells amazing."

"Wait till you taste it." Jesse watched while she took her first bite. He couldn't remember feeling nervous about anyone eating his cooking before.

Her eyes drifted shut as she chewed. "Mmm."

"You like it?"

"It's delicious." She dabbed her lips with a napkin. "It's the best homemade spaghetti I've ever tasted."

A knot of tension inside him dissolved. "You should try my lasagna."

Listen to you. Who's cocky now?

"Feel free to make it for us anytime. Seriously." There was a sparkle in those green eyes that hadn't been there when she'd gotten home.

Jesse could see she'd been crying. Her puffy eyes told him that. He knew how fucking much it hurt to want desperately to save a life—only to find yourself helpless. And when that life was a child's...

Don't go there, buddy.

She seemed to relax as she ate, shaking her head at the mess the twins made of themselves, spaghetti sauce on their faces from ear to ear. "Sometimes I wonder if they're getting any food into their tummies."

Jesse glanced under the table. "I can see why you worry."

Between the sauce on their faces and fingers—and the pasta on their bibs and the floor—it hardly seemed like they could have eaten enough to survive.

As they finished the meal, Jesse found himself wondering what it would be like to have a wife and kids, to sit down like this with them for dinner every night, to spend the evening with a family.

You're out of your fucking mind.

He wasn't a family man. The fact that he'd survived a handful of hours with two toddlers didn't change that. Besides, no woman in her right mind would want to take him on. He was only here because he had wanted to do his part. In fact, it was probably time for him to pack up his stuff and go home.

But he didn't. As the hours stretched on, he kept finding reasons to stay. Helping Ellie with the dishes. Playing dump truck with Daniel while Ellie gave Daisy her bath. Holding Daisy and reading her a story while her brother was in the tub, her blond head resting trustingly against his chest, one little hand wrapped around his finger, the sweet baby scent of her hair putting an ache in his chest.

He just couldn't walk away from that.

When the kids were asleep, Ellie walked back out to the living room, somehow managing to look tired, sad, and beautiful at the same time.

He stood. "Do they sleep all night?"

"Usually." She took his hand. "You did really well with them. I'm impressed."

"They're sweet kids." He was a little surprised to realize he meant that.

She stepped into his arms. "You were my hero today."

Part of him was pleased by this. At the same time, he wasn't sure he wanted to be anyone's hero. He'd tried being a hero before—and had failed.

She looked up at him. "Do you want to stay for a while?"

What he wanted was space, a little air, some time alone.

He drew away. "Not tonight. I've got to be up at four."

"Oh. Right. I probably ought to go to bed soon anyway. Thanks to a certain someone—that would be *you*—I didn't get much sleep last night."

So he wasn't the only one. He liked that.

*J*esse *tried to run, whitewater crashing against his thighs, dragging him down, making it almost impossible to move.*

The child screamed, arms flailing, her terrified eyes looking into his for a moment before the creek rolled her over like a toy and swept her beyond his reach.

He ran as fast as he could, but it was so hard, water slowing his legs, making him fight for every inch. He reached for her again—and again the creek took her.

"She's dead," Megs said from the embankment behind him.

No. She couldn't be. He wasn't going to let her die.

Goddamn it!

He kicked against the water, fought his way through it, searching.

*E*llie did some quick cleaning Thursday morning, then packed the kids in the car and drove down the canyon to Claire's house. Flowers and stuffed animals sat at the intersection where the school bus had been hit, but Ellie tried not to look. The roadside memorials reminded her of people she'd known or cared for and lost.

She didn't often take the kids to her sister's condo. The place was modernist with floor-to-ceiling windows on the west side that offered a beautiful view of the Flatirons, but it was also completely un-childproofed.

Ellie shut the bathroom and bedroom doors to limit the amount of damage the kids could do to themselves or her sister and brother-in-law's property, then settled the kids in the living room with the box of toys Claire kept for them.

She plopped down on the sofa across from Claire, who sat in the recliner where she could keep her injured leg elevated. "Dad said you're scheduled for surgery at St. Luke's Friday morning."

"I'm dreading it. You know me. I hate needles. I asked if they could skip the IV, but the doctor said no."

"I wish I could be with you." Ellie worked on Fridays, and St. Luke's was in Denver.

"Cedar is taking the day off, so he'll be with me."

Ellie realized Daniel was about to dig into the dirt of Claire's potted ficus tree with a plastic toy screwdriver. "Daniel, no! Don't dig in Auntie Claire's plant."

Claire told Ellie what the surgeon had said—how long she would have to be on crutches, how important physical therapy would be to her recovery. "Cedar and I are going to my office tonight to see whether we can adapt the treatment room so that I can give massages from a rolling saddle chair."

That didn't sound like it would be easy.

"Do you have a chair like that?"

Claire shook her head, pointed to Daniel. "We saw some online. They're not too expensive."

"Daniel, stop. No." Ellie got to her feet, picked Daniel up, and pulled him away from the plant once more. "If you do that again, I'll take the screwdriver away."

Daisy, meanwhile, was playing with a little toy that made animal noises, moos and quacks and oinks holding her attention.

Claire got that sly look on her face that usually meant she was about to meddle in Ellie's life. "Mom told me that Jesse babysat for you yesterday."

Ellie sat again, unable to keep a smile off her face. "He did a great job. When I got home, he had Daisy's tiara on his head. He'd forgotten it was there."

"Oh! I like this guy."

"He even made us dinner—spaghetti with homemade meat sauce."

Claire gaped at her. "He *cooked* for you? Please tell me you slept with him."

Ellie glared at her sister. "Could you maybe not talk about it quite so openly? Daisy repeats everything these days."

"Oh, sorry. Did you F-U-C-K yet?"

"No! But I wanted to." Ellie told her how she'd invited Jesse over for a glass of wine—and how that had led to other things. "He is the most amazing kisser. He really knows how to use his mouth."

"How far did you go?"

"Just second base."

"Awesome. Wait. Is second base…" Claire made a wanking motion.

"That's not second base. That's third base. Isn't it?"

"I thought third base was, you know…" Claire stuck out her tongue and wiggled it—at which point the conversation seemed so absurd that they both burst into laughter.

"We sound … like we're back … in high school," Ellie managed to say.

When the giggles subsided, Ellie lowered her voice. "We kissed and got under each other's shirts."

"And?" Claire looked at her expectantly.

"And what?"

"How was it?"

"It was *incredible*. Truly. I didn't sleep all night. I haven't felt this alive since…"

The words "since Dan was killed" hung, unspoken, in the space between them.

"When are you going to see Jesse again?"

"I don't know." Ellie and Jesse hadn't talked about it. "Soon, I hope."

Jesse skied slowly down Ashes to Ashes, towing a toboggan and doing his best to avoid the bumps that made the snowboarder he was evacuating scream. Travis skied down behind him, making sure Jesse didn't cut across the paths of other skiers.

"Traverse!" Jesse called out.

"Clear!"

Jesse snowplowed into the turn and cut back across the slope, using the edges of his skis to keep his speed under control, the weight of the toboggan pushing him down the fall line.

He hit a small bump.

"God*damn* it." The kid had taken a nasty fall off the halfpipe in the terrain park, and Jesse was pretty sure his radius was fractured.

"Sorry, buddy," he called back.

It had been a busy day so far, which was just as well. There'd been two calls for knee injuries, one for a fight in the lift line, and another about a couple fucking behind the ski patrol cabin at the top of Eagle Ridge. It had kept Jesse's mind off things he didn't want to think about—like Ellie, like the nightmare.

He'd had it again last night for the first time in maybe four months and had woken up covered in cold sweat, his pulse racing. He'd thought he was done with that shit. Hearing about the bus crash and that little boy's death had probably triggered it.

Hell, he didn't know.

But Esri would. She'd been the one who'd stopped the nightmares before. He couldn't go back to the way he'd been this past August, when he'd had that same nightmare four and five times a night, so he'd made an appointment with her this evening. He was probably overreacting, but he'd rather take action sooner than later.

He got the victim down, helped him out of the toboggan and walked with him into the First Aid Center. "They'll take good care of you."

He glanced at his watch. It was after one.

Time for his lunch break.

He skied to the Ski Patrol chalet, stepped out of his bindings, and stowed his skis in the rack, then walked in and cleared his break with dispatch. He took advantage of his time off the slopes to call Nate West and

set up a day to practice skijoring. They quickly settled on next Wednesday—
his next day off.

"I'll see if we can't create a mini-skijoring course up here to give you a
taste of what it's really like," Nate said.

Jesse would be impressed if they could pull that off. "Terrific."

"Matt tells me you served with the Rangers."

"That's right."

"So did my father. He did two tours with the Seventy-Fifth during
Vietnam. I imagine you two could find a lot to talk about."

"I bet we could."

"Matt also says you're a natural-born athlete, that you learned to climb
and made the Team in a handful of months."

"Matt has a big damned mouth."

That made Nate chuckle. "We'll see you up here next Wednesday. I'll
text directions to the ranch."

"Thanks." Jesse ended the call, feeling a little lighter.

Jesse walked into Esri's office, which occupied a set of rooms on the
ground floor of an old Victorian-style home on Second Street across from
Food Mart. The waiting area was decorated in shades of green, tan, and soft
blue—calming colors, he supposed. It had a little fountain in the corner, the
tinkling of water mixing with Japanese flute music. A mezuzah hung just
outside the front door, a cross hanging on one wall, a dream catcher on
another, while a smiling golden Buddha sat on the coffee table surrounded by
magazines.

Esri had all the bases covered. Or maybe she saw it all as part of her
heritage. What did she tell him she was? Tibetan and Jewish?

He sat, uneasy to be here again. It wasn't that he didn't like Esri. She was
kind. She was smart. She was also cute—maybe five-two with a feminine face,
shoulder-length dark hair, and big brown eyes. But when he was with her, he
felt transparent, naked.

He hated that.

The door to her inner office opened, and she stepped out, wearing an
oversized sweater that emphasized how petite she was.

She smiled when she saw him. "I didn't hear you enter. Come in."

The inner room where she met with clients was cozy, its walls a shade of ivory, the carpeting white, the plush armchairs a soft shade of gray.

She sat and waited for him to do the same. "How have you been? It's been more than four months since our last session."

"I've been good. Ski season has been busy. I helped save a skier's life last week after an avalanche buried him."

"I heard about that. It's not often you get a happy ending with an avalanche."

"No. It isn't." It wasn't natural for him to talk about feelings. Maybe some guys found it easy, but he didn't. Still, he'd had training for post-traumatic stress and knew damned well that there was no shortcut here. "I had the same nightmare last night—the one I used to have all the time."

"The dream where you try to save Kayla Fisher, and she gets swept away?"

He nodded. "I thought if we talked about it right away, maybe it wouldn't go back to being a nightly thing again."

God, he didn't want that.

"I don't know that we can guarantee that, but I think you made the right decision." She gave him a reassuring smile.

"There was a bus crash yesterday. A friend of mine—a woman—she's a nurse. She got called in to help with the casualties. A little boy she was taking care of died. I heard about it afterward. I wonder if that's what triggered the dream."

She seemed to consider that. "It could be. There are some similarities between what your friend went through and what you've been through."

That's exactly what he'd thought.

"I have a question for you. What kind of emotions do you feel when you're stuck in that nightmare?"

Jesse didn't have to think about it. "Helpless. I can't move fast enough. I just feel—yeah, helpless. And desperate. I would do anything to save her, but I can't."

That's how it had been in real life, too.

"I think anyone who'd been there, who'd gone into the water after her, would feel the same way. So there's nothing out of the ordinary about your emotions, either in the nightmare or in real life."

"Yeah." They'd talked about this before.

"What else has been going on in your life?"

"I kind of met this woman. She's got twins—a boy and a girl—that are almost three. Her husband was a pilot and was killed in Iraq." Hell, he'd probably told Esri enough for her to know which woman he was talking about.

Scarlet Springs was a tiny town, after all.

If she knew, she didn't give it away. "Are you dating?"

"I don't know that I'd call it that. I've never wanted to be a father. I'm not into kids, and she has kids, so that kind of rules out anything serious." He told Esri how he and Ellie had met, how Ellie had invited him over for a glass of wine, and how he'd babysat for her yesterday so she could help at the hospital.

"You babysat?" Jesse had never seen surprise on Esri's face—until now. "That's really stepping out of your comfort zone, isn't it?"

He nodded. "You could say that. Toddlers, little kids—they're so helpless."

Helpless.

The word echoed, reminded him of what he'd said a few minutes ago.

"What is it? You've got a faraway look on your face all of a sudden."

"Do you think babysitting could explain the nightmare?"

"What do you think?"

Until yesterday, he'd have said that the idea of babysitting *was* a nightmare, but it hadn't been that bad.

"It was strange. I could've gone home after she got back from the hospital, but I didn't. I grabbed some stuff out of my fridge—we're neighbors—and made dinner for them. I could have gone home after that, but I didn't."

"What does that tell you?"

"I don't know. That I really need to get laid?"

"Maybe it says that you were enjoying yourself, that you were getting something out of spending time with them that you didn't expect."

He remembered how it had felt to hold Daisy, to sit on the floor playing dump truck with Daniel, to see Ellie's face when she inhaled the scent of his meat sauce.

"Have the two of you been intimate?" At the expression on his face, Esri held up a hand. "I'm asking for professional reasons, not to gossip about it. Nothing you say to me goes outside this room."

"Not yet, but we did kiss and stuff." He would leave it to her to decide what "stuff" meant. "I care about her. I care about the three of them."

The moment he said it, he realized it was true.

Esri seemed to consider this. "Sometimes when we've shut off our emotions to try to stop feeling bad things, we stop feeling altogether. Then, when we let ourselves have good emotions again, we turn on the spigot and the dark stuff comes up, too."

Wasn't that just fucking convenient?

"So that's it then?"

"It's possible. You're looking for a one-on-one correlation for the nightmare, a single cause. You don't want to have that dream again. No one would. But I'm working on a puzzle, trying to help you put the pieces together, and there are a lot of puzzle pieces you haven't shown me."

Shit.

Chapter Ten

The bus crash had shaken Scarlet Springs to the core, and people were doing what they always did—coming together.

As Ellie drove to work Friday morning, she passed homemade signs of wood and cardboard that had been spray painted with the words, "Protect our kids from drunk drivers!" and, "Thank you, first responders!" Flowers were piled at the base of the flagpole outside Peaks Elementary School. Posters were tacked to utility poles announcing a benefit at Knockers tonight to help the Kirby family cover funeral costs. She would have to bundle up the kids and take them there for supper this evening.

Thinking of Carrie and Jim and little Tyler put a lump in Ellie's throat. But the outpouring of love reminded her why she'd moved back here after Dan's death. No, Scarlet wasn't a big town. It didn't have a shopping mall or a Starbucks or even a McDonald's. But it had a big heart.

She parked, walked in through the hospital's employee entrance, and clocked in. She'd gotten a text from Pauline this morning so she knew she'd be working in the pediatric unit, where every bed was full with children injured in the crash. She'd worn her special bunny scrubs and had brought a set of bunny ears to wear—anything to make the kids' stay in the hospital less scary and more fun.

She was one of two RNs on duty—the others were LPNs—which meant she was responsible for ten patients. Sebastian, 5, Room 201, had a broken arm that needed surgery. Ryder, 7, also in Room 201, was stable after surgery for a ruptured spleen. Ava, 9, in Room 202 had been kept overnight for observation for a concussion and would be discharged soon. Ava's little sister Emma, 7, had a broken femur and needed surgery, too, so she would be staying.

Ellie took as much time as she could with each little patient, making sure their pain was under control, letting them talk about what had happened, assuring them and their parents that they were getting good care and would be going home soon. She gave lots of hugs and held a lot of hands. Nursing wasn't just about giving meds, checking vitals, and treating the body. It was about healing the heart and mind, too.

She worked through her scheduled lunch break, *finally* getting a bathroom break and a few bites of her sandwich while charting at about one. Then her mother texted to tell her that Claire was out of surgery.

That was a relief.

By the middle of the afternoon, Ava had been discharged, Emma was out of surgery and in recovery, and little Sebastian was on his way to the OR.

Ellie was hanging a second bag of antibiotics for Ryder, who was sleeping, when her father walked into the room. "Hey."

She'd been expecting to see him. Most of the kids here were his patients, children he'd known since the day they were born. Though the children were in the care of hospitalists for the moment, he wanted to see them and keep up on what was happening with their treatment. He was just that kind of doctor.

He gave Ellie a side hug and walked over to Ryder's mother. "It looks like Ryder's in good hands. How are you holding up, Marie?"

Marie stood and accepted a hug, her voice quavering. "How could something like this happen? I feel terrible for the Kirbys."

"Sometimes there's no 'how' or 'why' in life. Bad things just happen."

Ellie got the antibiotics flowing into Ryder's IV, then went to check on Emma, who had just been wheeled back into her room. She and her father went room to room separately, each doing their job. They'd run into each other at the hospital many times before, but never under such awful circumstances.

Ellie was finishing the uneaten half of her sandwich when her father came up behind her, bent down, and kissed her cheek.

"I'm heading into my office. Keep me posted, okay?"

Ellie, caught with her mouth full, nodded.

"Have I ever told you what a damned good nurse you are?"

Ellie turned in her seat to look up at him. "Thanks. I guess the apple didn't fall far from the tree."

A moment after her father left, Kathy, one of the younger LPNs, hurried over to her. "Was that old goat hitting on you? He was totally hitting on you."

Ellie had just taken her last bite of sandwich and almost choked to death laughing. "That old *goat* is my father."

Jesse drove straight from the slopes to the rock gym, where he changed into climbing clothes and climbed laps up the wall, going for speed, building up a sweat. He told himself that he was working on endurance, but he really just wanted to get his heart pumping, burn off the frustration that had been eating at him all day, get his head straight.

He'd had his shit together until he'd let himself get distracted by a pair of pretty green eyes. Now he was having nightmares again. Why?

Hell, he didn't know. Because he enjoyed being with Ellie? Because he had feelings for her? Because he liked her kids? Because they'd talked about yesterday's bus crash and the little boy she'd lost?

For fuck's sake. None of that made any sense.

He self-belayed and took a breather, shaking out his arms. His cell phone buzzed in the pocket of his climbing pants. He pulled it out.

Megs.

"Moretti."

"Knockers is holding a fundraiser tonight to raise money for the Kirby boy's funeral. Hawke's having a pretty rough time of it today. He's the one who pulled the boy out of the wreckage. I thought you might want to stop by, do your part for the Kirby family, and maybe hang with Hawke. You know what he's going through."

Shit. Yeah. He did.

"I'm at the rock gym. Give me a few minutes to shower, and I'm on my way."

He hit the locker room, showered, and then headed off to Knockers. The parking lot was packed, forcing him to park down the street and walk. He pushed through the front doors. The Timberline Mudbugs were playing on stage, and the place was full.

"Jesse!" a tiny voice called.

He turned and saw Daisy running toward him, her mother standing with Daniel in her arms a few feet away. "Hey, Daisy."

Ellie smiled when she saw him. It was a genuine smile that reached her eyes, and it lit up something inside him.

He took Daisy's hand, walked over to Ellie. "You here for the fundraiser?"

She nodded. "I'm waiting for a table. We might have to go because the kids are pretty hungry, and there's a twenty-minute wait."

At that moment, Rain walked up and handed him a menu. "Hey, Jesse, the Team's back at the usual table. It looks like you've made a friend."

"This is Daisy, Ellie Meeks' little girl."

"Hey, sweetie."

"Can we get a couple of—I don't know—high chairs or whatever?"

Rain nodded. "You bet."

Jesse scooped Daisy up and headed toward the Team table. He glanced over at Ellie. "You coming?"

Everyone was here, several tables grouped together. The surprise on their faces when he walked up holding Daisy was priceless.

"Well, now I've seen everything," Megs said.

Hawke and Taylor got to their feet and said hello to Ellie.

Lexi waved. "Hey, Ellie."

Ellie said hello back, then explained for Jesse's benefit. "We know each other from high school. They were all in the same class as Dan."

"Oh. Right." Because everyone knew everyone, except Jesse, who after almost three years was still sometimes called "the new guy."

Rain walked up carrying two wooden high chairs. "Hey, Herrera, do you mind?"

"What?"

Jesse was more direct. "Move."

People scooted around the table to make room for them. Megs moved to a different seat entirely, opening up the spot next to Hawke. Jesse helped Ellie arrange the high chairs so that the twins could sit between them and so that he could sit beside Hawke. Only after they sat did he realize the disadvantage of this arrangement: He wasn't sitting next to Ellie.

Megs watched this with interest.

Jesse turned to her. "What?"

She got an innocent look on her face. "I just never thought I'd see you carrying a toddler. You must like her quite a lot—not the toddler, the mother."

Jesse ignored that and hoped that Ellie hadn't overheard. He hadn't come here to talk with Megs anyway. He turned to Hawke. "Hell of a day yesterday."

Hawke took a sip of scotch. "Yeah. You could say that."

"Ellie took care of the Kirby boy in the ER."

Hawke's gaze shifted to Ellie. "Yeah?"

"That's not something anyone should really know," Ellie whispered.

A server came to take people's orders. Jesse opted for a burger. Ellie wanted a salad for herself and chicken fingers, French fries and milk for the kids, plus crackers for them to munch on until the meal arrived.

Ellie glanced around the table. "So this is the famous Team."

"More like infamous," Conrad said.

While Ellie got into a conversation with Lexi about pregnancy, Jesse found himself talking with Hawke and Taylor and distracting hungry little Daniel with crackers.

"I guess if we need a babysitter, we'll call Moretti here," Taylor said.

This made everyone who'd heard Taylor laugh.

"Hey, laugh all you want. I babysat these two by myself yesterday."

Taylor stared at him. "No way!"

Ellie overheard this and came to his rescue. "He did a great job of it, too."

That shut them up.

The food had just arrived at the table, when the band fell silent and Caribou Joe—Joe Moffat, the pub's eccentric owner—got up on the stage and took the mic.

"I want to thank everyone for turning out tonight. Our town has suffered a terrible tragedy, and there are lots of families suffering this evening—families with kids who are still in the hospital, some still fighting for their lives. The Kirby family—Carrie and Jim—lost their firstborn, Tyler, who was only six. All of tonight's profits go to help with his funeral expenses. Anything above that will go into a fund to help cover hospital costs for the injured. There's also a two-gallon jar for donations at the bar. Let's fill it."

Cheers.

"I also want to thank this community's first responders. Eric Hawke—is he back there, hiding with the Team?"

Hawke looked startled at being singled out. He stood.

"Let's give a hand to Eric Hawke, our fire chief, and his crew at the firehouse. Our first responders did one hell of a job yesterday. They saved young lives. Their meals are on the house tonight."

More cheers.

Hawke waved, a tight smile on his face, then sat again.

"One last thing—for the love of God, don't drink and drive. You take your life into your hands and the lives of strangers, lives like little Tyler's, when you do. Thanks."

Jesse glanced over at Ellie to see tears on her cheeks.

Ellie traded places with Jesse so that she and Eric could talk more privately. She didn't know him well, but she could tell that Tyler's death had hit him hard. Eric's beautiful wife Victoria sat beside him, listening, her fingers twined with his.

"You did all the right things—large bore IVs opened wide, c-collar, ventilation, sterile dressing over his head wound. There was nothing more you or anyone could have done except go back in time and prevent that crash. He had massive internal organ damage, and we just couldn't get to all of it fast enough."

Eric seemed to take this in. "Must've been a hell of a day for the ER crew."

"It stretched our resources to the limit. I worked in pediatrics today, and we were busy." Ellie took a sip of her Coke, fighting her own emotions. "I'm hoping we'll use this as a way of revamping our response plans for mass-casualty events."

"I'd like to work with the hospital on that if I can. I'll give them a call, see if we can put something together with the sheriff's department and the ambulance services that responded. Maybe we can run through this and find ways to improve."

Ellie reached across the table, took Eric's hand in hers to comfort him just like she would anyone in her care who was grieving. "Please don't torture yourself. You guys did the very best you could for those kids. You saved lives. Tyler was beyond any of us."

It broke her heart to say it, but it was true.

A muscle clenched in Eric's jaw. "Thanks."

"How old are your twins?" Victoria asked.

"They'll be three in April." Ellie glanced over at the kids to find Jesse flying French fry airplanes covered with ketchup into Daniel's mouth.

"They're adorable."

Eric shook his head. "Don't go getting ideas."

"We agreed to wait for a few years, and I'm not changing that."

"Yeah?" Eric looked like he didn't believe his wife. "She and Lexi are best friends. As soon as that baby's here, I'm afraid Vickie is going to want one of her own."

Victoria laughed at this. "I will—eventually."

By now, Daisy had resorted to throwing French fries onto the floor—which meant that it was time to go.

Ellie took two wet wipes out of her handbag and cleaned the ketchup off the kids' fingers. "I need to get them home, bathed, and in bed. I work tomorrow. Did the server bring our checks?"

"I paid already," Jesse said.

Ellie stared at him. "You paid—for all three of us?"

"Yes, all three of you. You think I'd make the kids pay for themselves?"

She laughed. "Thank you. That was incredibly kind of you."

He shrugged it off. "It was nothing."

She leaned closer. "There's ketchup on your cheek."

"Oh. Yeah." He wiped it off. "Thanks."

She stood. "Nice to see you all."

"Nice to see you, too, Ellie," Hawke said. "Come around more often."

Ellie put the amount she'd planned to spend in the donation jar. Then Jesse helped her get the kids out to the car and into their car seats. For a moment they stood in the parking lot in awkward silence.

She reached out, took his hand. "Thanks for dinner. That's the second night you've fed the three of us."

He raised her hand to his lips, kissed it. "You're welcome."

"I'd invite you over, but I'm beat. I'm probably going to bed as soon as the kids are asleep." It was disappointing to have to admit it.

He nodded. "Yeah. I need to hit the sack early, too."

She stood on tiptoes and kissed him. "See you."

"Yeah." He turned and walked away.

She felt the pull of it, this parting, regret tugging at her. She turned toward him again just as he turned to face her, and they spoke at the same time.

"Maybe—"

"We could—"

They laughed.

"You first," he said.

"Maybe you could pop over an hour from now, and we could talk."

"I'd like that."

J esse finished brushing his teeth and stared at his reflection in the mirror.

What the hell are you doing?

God, he didn't know.

His life felt like it was spinning out of control, as if he was no longer in the driver's seat—which was absurd. No one was in control of his life but him. And yet...

In a period of two weeks, he'd helped Ellie get home, made out with her like a high school kid, babysat the twins, made her dinner, bought her dinner at Knockers. And now he was going to walk over just to talk.

Shit.

He didn't do relationships, especially not with kids in the picture.

If it quacks like a relationship and walks like a relationship...

Okay, so, this was starting to look a lot like a relationship. That's certainly what they'd left his fellow Team members thinking.

Maybe if he and Ellie had fucked that night, things would have stayed simple. They'd be living their own lives, hooking up a couple times a week to blow off sexual steam. He wouldn't be having nightmares or talking to his own fucking reflection in the bathroom mirror.

Get a grip.

He walked out of the bathroom, put on his snow boots, and grabbed his parka.

Maybe he was just horny and this desire to be with her was nothing more than lust. It had been a long time since he'd gotten laid, after all, and he had the same urges as any man. Then again, he'd never let the need for sex drive him. Repeated deployments meant that he was used to going long periods with just his right hand for company. It wasn't like he was going to come undone if he didn't get pussy.

Yeah, he wanted Ellie, but there was more to it than that. He enjoyed spending time with her, enjoyed listening to her voice, liked watching her interact with her kids. He admired her, too. She was smart, sweet, compassionate. He'd watched tonight when she'd spoken with Hawke and had seen the effect her words had had on him. She'd helped Hawke more than he ever could have.

Terra incognita.

Unknown territory.

That's what this was. He'd never been drawn to someone like this before, and a part of him was fucking scared to death. He had no plan of attack. There was no enemy. Or maybe there was. Maybe *he* was the enemy.

What are you going to do about it?

He could end this. He could call Ellie and explain that things had gotten out of hand. He could tell her that he was interested in sex, not a relationship. He could tell her that he'd be there for her as a neighbor but nothing else.

And then what?

She'd think he was an asshole, and she'd be right. Worse than that, it would make him a coward and a liar because he *did* want to be with her—and not just for sex.

He stepped outside into the dark and cold and walked through his
backyard down the mountain toward Ellie's house. Snow crunched under his
feet, the sky bright with icy stars, the golden light that spilled out from her
kitchen window drawing him.

She opened the door before he could knock. "Hey."

Jesse stared.

Jesus!

She stood there in nothing but a long nightgown of blue silk, its slender
straps baring her soft shoulders, her nipples making little points beneath the
fabric.

You're letting in cold air, idiot.

He stomped off the snow and stepped inside, then closed the door and
slipped out of his parka, still unable to take his gaze off her.

And then she was in his arms.

Chapter Eleven

Ellie kissed Jesse the way she'd been burning to kiss him, the way she'd fantasized about kissing him. His response was immediate, like a match hitting gasoline. He crushed her against him as he kissed her back, almost lifting her off the floor, ravishing her mouth with his.

God, yes.

She needed this, this raw male part of him, his strength, that hint of aggression he kept under such strict control.

Oh, he knew what he was doing. He sucked her lower lip into his mouth, traced the outline of her lips with his tongue, then claimed her mouth again, his scent an aphrodisiac, the hard feel of his body making her knees weak.

She slipped her arms around his neck and held on, molding her body to his.

One big hand cupped her breast, his thumb teasing her nipple through the silk of her nightgown, each flick heightening her arousal.

Hungry for him, she slid her hands beneath his shirt, drinking in the feel of him—soft skin, plains and ridges of muscle, the curls on his chest.

He backed her up against the table, jerked up her nightgown, and slipped a hand between her thighs, stroking her, sliding a finger inside her.

She moaned, the intrusion sweet.

It had been *so* long.

He moaned, too. "God, you're wet."

"I want you. *Now.*" She didn't want to wait. She couldn't wait. She'd already waited long enough for this—a lifetime it seemed.

"Impatient?" He lifted her off her feet, and sat her on the edge of the table—then dropped to his knees.

Her heart seemed to ricochet off her breastbone when she understood what he intended to do. "Oh, no, you don't have to do—"

"Don't distract me." He looked up at her, his eyes dark with lust. "I'm busy."

He pushed her thighs apart, and she watched his expression darken as his gaze fixed on her *there*, his brows drawing together. Then he parted her with his fingers and gave her a long … slow … lick.

Her head fell back, her hips giving an involuntary jerk, her fingers sliding into his thick hair.

"Mmm." Strong hands grasped her buttocks, dragged her closer to the table's edge, then his mouth closed over her.

Oh, God.

The hot shock of it made her gasp. She'd forgotten how good it felt to be taken by a man like this, one exquisite sensation after another shivering through her as he stroked her clit with his tongue, then drew her into the heat of his mouth and sucked.

Lost somewhere between bliss and oblivion, she lay back on the table, hands clenching into fists in his hair. "*Jesse.*"

Her breath came in moans now. God, she had missed this—the sweet ache, the urgency, the desperation. She was awash in desire, strung out on lust, lost somewhere between agony and bliss.

Then he pushed a finger inside her.

She came with a cry. "*Jesse!*"

Climax crashed through her, breaking the bars of the cage that had held her heart for so long, setting her free.

For a time—she couldn't say how long—she lay there, eyes closed, floating, her heartbeat gradually slowing.

She felt butterfly kisses on her inner thighs and opened her eyes to find him watching her, the intensity in his eyes sending a dark thrill through her.

He stood, holding her legs against his chest, and reached into his back pocket.

The condom.

He tore open the packet with his teeth, yanked down his jeans and boxer briefs, his erection straining toward her. She expected him to put on the condom and enter her, but he didn't. Instead, he slid two fingers inside her, stroking her, exploring her. "Can you feel how wet you are?"

She was still hypersensitive, the slick glide of his fingers both soothing and arousing. *"Yes."*

He found that magic spot inside her. "Do you like this?"

"Oh ... *yes.*"

He withdrew his fingers and stroked her moisture over the head of his cock, making himself slick with her essence, the act so erotic that it made her breath catch. Then, at last, he rolled on the condom.

He looked into her eyes. "Are you sure?"

He was truly asking her, giving her a chance to back out, to say no, to refuse him. But she wanted him. "Fuck me."

His gaze held hers as he entered her, his pupils going wide, his slow thrust making them both moan.

It had been so long since a man had been inside her, and it took a moment for her body to adjust to the thick, hard feel of him. But then he was moving, his hips thrusting, pushing his cock in and out of her, the sweet, slippery friction driving her crazy.

"God, you're tight." Big hands palmed her breasts, rubbing and pinching her nipples through the silk.

Needing him, wanting every inch of him, she drew her knees back, reached for him, her fingers digging into his lower back.

"God, yeah, open yourself to me, honey." His voice was rough, his face hard with the raw ache of sex.

He grasped her hips, drove into her faster, harder, each thrust bringing her closer to the bright edge of orgasm. Oh, God, the way he moved, so smooth, powerful, erotic, all that muscle in motion. He reached with one hand to stroke her clit. The combination felt *so* ... fucking ... good.

She was unraveling, coming undone, pleasure breaking her down. Little moans rolled from her throat with every exhalation, mixing with incoherent whispers. *"Jesse ... God ... Fuck ... Oh, yes..."*

Orgasm hit her with the force of a tidal wave, drowning her with more bliss than her body could contain. *"Jesse!"*

He wasn't far behind her. He pounded himself into her, then sucked in a breath and held it, his eyes squeezed shut as climax claimed him, the sexual anguish on his face relaxing into bliss.

Jesse stretched out in the big bed and drew Ellie into his arms, his body replete, his mind empty. They'd had sex again, this time in her bedroom, taking it slow, lingering over little details, the smallest pleasures.

She snuggled against him, her head resting on his shoulder, her fingers trailing through his chest hair. "Your heart is still pounding."

"So is yours."

There was sex a man forgot the moment it was over. There was sex he remembered. There was sex that blew his mind. Tonight had definitely been in the latter category, because … *damn.*

Her scent still filled his head, the taste of her lingering on his tongue, his mind and body shaken by the force of his response to her.

He kissed the top of her head. "I can't stay."

"I know."

Still, he couldn't get himself to leave her. He told himself that no one would want to climb out of a warm bed and hike uphill through the snow. But the truth was that he didn't want to leave *her.*

As they lay there together in the light of her bedside lamp, he began to notice things he hadn't when they were tearing each other's clothes off. The plush armchair in the corner. The photo of Ellie and Dan on their wedding day that hung on one wall. The pictures of the twins there on her nightstand. The portrait of Dan in his Ranger uniform that sat on her dresser.

She must have noticed the direction of his gaze. "Do the photos bother you?"

They did, though he couldn't say why. Seeing Dan's face again …

"He was your husband. He's Daisy and Daniel's father." That wasn't exactly an answer, but Jesse couldn't admit the truth—that seeing Dan's face left him feeling … what? Uneasy? Jealous?

You must be a special kind of asshole to be jealous of a dead man.

"Do you want to talk about this—about what happened tonight?"

He wanted to tell her there was nothing to talk about, that they were just neighbors who'd hooked up for sex. But when he opened his mouth, that's not what came out. "I'm not the man you think I am, Ellie."

"What kind of man do I think you are?"

"I'm not good with relationships or kids."

"You do a great job of faking it. I'll even give you extra points for the tiara." She raised her head and looked up at him. "Is this the part where you say, 'thanks for the sex,' and leave?"

That was more or less the gist.

"I just never imagined myself getting serious with anyone—or being a father, raising kids."

She rested her head on his shoulder again. "You get along well with the twins."

"I'm not saying that I don't like kids." Hell, he'd just fucked her senseless. She might as well know. "I grew up in a pretty screwed-up family. My dad wasn't really my dad. He married my mother when she was pregnant with me. He beat the shit out of me. I never found out who my real father was."

She turned onto her belly, her gaze soft with compassion. "God, Jesse, I'm so sorry. That must have been terrifying."

Yeah, but that wasn't the worst part. "My mother tried to protect me, but sometimes he beat her, too."

"Watching that must have made you feel so helpless."

"Yeah." How could he explain this? "I've always been afraid…"

"That you would be like him."

"Yeah."

She shifted in his arms, bringing her face even with his. "I'm a pretty good judge of people. Most nurses are. I don't think you have it in you to hurt women or children."

"I'm not a hero, Ellie."

She brushed her lips over his. "You might feel that way, but you're going to have a hard time convincing me of that. You're a combat veteran who saves lives for a living, shovels my sidewalk, watches my kids, and makes me scream."

He couldn't help but smile. "That last part is true."

It's a wonder she hadn't awoken the twins.

"It's all true." She settled into his arms again. "I'm okay with taking this one day at a time. Neither of us expected this to happen. Just promise me one thing."

"What's that?"

"Be honest with me."

That's what he'd been trying to do.

Jesse trudged uphill through the snow toward his cabin, fat flakes beginning to fall, a cold wind blowing from the northwest. Somehow, he'd fallen asleep, the alarm on his smartphone the only reason he wasn't still lying in bed beside Ellie. It had been hard to pull himself away from her—her warm body, all that feminine softness. For just a few minutes, he'd thought about calling in.

Hey, Matt, I was up most of the night fucking. Can I have the day off?

Yeah, no. That wouldn't go well.

Strangely, he wasn't tired. He felt energized, awake, alive. He'd told Ellie about his family. She hadn't shown him pity. She hadn't pulled away from him. She'd understood. She'd understood all of it.

Dan Meeks had married an incredible woman.

Jesse unlocked his door and stepped into his cold, dark cabin. He didn't have time for a shower, so he slipped into his warmest layers, put on his ski pants and parka, then made a lunch and headed to work, his mind full of Ellie. God, he could still smell her, her scent lingering on his skin, images of last night playing in his head. Ellie answering the door in that nightgown. Ellie lost in orgasm, pleasure dancing across her face. Ellie lying asleep beside him, eyelashes dark on her cheeks.

What the hell had he gotten himself into?

He didn't know, but he liked it.

He was so caught up in thinking about her that he almost missed the turn-off to the ski resort.

Get it together, jackass.

By the time he parked in the staff lot, the snow was coming down hard, wind creating near-blizzard conditions.

Inside the chalet, Matt was on the radio with someone from management. "We're looking at gusts of thirty to fifty miles an hour up here. Yeah. I don't think we have a choice."

Well, shit.

It took a hell of a lot of snow to shut a ski resort down, but wind was something else. Ski lifts couldn't operate safely in high winds. People could get blown out. Chairs could derail and fall, or swing into the support poles and crush someone. And a ski resort without operational lifts was a ski resort without skiers.

But that didn't mean it was going to be a slow day. Far from it.

At the morning huddle, Matt gave people their assignments, then added a word of caution. "We're seeing temps of minus forty with wind chill up at the top. Watch yourselves. Hypothermia is a sneaky son of a bitch. I don't want to lose anyone to the weather—not one of you and certainly not a guest."

With no lifts to carry them up the mountain, patrollers rode up on snowcats and snowmobiles. Jesse rode up to Eagle Ridge with Kevin and Ben and a load of explosives, snow swirling in the snowmobile's headlights, wind beating down on them. By the time they reached the top of the ridge, Jesse knew they were fucked.

He shouted to the others, wind biting into his face, the cold merciless. "We can't toss bombs. The wind will catch them. We'll blow ourselves up."

Jesse could tell Kevin wasn't happy.

E llie awoke to the beeping of her alarm at five. She stretched in the darkness, smiled to herself, and reached to feel the indentation Jesse had left on the pillow. He'd left behind other signs of his presence, too—his scent on the sheets and on her body, the salt and musk of sex in the air, the soreness between her thighs.

She crawled out of bed and walked naked to the bathroom, feeling as if she were floating on air. She stepped into the shower, her hands retracing the path his hands and mouth had taken last night, the memory turning her on.

She was no stranger to great sex. She and Dan had had a crazy, wonderful love life, cocooning when he was home on leave, trying to make up for lost time, screwing until they could barely walk straight. But last night with Jesse had been ...

Incredible was the only word that came to mind.

Jesse had been rough. He'd been tender. He'd overwhelmed her in the best possible way. How many times had she come? Four. No, *five*. It wasn't her record for one night, but it was only off by one. And she and Jesse barely knew one another. What would it be like once they'd been together for a while?

Don't lose your head over this.

She ignored that annoying voice. She wasn't a teenager. Jesse had been upfront with her. He'd told her that he wasn't good with relationships and had never planned to be a father. She'd heard him. If a week from now he ended it...

How will you feel then?

She would be fine. She would be better than fine. She knew something now that she hadn't known two weeks ago. She could *feel* again.

She woke the kids, got them ready to go, and drove through wind and four inches of new snow to drop them off at her parents' place.

Her mother answered the door. "There are my sleepy angels."

Ellie set the kids down just inside the door. "How's Claire?"

Her mother bent down to take off the kids' hats and coats. "I haven't heard anything since last night. She was in a fair amount of pain, but Cedar was taking good care of her. Haven't you called her yourself?"

"I went to the fundraiser at Knockers last night and got home late." Ellie omitted the fact that she'd spent the rest of the night having sex with her neighbor. "I'll call her on my lunch break if I get one. I'm in the ER today."

It was a slow day, slow enough that she was able to work on the SnowFest first-aid tent and spend a fair amount of time thinking about Jesse—his mouth between her thighs, his hands on her breasts, the expression on his face when he came.

"Don't distract me. I'm busy."

Good God!

You're at work, Nurse Meeks.

Scolded by her inner Nurse Ratched, Ellie sorted through the volunteer forms for the first-aid tent, matching them with the CPR certifications she'd received. She was missing only one—Jesse's. She'd left it at home on her kitchen counter.

They had a couple come in with their four-day-old baby. The poor little thing was crying and running a fever of 102.8. The doc on duty quickly diagnosed the cause—an infected circumcision. They gave him some IV fluids, piggy-backed antibiotics, and gave him oral medication for his pain and fever. Because he was so little, the doc admitted him. The mother, who was still recovering from giving birth, was clearly exhausted from being up all night.

Ellie did her best to support her. "The nurses will take good care of him. You should try to get some sleep."

Then it was lunchtime.

She walked down to the cafeteria, sat down with her salad, and called Claire. "Hey, sis. How are you feeling?"

"Better than last night, or maybe the Percocet is working. I can tell you already that I don't like walking on crutches or having my mobility limited."

They talked for a while about the surgeon's prognosis and the physical therapy regimen Claire would be starting in six weeks.

Then Ellie couldn't hold it back any longer. "Guess what I was doing last night—or maybe I should say *whom*."

There was a moment of silence—and then Claire squealed. The sound pierced Ellie's eardrum. She jerked the phone away from her ear.

"Oh, my God! You were with Jesse, weren't you?"

"Yes." Ellie had no sooner said this than she got a page from the ER. "I need to go, Claire. We've got an ambo coming in."

"What? Oh, no you don't! You can't call me, tell me you slept with a super-hot guy, and then hang up on me."

Ellie laughed, but the situation was serious. "I'll call later. Love you. Feel better."

She hurried from the cafeteria to the stairs and down to the ER.

"We've got two injured parties coming in—shrapnel wounds. Apparently, there was an explosives accident up at the ski resort."

Ellie's heart gave a hard knock.

Explosives accident at Scarlet Mountain Resort?

Handling explosives was Jesse's job.

Chapter Twelve

"Can't you turn the siren off?" Jesse called up to Chloe Rivas, who was driving. They were making a big fucking deal out of nothing. "No one's dying here."

Hawke, who'd ridden up with the ambulance when he'd heard the call, pressed sterile gauze against the cut in Jesse's forehead, his hands in sterile gloves. "We like the sirens. They make us feel important."

He gave Chloe a nod, and she cut the noise makers.

Jesse looked over at Ben, who lay on the gurney, still pale as a sheet, an IV running wide open in his arm. "You hanging in there, buddy?"

"I'd be dead now if it weren't for you."

"Yep." Jesse wasn't going to sugar coat it for him.

The kid had fucked up, nearly killing them both.

They'd gone back to Eagle Ridge when the wind had died down to toss a few bombs. Jesse had thrown his on the count of three, as they usually did. He'd started to ski away. "Fire in the hole!"

But Ben had stood there, live charge still in his hands.

"What the fuck are you doing?"

"The fuse went out."

Jesse had reacted on instinct. He'd grabbed the charge out of Ben's hands and hurled it as hard as he could, throwing himself on top of Ben, knocking him to the ground, and covering his own ears.

BOOM!

The blast wave had shaken the ground beneath them, the negative air pressure making Jesse's eardrums pop, hot shrapnel from the canister slicing through his ski pants and parka and striking him in the forehead. For a moment he'd laid there, stunned.

Kevin had radioed for a rescue. Jesse had sat up, blood streaming down his face, and started first aid. From there it had become a circus.

A helicopter. A ride down to the lodge. Every patroller at the resort standing around looking like someone had died. Half a dozen Team members in the parking lot ready to help with a rescue. Ben babbling and bleeding and in shock.

Fuck.

Jesse had insisted he could drive himself and Ben to the ER, but Matt, worried about possible concussion or internal injuries from the blast, had insisted on an ambulance. And here they were.

Hawke leaned in and examined the laceration on his forehead. "Looks like you've got some debris stuck in there. You need stitches."

"Yeah?" Jesse didn't know how to say it without sounding like an asshole, but he'd seen much, much worse. "I can do this myself, you know."

"No headache or dizziness?" Hawke asked.

"For the fifth time, no."

"Anyone ever tell you that you're grumpy when you're bleeding?"

They pulled into the ambulance bay and stopped, and Jesse caught a glimpse of a team in green scrubs waiting for them.

Ellie.

The doors opened, and there she was. Her gaze met Jesse's, emotion in her green eyes. Had she been worried?

Okay, so maybe there was an upside to being fussed over like this.

The other EMT whose name Jesse didn't know jumped out and pulled Ben's gurney out of the ambulance. "Shock and lacerations."

Ellie walked alongside Ben's gurney, glancing over her shoulder at Jesse as she walked through the automatic doors.

Lucky bastard.

Hawke held Jesse back. "I think they're bringing a wheelchair."

"I don't need a wheelchair, for fuck's sake." Jesse grabbed the gauze out of Hawke's hand and stepped to the ground, still in his ski boots, doing his best to maintain direct pressure.

He tromped inside, passing the person with the wheelchair, Hawke following along beside him.

"Where do you want this one?" Hawke called out. "He's a pain in the ass."

"Put him there." Ellie pointed to the bed next to Ben, her expression serious. "If he gives you any guff, call security."

"You got it." Hawke grinned. "Hear that, tough guy? Get in the nice bed, or I'm calling security."

Ellie took Jesse's vitals again. Blood pressure, pulse, blood oxygen, temperature—they were all normal for an extreme athlete. She wrote down the results, stuck the pen and paper in her pocket and poked at the laceration on his forehead with a gloved finger. "Are you feeling numb yet?"

The doc had spread lidocaine gel on it about thirty minutes ago. They were going to have to clean the wound before they sutured it.

"A little." Jesse sat up in the bed wearing only his boxer briefs, looking far too sexy for a patient in the ER, a sheet drawn casually across his lap.

They had already cleaned the dozen or so small lacerations on his back, his legs, and the back of his head. None of those had required stitches. But the laceration on his forehead was jagged and deep.

Ben, the other ski patroller, had already told her what had happened, breaking down in tears while she'd cleaned him up. His story had left a sick feeling in Ellie's stomach. Jesse had come close to being killed today.

The logical part of her brain, the one that was helping her maintain a professional demeanor, kept reminding her that Jesse was fine, that he'd saved not only his own life, but Ben's too. Still, something inside her couldn't shake a sense of panic.

"We'll let the lidocaine sit a little longer." She turned to walk back to the nurse's station, but he caught her arm.

"Hey, are you okay?"

"*No*," she whispered. "You were almost killed."

He brought her hand to his lips, kissed it. "Just one of the risks of the job."

She yanked her hand away. "Getting blown up is a risk of your job? Well, then, I hate your job."

Perilously close to tears, she turned and walked into a nearby conference room, shut the door, and leaned back against it, taking deep slow breaths.

The door opened, and Jesse stepped inside, long underwear drawn over his boxer briefs. "Hey, come here."

She knew this wasn't the time or the place for personal feelings, but when he reached for her, she went to him.

He drew her against his bare chest, one big hand stroking her hair. "It's okay. It was just a freak accident. It won't happen again—not on my watch."

She fought not to cry, knowing that she shouldn't be here with him like this. "You're supposed to be in your exam bed. Patients can't just run around hugging nurses."

"Shhh."

For a few minutes, he held her, strong arms enfolding her, his familiar scent and the warmth of his skin reassuring.

"I should get out there." She pulled away. "I'm on the clock. I can't be getting emotional like this."

He searched her face, running his thumb over her cheekbone. "It's okay."

She narrowed her eyes, glared at him. "Next time you try to tell me you're not a hero, I'm going to throw this in your face."

He chuckled. "Okay. That seems fair."

"Now get back in bed. Doctor Warren is going to be here to clean that out and stitch you up soon."

"I could do that myself, you know."

"This isn't Iraq where you have to fix everything with duct tape. Get back in bed before you get me in trouble."

"Yes, ma'am."

"I didn't think the fuse was lit," Ben told Julia Marcs, a sheriff's deputy. "I didn't see any smoke. I thought it had gone out."

Jesse offered the only explanation he had. "Must have been the angle of the light."

"You saw the smoke?" Deputy Marcs was conducting the official investigation on behalf of the sheriff's department.

Jesse nodded. "Yeah, I did."

Both he and Ben were waiting to be discharged, a process that seemed to take longer than stitching his head back together.

"What happened then?"

"I didn't have time to do anything but react. I skied over to him, grabbed it and threw it. I knew we didn't have enough time to get away, so I knocked Ben to the ground, hoping the blast wave wouldn't catch us."

"It could have blown your hand off." Ben was still coming to grips with what had happened. "It could have killed you."

Jesse didn't mince words. "If it had gone off in your hand or mine, it would have killed both of us. No question."

Across from the little room where Deputy Marcs was interviewing them, Ellie was still busy. A woman had come in with a migraine. A middle-aged man had arrived in an ambulance having chest pain. Then a homeless man had been brought in by Scarlet PD, who'd found him outside Food Mart suffering from hypothermia.

A part of Jesse liked watching her work. She was good at her job—professional, compassionate, skilled. Every once in a while, she looked over at him, and he could see in her eyes that she was still upset.

Yeah, she was still upset. He got that. He just didn't understand why—not when everything had turned out all right in the end.

"You say you just reacted?"

It took Jesse a moment to realize Deputy Marcs had asked him a question. "There wasn't time for anything else."

"How long have you been working with explosives?"

"Well, ten years in the Rangers, plus a couple of years at the resort."

Marcs stopped writing and looked up. "You were an Army Ranger?"

"Ten years of sustained combat ops with the Seventy-Fifth Ranger Regiment."

Deputy Marcs closed her notebook and stood. "That experience came in handy today. I'm glad that I'm talking to you instead of waiting for the coroner's report."

Ben looked like he wanted to puke.

Ten minutes later, Jesse got his discharge papers. Ellie went through the instructions with him line by line and then had him sign. He was free to go.

He stepped into his ski boots and found himself wondering what the fuck he was supposed to do now. Ben, who was still shaken, caught a ride home with a roommate. But Jesse's vehicle was still parked up at the ski resort.

He tromped across town to The Cave—a ten-minute walk in ski boots.

Megs sat in the ops room doing paperwork. She looked at his boots and pointed west. "The lift line is that way."

"Funny." He glanced around, hoping to see Hawke or Taylor or one of the other guys. "Anyone around who can give me a ride back up to the resort?"

"Belcourt's in the back. You might be able to bribe him."

Jesse started to go, then remembered. "Hey, can I borrow one of the UTVs for SnowFest? I'm volunteering for the first-aid tent, and they need a way to cover the event grounds in case someone needs transport."

"Fine with me. Fill out the paperwork."

"Thanks." He headed for the door to the bay.

"Hey, Moretti, good job up there today. I'm not sure what we would do without you." For Megs, it was an emotional outburst.

"Thanks."

Jesse found Belcourt sharpening the spikes on crampons—a tedious but necessary chore. "Hey, man, can you give me a ride up to the resort?"

"Sure thing." Belcourt's gaze took in the bandage on Jesse's forehead and the ski boots on his feet. "You look good for a man who got blown up."

Jesse filled Belcourt in on what had happened as they walked out to the parking lot and climbed into Belcourt's beat-up, piece-of-shit Ford.

They were about ten minutes up the road when Jesse just had to ask. "Do you understand women?"

Belcourt looked surprised by the question. "Do I understand women? That's like asking me if I understand the wind. Why? You having problems?"

"No. Kind of. Okay, yes."

Belcourt waited for him to go on.

"There's a woman I'm kind of seeing."

"The woman with the twins who came to Knockers?"

"Yeah." Jesse had forgotten that most of the Team had already seen him with Ellie. "She's a nurse. She was working in the ER when I was brought in. Rather than being happy I'm not dead or injured, she seems angry. She told me she hates my job."

Belcourt nodded, a thoughtful frown on his face. It took him a full two minutes to say anything. "I got into a car accident late one night when I was sixteen. When I got home, my granny hugged me and then started yelling. I think she was just scared at the thought of me getting hurt. People show love in strange ways."

And damned if adrenaline didn't shoot through Jesse's bloodstream. "Wait, wait, wait. Nah, man, it's not like that. We've only just connected. I've known her for only two weeks. We probably haven't even spent twenty-four hours together."

He waited for Belcourt to say something. Instead, Belcourt glanced over at him with that "I have spoken, and it is so" look on his face.

"I shouldn't have asked you."

That made Belcourt grin. "Ellie Meeks—she's a widow, right?"

"Yeah. Her husband was a Black Hawk pilot. He was killed in Iraq."

Belcourt nodded but said nothing.

And then it clicked.

Ellie had lost her husband, and the first man she'd hooked up with since then, the first man she'd trusted, had almost been killed on the job today.

Moretti, you idiot.

Ellie stopped at the grocery store on her way home. It had been an exhausting and irritating day. If it had been up to her, she would spend the rest of the night soaking in a hot tub and sipping wine in front of Netflix, trying to forget the world—and the fact that Jesse had almost been killed today.

He acted like it was no big deal, but it was.

Why did some men find it necessary to take risks? Dan had already been an army helicopter pilot by the time she'd gotten together with him, but why had he fought so hard to make it into the 160th? There were other important jobs he might have done. When she'd asked him, pleading with him to do something less dangerous, he'd told her that someone needed to do this job, and it might as well be him.

She had appreciated his sense of duty, but it had cost him his life. She'd lost her husband, and Daniel and Daisy had lost their father.

To hell with that.

Not wanting to cook, she grabbed a roast chicken and some mashed potatoes from the deli, then picked a few other things she needed—diapers, wipes, toothpaste, milk. She was about to head to the checkout lane when she decided she needed something else.

Condoms.

She made her way to the aisle near the pharmacy and stared at the selection. It had been a decade since she'd bought condoms—maybe longer—and the selection had definitely changed. She had no idea what Jesse would prefer—ribbed, extra lubricated, deep grooved, flavored, spiral pleasures. What the hell did that even mean?

"Good grief." She grabbed a variety pack and tossed it into her cart.

A voice came from behind her. "Ellie."

Ellie turned to find her father standing there with a basket on his arm. "Dad."

Oh, God.

Her father looked into her cart, saw the box of condoms. "I won't ask."

"I won't tell." She pushed her cart down the aisle, her cheeks blazing.

But life wasn't finished humiliating her.

Rose came up behind her in the checkout lane. "It was a boy."

A boy?

"Oh! Yes." Rose was talking about the birth she'd attended. "Wonderful."

Rose's gaze landed on the condoms in her cart, her face brightening. "Oh, Ellie. I'm so glad you're moving forward. It's time."

The temper Ellie had held in check all day exploded. "Oh, for God's sake! Can't a woman buy condoms without half the town commenting on it?"

A hush fell over the store.

Only then did she realize she had shouted the words.

E llie drove to her parents' house, picked up the kids without staying to talk and drove home, wishing the earth would swallow her whole. Or maybe she could just go back in time and stick a sock in her mouth. Or perhaps she should pack up the kids in the car and drive to Timbuktu.

Now word would be all over Scarlet that Ellie Meeks had met a man, and soon they would figure out who that man was. They would have opinions, of course, just as they'd had when she and Dan had gotten together.

"You can do better than that. Your father is a doctor."

"Why marry a soldier? He'll never be home."

"You're going to spend a lot of time alone."

To hell with all of them.

Ellie changed into jeans and a T-shirt, then went about getting dinner ready. She steamed some green beans to go with the roast chicken and mashed potatoes and set the food on the table. She did her best to focus on the kids throughout the meal. They were what mattered, not what Rose or anyone else in Scarlet thought of her.

She'd just gotten the kids out of the tub and into their pajamas when Claire called.

"I heard you bought condoms." Her sister sounded amused.

"Oh, God." Had it gotten around town already? "Who told you?"

"Mom. She heard it from Dad, who says he caught you in the act. He also heard you shout at Rose." This made Claire laugh. "I would've paid money to see that."

But Ellie wasn't laughing. "Today was awful."

"Oh, come on. It's not all that bad."

But Claire didn't know.

Ellie told her about the accident at the ski area and how Jesse had come within a couple of seconds of being killed. "If he hadn't reacted so quickly, he would have been blown to bits."

"God, Ellie, how scary."

Ellie had followed the kids into their playroom. She leaned against the wall and sank to the floor, her throat going tight, panic rising inside her, words she'd held back all afternoon spilling out of her. "I can't do this, Claire. I can't. I can't be with another man who goes and gets himself killed."

"That's not going to happen this time." Claire sounded so certain.

"It almost happened today."

"I know."

While the kids played, Ellie told Claire about last night, finding creative ways to talk about S-E-X. Then she told Claire how afraid she'd been when she'd heard there'd been an explosion at the ski area. Claire listened and sympathized, talking Ellie down the way she'd done in the weeks and months after Dan had died.

By the time the conversation drew to a close almost an hour later, Ellie was laughing again. "You should have seen Rose's face."

Claire laughed, too. "I wish I had."

When she ended the call, Ellie's panic was gone. She read the kids a bedtime story, tucked them in, and went to pour herself a glass of wine.

She'd just pulled the cork out of the bottle when a knock came at her back door, making her jump.

Jesse.

He stood on her back deck with wet hair, his face clean shaven, the gash on his forehead hidden behind a bandage.

She opened the door. "Hey."

"Hey." He stomped the snow off his boots and stepped inside, shutting the door behind him. "I just wanted to say I'm sorry for putting you through that today."

"You shouldn't apologize. It wasn't your fault." Then she stepped into his embrace. "Oh, Jesse."

Chapter Thirteen

Jesse held her, all the stresses of the day seeming to melt away. She felt fragile in his arms, sweet and soft. "Are you okay?"

"Am *I* okay?" She gave a little laugh and leaned back to look up at him, a vulnerability in her eyes that tugged at him. "You're the one who almost got blown up and had to have stitches."

He took her face between his hands. "I know that what happened today scared you. You don't have to pretend with me."

Her gaze searched his, a pleading look in her eyes. "Why do you have to work with explosives? Why can't someone else do that job?"

"I'm good at it, Ellie. I'm the reason two people didn't die today."

"I have no right to question your life. I'm sorry." She drew away from him, clearly still unhappy. "Would you like a glass of wine?"

He let it go. "After today, I'll take some of that scotch you mentioned."

She opened a cupboard and was about to scoot a stepping stool over so that she could reach the amber bottle.

"I've got it." Jesse reached over the top of her head, took the bottle down from the shelf, and read the label. "Old Pulteney twenty-one. You know your scotch. This stuff is expensive. Are you sure you want me drinking it?"

"That's what it's for." She handed him a tumbler, a sad smile on her lips. "It was Dan's favorite. I hope you enjoy it."

Jesse was touched that she would share it with him. He poured out the equivalent of two shots, capped the bottle, and put it back in the cupboard. He took a sip, the taste exploding across his tongue. "*Mmm.* Damn."

They sat together on the sofa, Ellie leaning back against his chest.

"It can't have been fun to take a shower," she said.

It hadn't been. The water had stung every nick and cut, but it had felt good to wash away the blood and reek of pentolite.

"I've dealt with worse." He kissed her hair, trailing his fingers up and down her arm. "How was the rest of your day?"

She gave a little moan. "You don't want to know."

"I think I do."

By the time she finished telling him what had happened at Food Mart, he was clenching his jaw and holding his breath in the effort not to laugh.

"Everyone in the store heard me. I wanted to die. You're laughing."

"No." He coughed, choked. "Does this mean I can expect your dad to show up at my door with a shotgun?"

She craned her head to look up at him. "How could he know you're the one?"

He smoothed the hair from her cheek. "Half the town saw us together at Knockers, remember?"

"Oh, right. God, I'm sorry."

"Hey, don't apologize. People can gossip all they want. Actually, I find the whole thing kind of sweet."

"Sweet?"

"Yeah." He nuzzled her ear, nipped her earlobe, and felt her shiver. "It means you were thinking of me today, just like I was thinking of you."

She smiled at this, her eyes drifting shut. "I guess it does."

He found the side of her throat, licked that sensitive spot just below her ear, then kissed her, his lips brushing over the flutter of her pulse.

She let her head fall to the side, the wine glass tilting in her hand.

He took the glass from her and set it down on the coffee table. "Come."

He helped her to her feet, then scooped her into his arms.

She gave a little gasp and grabbed onto him, her arms sliding behind his neck.

He kissed her forehead. "I'm not going to drop you."

He carried her down the dark hallway to her bedroom, then lowered her to her bed and stretched himself out above her.

Everything else faded from his world as he kissed her, nothing in his mind but Ellie—her scent, her taste, the softness of her skin. He peeled off her T-shirt, unhooked her bra, then sat up and tore off his own shirt. For a moment, he stayed upright like that, letting her play, watching while the feel of his chest and abdomen turned her on.

It turned him on, too, the arousal on her face making him rock hard, his resolve not to rush this time fading fast. He reached down and cupped both of her breasts, teasing her nipples with his thumbs, watching as they puckered at his touch. Unable to stop himself, he caught her wrists in his hands, stretched her arms above her head, and lowered his mouth to taste her.

He teased first one tight crest and then the other, flicking them with his tongue, tugging on them with his lips, sucking them into his mouth.

She writhed beneath him, her eyes shut, little moans rolling from her throat with each exhalation.

He released her wrists and kissed his way down her belly to the waistband of her jeans. "These have to go."

"*Yes.*" She wriggled out of her jeans and then her panties.

He yanked them over her ankles, tossed them aside, then made short work of his jeans and boxer briefs. Naked now, he let himself feast on the sight of her.

She tensed, her hands moving to shield her lower belly. She'd done that last night, too. He'd noticed but hadn't said anything.

He stretched out beside her again, slipped his hands beneath hers, tracing her C-section scar with his fingers. "You're beautiful, Ellie. You don't have to hide anything from me."

And then it struck him.

No other man had seen her scar and her stretch marks, not even the man who had caused them.

The thought brought a hitch to his chest.

"Your scar is a warrior mark." He repositioned himself, kissed his way along the thin silver scar, wanting her to know that it didn't bother him. What kind of shitheel could be bothered by something like that? "I have scars, too."

And then he couldn't resist, his hand finding its way between her thighs, exploring the hidden treasures there. But it wasn't enough. Drawn by her scent, he knelt at the side of the bed, pushed her thighs apart, and let himself feast.

Her fingers curled in his hair. "Oh, fuck, yes."

She had a dirty mouth when she was turned on, but Jesse liked it. He loved seeing her on the edge and knowing he was the one who'd put her there.

He gave her no quarter, taking what he wanted, her scent filling his head. He suckled her clit, penetrated her with his fingers, her cries growing more frantic, her breathing ragged, her thighs trembling.

"*Jesse!*" She arched off the bed, pleasure shuddering through her as she came, her pussy contracting around his fingers.

He waited for her climax to pass, watched the tension leave her. Then he kissed his way up her body and straddled her. "So where are these condoms?"

Eyes still closed, she pointed toward her nightstand.

He found the box—a variety pack. He read them off. "Extra Lubricated. Well, we don't need that. Ribbed. Deep Grooved. Chocolate. Spiral Pleasures. Do you have a preference?"

She opened her eyes, took hold of his cock, stroked him. "Fuck me."

"Yeah." *Jesus.* He grabbed one of the ribbed ones, tore it open.

She took it from him and rolled it onto his length, then got onto her hands and knees, looking back at him over her shoulder, her bare, beautiful ass wiggling back and forth in blatant invitation.

Holy fuck.

He grasped her hips with his hands and nudged himself inside her, the two of them moaning in unison. "God, Ellie."

Determined to last, he started slow, pacing himself, moving in and out of her in an easy rhythm. She felt so incredibly good, and it just kept getting better, her slick pussy gripping him like a fist. He reached out, brushed the hair away from her face so he could watch the effect he had on her. Her eyes were shut, her lips parted, her breath coming in erotic little moans.

He bent down and pressed kisses to her spine, reaching around with one hand to stroke her swollen clit. He couldn't remember ever wanting a woman like this. He was burning for her, burning up inside her, orgasm building at the base of his spine.

He was pounding into her now, her gorgeous ass bouncing with every thrust, her hands fisting in the sheets.

"Ooh... Fuck, yeah... Jesse... *God.*" Her breath broke on a cry, and she arched, her inner muscles clenching around him as she came.

He kept up the pace until her climax had passed. Then he let himself go, grasping her hips and driving himself into her until bliss carried him away.

Ellie lay in the darkness of her bedroom, her head resting on Jesse's chest, her body languid. "What have you done to me?"

He kissed her hair. "I was going to ask you the same thing."

Ellie was deep in a dreamless sleep when the sound of crying woke her. It woke Jesse, too. "What's wrong?"

"She probably just had a bad dream." Ellie had just started to get out of bed when Daisy ran into the bedroom and scrambled up into the bed.

"Mama!"

Jesse sat up, clutching the sheet to his chest, looking like he might bolt.

Ellie fought not to laugh. "Don't worry. She's too little to understand anything."

Daisy crawled into the nonexistent space between Ellie and Jesse, tears on her cheeks, apparently unfazed by his presence in the bed.

"Hey, sweetie, what's wrong? Are you scared?"

Daisy nodded but didn't say, either because she wasn't sure or because she didn't have the words to explain.

"It's okay, baby girl. You're okay." Ellie held her daughter, glancing over at Jesse, who had turned onto his side, one hand still holding fast to the sheet.

Daisy turned her head to look at him. "Jesse seepy?"

Jesse's lips quirked in an amused grin. "I'm sleepy, too."

"Come here, honey. Just close your eyes." Ellie cradled Daisy's head against her bare breast, kissed her forehead and hummed her favorite lullaby. *"As I was a-walking for my recreation/A-down by the gardens I silently strayed."*

Ellie glanced over to find Jesse watching her, a mix of gentleness and intensity in his gaze. He reached out, lifted a strand of hair from her cheek, the tenderness of the gesture reminding her of the way he'd kissed her C-section scar and stretch marks. She'd gotten tears in her eyes then, tears she'd hidden from him, afraid she'd spoil the mood.

"The blackbirds and thrushes sang in the green bushes/The wood doves and larks seemed to mourn for the maid."

Daisy's eyes were closed, her little face relaxed.

Ellie hummed for a minute or two longer, then stopped. She sat, scooped Daisy into her arms, and carried her back to her bed, staying with her for a few minutes just to make sure she was truly asleep.

She walked back to the bedroom to find Jesse already wearing his jeans and pulling his T-shirt over his head.

She felt a stab of disappointment. "You're leaving?"

"It's almost four."

"Already?" How could that be?

"The night flies when you're having fun."

"I'm sorry she woke you. I hope that didn't make you too uncomfortable." He'd probably never sleep over again.

"Hey, don't apologize." He closed the space between them, drew Ellie into his arms. "It just took me by surprise. I've never been in bed with a naked woman and her toddler before."

When he put it like that...

"So that means Daisy hasn't scared you away, that I'll see you again?"

His hands slid down her back to pat her bare ass. "Damned straight."

She slipped into her bathrobe and followed him down the hallway, smiling to herself when he stopped to glance in Daniel's and Daisy's bedrooms.

"They're so ... little and helpless," he whispered.

They turned and walked toward the kitchen together.

"If you think they're little and helpless now, you should have seen them when they were born. They were just over six pounds each."

He shook his head as if this were crazy. Then he stopped and turned toward her, reaching down to rest one big hand on her lower abdomen. "That means you were carrying more than twelve pounds of baby in there."

There was an intimacy to this, to sharing memories of her pregnancy with him. "It got pretty uncomfortable toward the end. I looked like an elephant."

"I bet you had a cute waddle."

They finished the short walk to the back door, Ellie watching while he put on his boots and slipped into his parka. "I wish you didn't have to go. I wish neither of us had to work today. I can't believe they expect you to work after what happened yesterday."

"Ben was rattled and needs the day off. They can't afford to be down two patrollers on a Sunday. But, hey, I have an idea. Why don't you pack up the kids and come up to Cimarron Ranch with me on Wednesday?"

"The Cimarron?"

"You've heard of it?"

"Who hasn't?" The West family were among the biggest landowners in the state and ran cattle on their ranch. They also bred champion quarter horses. "What are you doing up there?"

"Nate West and I are partnering for the skijoring race."

Of course, they were, because if there was some crazy way to get killed, Jesse was in. "I don't want to watch you break your neck."

"I'm not going to break my neck. I promise. I bet the kids would like to see the horses."

"I'm sure they would." She took hold of the front of his parka. "Please be careful up on the mountain today."

"You know it." He slipped an arm around her, kissed her.

Then she remembered.

"I have something for you." She pulled away, retrieved her extra key from the drawer, and held it out for him. "In case you need it."

He took it from her then tucked it in his pocket. "Thanks. See you tonight."

Then he turned, opened the back door, and disappeared into the darkness.

"Let me get this straight. You want me and Cedar to come sleep at your house Tuesday night so that you can stay over at Jesse's place?"

Keeping her voice down, Ellie told Claire how Daisy had come into the bedroom, waking them up and making Jesse uncomfortable. "I just want an uninterrupted night with him. You can come over at nine after the kids are asleep, watch TV, have some wine, and then just sleep in my bed. I'll be only a few minutes away if you need anything. I'll come back early in the morning so you can get home and get to work."

She'd been assigned to the ER again today. The only patient was down the hallway getting X-rays for a possible wrist fracture, giving her just a few free minutes.

"You do remember that I'm on crutches, right?"

"Yes, but you won't have to chase the twins around." Ellie lowered her voice to a whisper. "You can be on crutches at your house, or you can be on crutches at my house so that I can get laid."

"But you've gotten laid. You've gotten laid more than I have this week."

"Please, Claire."

"Let me talk to Cedar. It's a long commute down the canyon. I don't want to make problems for him at work. And you'll have to put clean sheets on your bed. I'm not sleeping in your sex funk."

"Of course I'll put clean sheets on the bed." Ellie glanced up from the nurse's station and saw Pauline walking her way. "I really appreciate your volunteering to help unload the supplies. It would be a big job without you."

"What? Ellie—"

"Thanks for calling." Ellie ended the call. "Hey, Pauline."

"I saw the supplies for the first-aid tent have arrived."

"I hope to get time this afternoon to do an inventory." She wanted to make sure everything she'd ordered was there.

"If you can't get it done today, you can always come in on one of your days off."

That crossed a line.

Outside of emergencies, Ellie refused to let the hospital chip away at her time with her kids. She was their only parent, and she wouldn't let them grow up without her. "I'm happy to volunteer free time from home, but I will not bring the twins to the hospital."

Pauline's smile went tight. "I'm sure you'll work it out."

Damned straight she would.

When it was time for her lunch break, she grabbed the supply list and went down to the loading dock. She'd never been down here before, so she had to ask one of the janitors for help finding the right room. She opened the door, stopped, and stared, her heart sinking.

How was she supposed to inventory this?

The supplies weren't organized or sitting in neat piles. Everything was stacked chest-high on three large pallets and wrapped tightly in plastic. It would take Ellie hours to break the stacks down, separate everything, do an inventory, and load up the pallets again. There was no way she could do this on her lunch break.

Pauline had said to delegate, but who had time for this? Every single person who'd signed up to volunteer had jobs. Most had families. She couldn't just dump this mess in someone else's lap.

Her cell phone buzzed.

A text from Jesse. He'd sent a photo.

She clicked, her pulse skipping at the sight of his face. It was a selfie of him riding the chair lift, a big smile on his face. A text message followed.

SITREP: IT'S AFTERNOON, AND I'M STILL ALIVE. HOW'S YOUR DAY?

Her heart melted.

She typed back.

I'M GLAD YOU'RE IN ONE PIECE.

She told him about the inventory issue and how it was all stacked high and wrapped in plastic and how she was going to have to come in on a day off this week to get it done in time.

I HAVE AN IDEA. HANG ON...

She waited for another message, but nothing came. Figuring he'd gotten caught up in something on the job, she headed back up to the ER. She'd just reached the nurse's station with her lunch when her phone rang, the number unknown.

"Hey, Ellie. It's Megs. Jesse tells me you've got a shitload of medical supplies that need to be inventoried before SnowFest this weekend."

"That's true."

"If you tell me what time we should be there, I'll ask for volunteers to come and help. I have an army of them, and they're always trying to suck up and get on my good side. And, honey, we do inventory like nobody's business."

Chapter Fourteen

Jesse had just started his end-of-day sweeps when he got a page from Megs. He slid to a stop and scrolled through it.

MORETTI'S GF NEEDS HELP WITH INVENTORY OF SUPPLIES FOR SNOWFEST. MEET AT 1800 HRS AT HOSPITAL LOADING DOCK.

Moretti's girlfriend?

That should have bugged Jesse, but it didn't. What else could he call Ellie? She wasn't just his neighbor. They'd fucked each other's brains out. They'd slept together—actually slept—in her bed. He'd watched her sing her little girl to sleep, and it had melted his heart, the image of Daisy snuggling against Ellie's breast burned into his memory. It was the purest expression of femininity he'd ever seen.

You're falling for her—falling hard.

Nah, man, that was crazy. No way. He'd only known her for two weeks.

In that time, you've gone from never having spoken with her to having the key to her house. What does that tell you?

So he liked her. He liked her a lot. But falling in love? No.

He shoved the pager into his pocket and pointed the tips of his skis downhill, determined to put her out of his mind for a while.

But what if he *was* falling for her? Shouldn't he do something to stop himself?

Yeah? Like what?

He could end it. He could return Ellie's key. He could tell her it was just sex.

But it wasn't just sex. It had never been just sex—not with Ellie. And why would he want to end it when being with her made him feel … happy?

And he *was* happy when he was with her. Here he was skiing by himself through some of the most beautiful terrain on the planet, and all he could think about was Ellie. And the worst part was that he was okay with this. He was smiling about it, grinning ear to ear. Because *that* is what she did to him.

You're hopeless, Moretti.

He spotted a couple of snowboarders about to drop into an out-of-bounds shoot on the other side of the orange plastic security fence. "Idiots."

Did they *want* to die in an avalanche?

He skied through a gap someone had cut in the fence. The two were smoking a joint, so they didn't see him coming up behind them until he slid to a stop. "Don't even think about it."

He confiscated their pot and their season passes and asked whether they had cut the fence—a crime.

"No, man, it was already like that," said the taller of the two. "That's why we crossed. We figured maybe it was okay."

"You figured wrong." He skied with them down the slope, ignoring their whining and yammering and all the names they called him.

"Bastard fuck."

"Loser."

"Pencil prick."

When they reached the lodge, he held up their passes. "You can pick these up at the main office in two weeks—unless we catch you breaking in or skiing out of bounds in the meantime. If that happens, you're out for the season. And leave the weed at home. It's legal, but not here. Got it?"

"Way to be an asshole, man," one of them muttered as they walked away, carrying their snowboards. "Weed thief."

Jesse skied to the ski patrol chalet, stepped out of his skis, and carried them inside together with the joint and the bag of weed.

The moment he stepped through the door, the chalet exploded into cheers and applause.

Hell.

It was an ambush. All the patrollers were there. Even the resort's general manager, a former patroller named Brent Arthur, had come.

Arthur shook his hand, then saw the weed. "Looks like you came ready to party."

Jesse was about to say that it wasn't his weed, that he'd taken it from a pair of snowboarders when Arthur pointed at him and laughed.

"Look at his face. He thought I meant it."

Everyone seemed to find this hilarious.

"I just wanted to thank you for saving lives yesterday, including your own. You did one hell of a job. I've never lost a patroller, and I aim to keep it that way."

More cheers and applause.

Jesus.

"On behalf of Scarlet Mountain Resort, I want to give you this." Arthur held out a piece of paper that turned out to be a gift certificate for an overnight stay in one of the lodge's luxury suites. "Kick back and relax a bit. That's an order."

"Thanks." Jesse's gaze fixed on the words *hot tub*.

And, damn, if that didn't give him some ideas.

Ellie walked toward the back door that opened onto the loading dock with the six-page supply list and a pen in hand. She'd told her mother not to expect her until after nine. Even if Megs turned up with a few people, it was going to take a long time to sort through all this stuff.

She pushed open the back door—and stared. "Wow."

A dozen Team members, all wearing bright yellow Rocky Mountain Search & Rescue Team T-shirts, stood in groups of twos and threes, talking and joking with one another. They stopped when she stepped out, heads turning. She knew some of them—Megs, of course, and Austin and Eric. The others she recognized from the benefit at Knockers. Sasha Dillon. Harrison Conrad. Creed Herrera. Mitch Ahearn. Nicole Turner. Malachi O'Brien. Kenzie Morgan. Chaska Belcourt.

"I think she's happy to see us," Megs said.

"You have *no* idea."

Jesse came around the corner, yellow T-shirt stretched over a black turtleneck, his hair windblown from a day on the slopes. "Sorry, I'm late."

"Yeah, what's with that, Moretti?" Creed joked.

Ellie led them to the storage room, flicked on the lights, and explained the situation to Megs. "The supplies for the first-aid tent are on these three pallets. Once they're inventoried, they have to be put back on the pallets and wrapped up again, because that's how they're going to be transported."

"May I? It goes faster this way." Megs took the inventory sheet from Ellie and plucked the staple out of the corner, turning it into six separate sheets. She handed one to Ellie, kept one for herself, and gave the other four to four volunteers.

Ellie was confused.

"Listen up, folks." Megs raised her voice to be heard over the chatter. "This stuff needs to go back on the pallets just the way we found it. Stack each pile in reverse order so that we don't have trouble later. Otherwise, it's just like we do it at The Cave. Got it?"

Megs turned to Ellie. "They'll call out each item as they remove it from the pallet and wait till they hear one of us repeat what they've said and say 'Check.' The hardest part is just keeping up with them. Okay. Let's roll."

Jesse, Austin, and Eric ripped the plastic off the three pallets, and the Team went to work. Ellie was afraid it would be chaos. In truth, it was efficient and fast.

"Exam gloves, nitrile, five-hundred count."

Ellie searched her page, but it was Megs who answered. "Exam gloves, nitrile, five-hundred count. Check."

"Adhesive bandages, three-eighths by one-and-three-quarters."

"Adhesive bandages, three-eighths by one-and-three-quarters. Check."

"Alcohol prep pads."

Ellie found that on her list. "Alcohol prep pads. Check."

"Emergency hand warmers."

"Emergency hand warmers. Check."

They quickly fell into a rhythm, and in far less time than she had imagined, the pallets were bare, supplies piled neatly beside them.

She, Megs, Mitch, Harrison, Kenzie, and Nicole, went over their lists to make sure they had accounted for everything.

"Blankets?" Nicole asked.

No one had seen that. The AEDs weren't there, nor were any of the oxygen supplies she'd ordered or the IV fluid warmer or the heating pads or the cots.

Jesse peered over her shoulder. "So, apart from the important stuff, it's all here."

"Looks like it." Ellie would have to get on this first thing tomorrow.

"All right, folks," called Megs, her voice rising over the joking and the chatter. "Let's put it back just the way we found it. Sasha, this isn't the rock gym."

Ellie glanced up… and her pulse skipped. "Holy shit!"

Sasha had climbed an I-beam almost to the ceiling.

Megs shook her head. "I can't take them anywhere."

But beneath Megs' deadpan exterior, Ellie could see the deep affection she felt for every member of the Team and her pride in their abilities.

Fifteen minutes later, the pallets were piled high again, Jesse, Austin, and Eric wrapping them tightly with plastic wrap they took from a big dispenser on the wall.

From start to finish, it had taken less than an hour.

Ellie looked around the room. "I am so grateful for your help. Thank you all. Thanks, Megs."

"Thank Jesse. He's the one who sent up the flare."

He stood near the door with Austin, Eric, and Creed, laughing about something.

"I will." Oh, she most definitely would.

Jesse came home, hit the shower, then put a steak in the oven on broil. He nuked a potato to go with it, grabbed some leftover salad out of the fridge, and called it good. By the time he had cleaned up, it was just after eight. He turned on the news but was too restless for that. He popped in a climbing DVD, watched the Stone Monkeys fuck around on El Cap for a while, but even that couldn't distract him.

He wanted to be with her.

The past two nights when he'd gone over, he'd waited until after nine to make sure the twins would be asleep. But what did it matter whether the kids were asleep? What was the worst thing two little kids could do? Cry? Throw up? Poop on him? Give him strep again? He could deal with that. And if they were going to crawl into bed with him and Ellie in the middle of the night anyway…

He sent her a quick text.

ON MY WAY.

He'd just started for the back door when she replied.

GIVE ME FIVE MINUTES.

Okay.

He gave her eight just to be sure, then followed the well-trodden path through the snow to her back door. The house looked dark, except for a faint light coming from the kitchen. He was about to knock when he noticed a note stuck to the door.

Use your key and come inside where it's warm.

He unlocked the door, stepped into the kitchen, and took off his boots and parka. Ellie wasn't there. She'd lit candles and set them on the table, their flickering light falling on a tumbler of scotch, which sat on a second note.

I'm waiting for you.

His heart gave a knock, blood rushing to his groin.

Holy fuck.

He took a sip of the scotch—damned good stuff—then walked back to her bedroom, anticipation putting his senses on high alert.

She lay on the bed in a black lace bra and tiny panties that revealed more than they concealed, her skin gleaming in the candlelight.

"*Jesus.*" Some primitive part of him wanted to fall on his knees to worship her—erotic dream-come-true, angel, goddess.

She sat up, got gracefully to her feet and walked toward him, her breasts swelling above the bra, her nipples just visible. "You've been a very good boy."

He opened his mouth to say something, but no words came out.

She undressed him, his erect cock springing free, doing the talking for him.

She stroked the length of him, then pointed to the bed. "Lie down."

He obeyed, part of him rendered stupid by lust, the rest of him curious to see what she planned to do.

She straddled his legs, took his cock in her hand, gave it a few exploratory strokes, a hint of vulnerability in her eyes. "Tell me what feels good, okay?"

This felt good—so far all of it felt good. "Yeah."

Then she bent down and took him into her mouth.

Pleasure shot through him, making his hips jerk. "Christ."

She teased the sensitive head with her tongue, flicking him just beneath the rim, swirling circles over him, sucking on the tip. If she was trying to drive him crazy, she was doing one hell of a job, the stimulation a sweet kind of torture.

Not wanting to miss a thing, he reached down, slid a hand into her hair, and moved the strands aside. God, she was beautiful, the sight of her mouth on his cock stunningly erotic. "*Ellie.*"

He didn't know whether to beg for mercy or to beg for more, his cock aching for her, aching to be inside her. He reached with his free hand, undid the clasp on her bra, watched her breasts fall free. He palmed them, the feel adding to his arousal. But, God, what she was doing with her lips just now, nibbling him ...

As if she knew he couldn't take much more, she tightened the grip she had on the base of his cock and took all of him into her mouth.

"*Jesus, Ellie.*"

She moved her mouth and hand together up and down his length, one sensation colliding with the next. The swirl of her tongue. The tight sheath of her hand. The wet heat of her mouth. He was lost now, lost in sensation, lost just knowing that *she* was doing this to him.

Ah, God, it felt good, so damned good, so fucking perfect.

His entire body was rigid now, both hands clenched in her hair, his balls drawing tight as she drove him closer to the edge. He fought to relax, tried to make it last, but she was merciless. Tighter. Faster. She was too damned good at this. He gave himself over to the inevitable, let pleasure carry him away.

Climax blasted through him in a scorching wave of white hot bliss, the breath leaving his lungs in shudders as she finished him with her mouth.

He lay there for a moment, somewhere between life and death, heart thrumming in his chest, his body relaxed. He opened his eyes to find her stretched out beside him, watching him, her gaze soft, a little smile on her wet, swollen lips.

His heart went soft, the tenderness he felt for her overwhelming him. He reached up, cupped her cheek. "Have I ever told you how much I love your dirty mouth?"

Ellie snuggled against him, feeling insanely aroused, but knowing Jesse was spent for now. "Did I surprise you?"

"Did you surprise me?" He chuckled, a soft deep sound. "Honey, you blew my mind. You almost killed me."

"Good." It had been amazing to see all of that muscular, powerful male rendered helpless and desperate—and to know that *she* had done that to him.

"Just so you know, I would never expect a woman to swallow." His fingers trailed up and down her spine. "I asked myself a long time ago whether I would want to swallow my own cum, and the answer was no. Don't think you have to."

God, he was sweet. "Don't worry about me."

Then she remembered. "My sister Claire and her husband Cedar have offered to stay overnight Tuesday night. I thought maybe we could spend the night at your place. We won't have to worry about waking the kids up."

Or having them toddle into the bedroom and catch them in the act.

"My place? I have an even better idea. What if I get us a room at the Scarlet Mountain Resort lodge—one of those luxury suites with a hot tub."

"Wouldn't that be expensive?" The luxury suites had cost about five hundred bucks a night the last time she and Dan had talked about staying there. That had been years ago.

"It wouldn't cost either of us a dime." He told her how the general manager had given him a gift certificate for a free night in thanks for the way he'd handled the explosives accident. "All I need to do is book the room."

A luxury suite at the Scarlet Mountain Resort lodge.

"You said the room comes with a hot tub?"

"A *private* hot tub."

She wriggled against him, feeling very hot and bothered. "I can't wait."

They raided the kitchen after that, nibbling on chunks of cheese, walnuts, and olives, Jesse in his boxers and Ellie in her bathrobe. They talked about everything and nothing—how they were due for more snow, how quickly inventory had gone at the hospital, how embarrassed Jesse had felt by the attention at work.

"You're kind of a big deal, you know." Ellie got to her feet to put the olives and the wrapped block of cheese back into the refrigerator. "You might as well get used to it."

She'd no sooner closed the refrigerator door when a strong arm caught her around the waist and drew her backward.

Jesse pulled her into his lap, turning her to face him, forcing her to straddle him, his fingers finding her, exploring her, stroking her clit. "Mmm. You are so wet."

She held onto his shoulders, looked into his eyes, unashamed of her body's response to him. "Giving you head turned me on."

"Is that so?" He pressed kisses to her forehead, nuzzled her ear, taking his time, his fingers touching her right where she needed it most. "Does this turn you on?"

"Yes." She had already been horny, but now she ached for him.

He knew what she wanted, but he didn't give it to her, not right away, one finger making maddening circles around the entrance to her vagina.

"Please."

Finally, *finally*, he penetrated her, two fingers sliding inside her.

Her head fell back on a moan, her fingers digging into his shoulders for support.

She couldn't hold still, her hips matching the rhythm of his thrusts, his fingers working magic inside her, making that inner ache worse.

He stopped, making her moan in protest.

"I would give money for a condom."

Ellie brushed her lips with his. "How much money exactly?"

"My whole goddamned fortune."

"Done." She reached into the pocket of her bathrobe, pulled out a condom—Spiral Pleasures.

He took it from her, tore it open with his teeth, reaching down between them to roll it onto his cock. Then he took hold of himself, rubbing his cock over her clit again and again until she was going out of her mind and ready to scream.

"*Now!*"

He raised her hips, guiding her as she sank onto him, spearing herself on his cock, taking him deep inside her.

She rode him while he drove into her from below, his hands grasping her hips, his cock filling her, stretching her, stroking her. She came fast and hard, the tension inside her shattering into bliss. He caught her cry with his mouth, pounding her pleasure home with deep thrusts and following her over the edge.

Chapter Fifteen

J esse ran as fast as he could, churning water making it almost impossible for him to move. He fought for every inch, knowing she would die if he didn't get to her. He reached for her again—and again the creek took her, the child's hands reaching skyward, her terrified little face disappearing from view.

"Jesse, it's okay."

He jerked awake, his heart slamming, a sick feeling in the pit of his stomach.

"It's okay. It was just a dream." Ellie sat beside him, her face lined with worry. "You're here with me. You're safe."

He yanked off the sheets and sat up, putting his feet on the floor in an attempt to find something solid, the nightmare still dragging at him.

She scooted up behind him, wrapped her arms around him, resting her cheek on his shoulder. "Just breathe. Deep breaths."

He fought the urge to lash out at her, to shove her away. "I'm okay."

But he wasn't, not really.

Fuck. Fuck. Fuck.

"Breathe." Ellie stayed with him, holding onto him, her warmth seeping in through his skin, the horror of the dream fading as he tried to do what she said.

In. Out. In. Out.

He gave her hand a squeeze. "I need to take a leak."

He got up and walked to the bathroom, took a piss, then washed his hands and splashed his face with cold water. He didn't want her to see him like this. He didn't want her to see the shattered side of him.

He dried his hands and face and walked back to the bedroom to find her sitting with the lamp on. Some part of him wanted to fold himself into her, to take all the warmth and gentleness she could offer. But the rest of him wanted to grab his things and head up the hill to his own bed.

He crawled into bed with her again and lay back on the pillow, staring at the ceiling, his arm bent behind his head.

"Do you want to talk about it? Sometimes that helps. Dan had nightmares, too."

He'd already talked with Esri about the dream so telling Ellie didn't seem like such a huge leap. Besides, he'd already told her about his father.

Would she think him weak, a coward, a loser?

"Last summer, I responded to a call about a rollover MVA in the canyon. The vehicle, a little Honda, had been struck by some idiot who'd crossed the double yellow to pass a slow driver. The Honda had rolled into the creek and was sitting upside down in the middle. The water was running high. I got there first. I could see that there were people in the car—a mother and her kids."

"God. How awful."

"Standard operating procedure at this kind of rescue is to wait until ropes are in place so that rescuers don't get swept away. We rope up, maybe create a Tyrolean traverse, then take out the survivors. No ropes, no rescue."

"That makes sense. If you lose the rescuers, everyone dies."

He nodded. "A little girl had taken off her seatbelt. I think she was worried about her mother, who was semi-conscious. Water was pouring into the car's open windows, getting deeper. I shouted to the little girl to stay where she was, not to move. The current washed her out like she was a cork, took her right out of that car while I stood there waiting for the rest of the Team."

He could still remember the dread that had taken him, his mouth going dry, his heart slamming against his breastbone.

"You went in after her."

"Yeah. I ran down the embankment and jumped in, trying to get downstream of her so that I could catch her. I didn't move fast enough. The current carried her right past me. I reached for her…" He swallowed the lump in his throat. "It was no good. I felt so fucking helpless."

"I'm so sorry, Jesse." Ellie's voice was soft, calling him back from the edge. "I've lost people, too. I know it hurts. You did everything you could."

"It wasn't enough."

"I know it feels that way, but from where I'm sitting, you did more than most people would have. You risked your life for hers."

"I was the last person to see her alive. They finally got her body out of the water on the east side of Boulder. I can still see that terrified look in her eyes, her little hands reaching for me. I couldn't save her. I couldn't."

Ellie drew him into her embrace, cradling him against her bare breast the way she'd held Daisy, pressing kisses to his hair.

And for the first time in his adult life, Jesse wept.

Ellie called Central Supply at the hospital first thing Monday morning to ask about the AEDs, oxygen equipment, and other supplies she'd ordered that hadn't yet come in. The clerk who answered the phone had no idea what Ellie was talking about and had put her on hold ten minutes ago, the background music grating on her nerves.

Daisy and Daniel sat on the living room floor together playing with wooden puzzles, sticking farm animals and zoo critters into their respective slots and taking them out again. Ellie was grateful that they were occupying themselves because she didn't have much in the way of emotional resources this morning.

Jesse was pulling away from her. She'd felt it last night in the way he'd turned off his emotions like shutting off a faucet. He'd left without kissing her goodbye. She'd texted him this morning to wish him a good day, and he still hadn't replied.

He'd broken down last night, and it had scared him.

"Who are you holding for?" a voice said in her ear.

"I've been on hold for almost fifteen minutes now waiting to talk to someone who can tell me what happened to the remainder of the supplies I ordered for the SnowFest first-aid tent."

"Let me see who's handling that. I'll just put you on hold."

"No, please—" And the background music was back. "Damn it."

"Damn," Daisy said.

"Shit." Ellie needed to watch her mouth.

She walked to the laundry room and moved the load of bed sheets from the washer to the dryer and tossed clothes in the washer.

"Ma'am?"

Oh, thank God. "Yes."

"Can you give us the order number?"

Oh, come on! "Does no one there know what I'm talking about?"

This wasn't a big city hospital. This was Scarlet Springs. There was only one SnowFest, and she'd placed one order.

"If you give us the number, we can look it up and figure out what's going on."

"Hang on a moment, and don't you dare put me on hold again." Ellie hurried to the kitchen, found the right file, and took out the form. She read the number over the phone. "I didn't get the AEDs, any of the oxygen equipment, or the heating pads—and those are the body-length pads used to treat hypothermia. The cots weren't there either."

"What's a good number for me to call?"

Ellie gave the woman her cell phone number. "Please understand that SnowFest is two weeks away, so I need these supplies within the week."

"I'll look into it and get back to you."

Ellie ended the call, her frustration soaring.

She sank onto the couch, wondering what to do now. Should she give Jesse space, let him find his way? Should she text him again, tell him that she cared? Should she assume they were off for Tuesday night and cancel with Claire?

Damn it.

She'd forgotten how miserable romance could be.

Oh, Jesse.

Her heart had broken for him last night. She'd known the story, of course. The Fisher family had lived in Scarlet Springs for a few generations, and Ellie's father had been the family's pediatrician. Everyone in town had been heartbroken over the tragedy, and most had turned out for the funeral in a show of support.

But it was still tearing Jesse apart. He'd broken down in her arms, his tears bringing tears to her eyes. It had lasted only a moment. Then he'd shut himself off, pulled out of her embrace, and laid back on his pillow. He'd held her, his fingers tracing a line along her spine, but he hadn't spoken again—not a word.

Daisy burst into tears because Daniel had taken apart the puzzle she'd been putting together.

"Okay. Let's put the puzzles away. It's time to play outside. Do you want to make a snowman?"

Jesse left a voicemail for Esri on his lunch break. "I really need to see you today. Give me a call or text me with a time, and I'll be there. Sorry for the short notice, but it's really important. Please call."

Goddamn it!

He shoved his phone back into his pocket, stared down at the burrito he'd bought from the cafeteria, not the least bit hungry. His body needed fuel, so he ate anyway, doing his best to relax, trying to tune out the maelstrom inside his head.

He'd fallen the fuck apart last night. He'd let Ellie hold him like a baby, and he'd shed actual fucking tears. He'd thought that crying was supposed to make a person feel better. Instead, he'd wanted to punch something. He'd been a weak fuck and dumped all of his shit onto Ellie. What must she think of him now?

It was a good thing she'd already seen his balls because after last night, she might otherwise have wondered if he had any.

Jesus!

She had texted him this morning first thing.

HOPE YOU HAVE A GOOD DAY.

She'd added a little heart on the end, her concern for him coming through. He hadn't texted back, not because he didn't want to talk to her but because he didn't know what to say. Should he pretend everything was normal? Should he apologize?

He hoped to God Esri had an opening this evening. If he couldn't see her soon, he might come out of his skin.

"Hey, Jesse." Ben sat down across from him, looking a lot better than he had on Saturday. "How are you?"

Jesse didn't feel like talking. He wanted to tell the kid to get lost, but he knew Ben would take that the wrong way. "I'm fine. You?"

"I just wanted to thank you for what you did Saturday."

"You mean saving your life?" *Tone it down, asshole.* "You're welcome."

But Ben hadn't finished. "I've asked Matt to take me off explosives. I'm just not right for it. He said he would talk to you and Kevin about it."

Jesse couldn't deal with Ben's shit right now. "Okay then."

"That means you'll ask him to take me off explosives?"

"Jesus, Ben. Can I just eat my lunch?"

"Sure. Yeah. Sorry."

Jesse finished, carried his tray to the counter, and walked out into the afternoon sunshine. He stepped into his skis, skied over to the lift line, and rode the chair to the top of the mountain.

The sky was blue and wide as only a Colorado sky could be, the high peaks gleaming white with snow. The mountains had saved his life when he'd come here from Louisiana. But today the beauty and vastness couldn't touch him.

He skied out to the back bowls, an out-of-bounds feature that attracted freeriders who wanted to risk their lives for a few minutes of adrenaline. There were no rule-breakers today, the snow pristine and untracked apart from the little trails left by pinwheels—little snowballs that were often the precursor to an avalanche.

Jesse could understand why people risked their lives out here. He could understand the need to throw everything inside you into a single moment, to test your mettle, to pit yourself against nature and see who won. Some part of him wanted to do that now, to point his tips down the fall line, forget everything but the rush of it, to throw himself at the mercy of the mountain.

How do you think the Team would feel digging your frozen, dead ass out of an avalanche? How would Ellie feel if you killed yourself on the job?

What the fuck was he thinking? This wasn't like him.

Neither is crying on your girlfriend's chest.

He needed to get a grip. "Forty-two to dispatch."

"Forty-two, go ahead."

"I've spotted a couple of skiers headed for the back bowls. I'm going to check it out." He'd never made a bogus call before.

"Forty-two, copy."

Jesse skied to an outcropping of rock and stared down at the slope below, the mountain calling him.

Ellie had just put the kids down for their afternoon nap when her cell phone buzzed. She almost tripped over her own feet in her rush to get it.

Jesse.

Her heart skipped a beat.

He'd sent another photo, this one of a breathtaking view of the Indian Peaks Wilderness—Navajo, Apache, and Shoshoni Peaks gleaming under a bright blue sky. A message followed.

TODAY'S VIEW FROM THE OFFICE.

She let out a relieved breath, texted back.

BEAUTIFUL. THANKS FOR SHARING.

Jesse was okay. He was okay.

Jesse sat down across from Esri, fighting to keep his rage and agitation in check. He didn't know how to talk about this. "I care about the woman I'm seeing. I don't want to fuck this up. I don't want to hurt her. I had the nightmare again last night while I was sleeping at her place and fell the fuck apart."

He had decided he wouldn't tell Esri what had happened on the mountain today. In the end, he hadn't done anything besides make a bogus call, and he was far from the first patroller to do that. He didn't want to risk his job or his place on the Team by having Esri flag him as being a danger to himself or some damned thing.

"When I last saw you four days ago, you hadn't yet become intimate with this woman. Your relationship has clearly deepened."

Jesse nodded, thinking of Ellie taking some of the edge off. "I care about her. But last night, I lost it. I told her about the nightmare, and I cried. I've never cried in front of anyone, not even as a kid."

"It sounds like you moved outside your comfort level again. But tell me—do you think it's bad for a man to cry?"

Jesse stared at her, his mind torn between the answer he knew he was supposed to give and his true feelings. "Even if it's okay for men to cry, I don't."

"Why do you think you cried last night?"

Jesse fought not to shout. "If I knew, I wouldn't be here talking to you."

That made Esri smile in her irritating oh-so-Zen way. "Sometimes when we feel truly safe with someone, emotions surface that we wouldn't ordinarily share. Do you feel safe with Ellie?"

He'd never considered that. Did he feel safe with Ellie? Of course, he did. He felt safe with her. He cared about her. He felt protective of her and the twins. When he was around her, he felt whole.

Until last night.

"Yeah, I guess I do. But now…" Regret cut through him, the pain almost physical. "I feel like damaged goods. I feel like I ruined everything, like I destroyed what was clean and beautiful. I feel naked. I feel…"

"Exposed?"

That was the word. "Yeah."

"Did she say anything to make you believe that she thinks less of you?"

He shook his head. "No, but Ellie's a nurse and…"

Shit. He'd said her name.

"Ellie's a nurse and…" Esri prompted him.

"She has a lot of compassion for people."

"Is it wrong if her compassion includes you—a man she obviously cares about?"

"I guess not."

"Do you feel you're worthy of compassion, Jesse?"

That question stopped him cold. "I don't know."

"Consider this for a moment: She believes you're worthy of comfort and compassion even if you're uncomfortable receiving it."

They talked for a while about the dream, about the terrifying sense of helplessness he felt watching the little girl get swept away. But they'd been through this before, and the minutes were ticking by.

Jesse cut Esri off mid-sentence. "You said last time you needed more pieces of the puzzle. I do *not* want to fuck things up with Ellie. What pieces do you need?"

He was ready to cut himself open and lay himself out for Esri right here and now if only it would make the darkness inside him go away.

Esri watched him for a moment. "Your childhood. Your combat experience. Any major traumatic events, especially those that made you feel helpless."

He steeled himself.

"My dad was a dick. He beat me when I was little—not all the time, but often enough. He beat my mother sometimes, too, usually when she got in between the two of us. Also, he wasn't really my dad. He married my mom when she was pregnant. My sister is his child, but I'm not. As for my combat experience—I killed the enemies of my country without remorse, and I watched good people die."

"That's a lot to tell me all in one go. Do you mind if we sift through this?"

He glanced at the clock. "I can't leave here until…"

Until I feel worthy of Ellie again.

She seemed to understand his urgency. "How did it make you feel to see your father hurting your mother, especially when it involved you?"

He looked into Esri's brown eyes. "I felt guilty. I felt so angry. I hated him. I felt … helpless."

That word again.

"How scary for a little boy to see someone he loves—his mother—being hurt. Did you ever try to stop him?"

"Yeah. Of course." Memories Jesse had tried to bury drifted through his mind. "I jumped on him, started hitting him. He knocked me to the ground and kicked the shit out of me. Afterward, my mother told me never to do that again."

"So you tried to save her, but you couldn't. You were overpowered by a stronger force, and you felt helpless."

Jesse wasn't a therapist, but even he could see the parallel. "Like in the dream."

"Like real life. You tried to save the little Fisher girl. You were overpowered by the rushing water, and you felt helpless."

They talked about this for a while, Esri allowing their appointment to go over by thirty minutes.

"I want you to think about something over the next few days," she said. "Your job with ski patrol and your volunteer work with the Team—it's all about protecting people, saving lives. You've told me before that saving lives gives you a high." She held up a hand to stop the objection she knew he was about to make. "Yes, I think anyone would feel good if they saved a life, but you've told me your work with the Team holds you together. Why is it so important for you to take on the role of guardian? Why is it so important to you personally to save people?"

Chapter Sixteen

Ellie was late getting dinner on the table. She'd decided at the last minute to invite Jesse to eat with them. She'd called him and left a voicemail and then made a mad dash to Food Mart with the kids to get everything she needed to make coq au vin. It was one of the few fancy meals she made, and it was easy.

Now dinner was finally ready, the twins were hungry and grumpy, and she still hadn't heard back from Jesse. She told herself that he'd probably gotten busy at work or been called out with the Team, but she couldn't shake the fear that something was wrong. He'd only been a part of her life for two weeks, but the thought of losing what they had together—whatever it was—left a bleakness inside her. She cared about him, truly cared about him. She didn't want it to end.

She cut a piece of chicken into bites for the kids and put it together with buttered pasta and peas on their plates. "Here you go, sweeties. Daisy, don't throw your fork."

She'd just given them each a sippy cup of milk when a knock at the front door made her jump. She hurried to open it, relief and joy pushing away the cloud of anxiety she'd been carrying all evening.

Jesse stood there in his ski pants and parka, looking like he'd just gotten off work, his hair windblown, the bandage on his forehead gone to leave the stitches exposed. He looked drained, but he smiled when he saw her. "Am I too late?"

"Jesse!" said the twins, Daisy first and then Daniel, and it was clear they were both happy to see him.

"Not at all. You're right on time." She stood on her toes and kissed him. "I'll fix you a plate."

He took off his boots and his parka and followed her to the stove, hands coming to rest on her hips as he looked over her shoulder. "That smells incredible. What is it?"

"Coq au vin. It sounds fancy, but it's very easy to make."

There was so much Ellie wanted to say to him, but now wasn't the time. They talked about little stuff while they ate—her attempts to get the missing supplies delivered in time, his day on the slopes, Daisy's new knack for profanity.

"She said it as clear as a bell—D-A-M-N."

Jesse looked into Ellie's eyes, a sexy smile spreading across his face. "I guess she takes after her mother."

Ellie felt her cheeks burn.

After supper, she let the kids play for a while, then plopped them one at a time into the tub. Rather than sitting in the living room and keeping his distance, Jesse helped, entertaining whichever child was in the tub with tub toys, tossing rings onto the floating octopus' tentacles, pouring water through pipes of the waterworks set, and ensuring that neither child wanted to come out of the tub when it was time.

"I think you like those toys more than they do." Ellie lifted a protesting Daniel out of the water. "Should I bring them with me tomorrow night?"

He chuckled, plucked Daniel out of her arms, and turned him into an airplane for the short journey to his bedroom. "Vrooom!"

"For a guy who's not good with kids, you're really good with kids."

"Thanks." His gaze met hers, a hint of sadness in his eyes. "File that under 'Things I never thought I'd hear a woman say.'"

Jesse read them bedtime stories, the sight of him holding Daisy and Daniel on his lap and reading Dr. Seuss making Ellie's heart squish. He might not have planned to be a father, but she had no trouble imagining him in that role.

When the kids were finally asleep, Ellie and Jesse sank onto the sofa together, facing one another. For a moment, they sat in silence, their fingers twining, the contact somehow reassuring.

He spoke first. "Ellie, I ... I'm sorry about last night. I've never done that before."

"It's okay, Jesse. When I said you were safe with me, I meant it. I don't think any less of you because of it. Tears are not a sign of weakness in a man."

The hard set of his jaw told her that he couldn't buy that.

"I saw my therapist today. Well, she's not really *my* therapist. She's the Team's therapist, but I've been seeing her off and on since ..."

"I'm glad." Ellie was relieved. "I think anyone who'd been through what you went through that day would be facing some post-traumatic stress. I said it takes courage to face your emotions. It takes even more courage to get help."

"I'm damaged goods, Ellie. Are you sure you want this in your life?"

"Is that how you think of yourself?"

The desolation in his eyes answered for him.

"When I look at you, I see a man who has served his country, who helps his neighbors and volunteers in his free time to save lives. In my book, you're a hero. You've gathered some scars along the way. That happens to everyone, but it especially happens to heroes."

He seemed to consider this. "I did something today I've never done before. I made a bogus call to dispatch. I told them I'd seen some skiers out of bounds, but I hadn't. I just needed to get as far away from people as I could to think, to clear my head."

"I bet you're not the first patroller to do that." She laughed.

He didn't. "I stood there, looking down. There were pinwheels rolling everywhere. The slope was primed to slide. A part of me wanted to drop into that powder, shoot for the bottom, and let the mountain decide whether I lived or died. How fucking heroic is that?"

Her stomach fell to think of him on the brink like that. He was talking about suicide here, taking risks not for the thrill of it, but for a chance to end his life. "But you didn't do it."

"Do you know what held me back?"

She shook her head.

He reached up, ran his thumb over her cheek. "You."

Her throat grew tight. "I'm glad."

"Plus, I didn't want my buddies on the Team to have to dig me out."

She laughed through the lump in her throat. "Megs would kick your ass."

"What did I do to deserve you?"

"Oh, Jesse." It hurt to think that he couldn't see himself as she saw him. "Do I have to list it all? You helped me when my car broke down, shoveled my walk, watched my kids—and you fuck like a god."

"Yeah?" He moved in on her, one smooth motion bringing his face to hers, his lips catching her lower lip, giving it a little tug. "What do you say to a little worship in the bedroom?"

"Hallelujah."

Jesse carried Ellie to the bedroom, the two of them rolling together on her bed, hands tearing at clothing, searching for soft flesh. He fucked her hard and fast, reveling in her moans and cries. Tears slid down her cheeks when she came, the tenderness he felt for her an ache in his chest. A few thrusts later, he followed her into paradise, climax washing through him as bright and pure as salvation.

They held each other in the darkness afterward.

"Promise me you won't do it—that you'll never try to kill yourself."

He kissed her hair. "I promise."

Ellie spent Tuesday cleaning the house and getting ready for her night with Jesse. She vacuumed, mopped, cleaned the bathrooms, dusted, and put clean sheets on the bed—again. In between, she played with the kids and packed an overnight bag.

Tonight would be her first night away from the twins, her first night completely alone with a man for almost four years. She found it exciting—but it also made her nervous.

While the kids took their afternoon nap, she showered, shaved her legs, and gave herself a pedicure. Then she called Claire, needing advice.

"I want tonight to be special, but I don't know what to do."

"Lingerie?"

"I did the sexy-bra-and-panties routine already. I do have some other lingerie. I just haven't worn it in years."

"Fruit and whipped cream?"

"That doesn't sound sexy to me."

"You don't want him to eat grapes out of your—"

"No!"

"I don't know what to say, sis. Tie him up. Let him spank you. It's your love life. Do whatever floats your boat. Just be sure to tell me about it—in detail."

"You are no help."

"Not true. I'm taking care of your kids tonight, remember?"

"Oh, right."

"Are you going to the Kirby boy's funeral Thursday?" That was an abrupt change of subject. "I think Mom and Dad are going."

"I'll be there. I helped care for Tyler. See you later."

Ellie ended the call, opened her bottom drawer, and looked through the lingerie she hadn't touched in four years. There was a white lace body suit with a neckline that plunged all the way to her navel. She'd bought it for what had turned out to be her last Valentine's Day with Dan. There was a silky pink baby doll gown she'd worn on their honeymoon. There was the teddy she'd bought to surprise Dan for his birthday their first year together.

She couldn't wear any of these. They were tied to Dan, tied to her past. Jesse was part of a new chapter in her life. If she wore lingerie, it had to be something she'd bought just for him. And since there was no time for that…

She saw a Victoria's Secret bag lying on the bottom of the drawer. She pulled it out, opened it, and found a red lace bustier with garters and a matching red thong. Red lace stockings lay folded in an unopened plastic package. She must have bought all of this to surprise Dan at some point, but she'd never worn it. *Perfect.*

Her cell phone buzzed.

It was the hospital.

"Hey, this is Sharon, manager of Central Supply. I found the missing stuff. It's here. It's in an adjacent room. I'm not sure how it ended up there, but it's all together now."

This was good news. "Thanks so much."

At least that was resolved.

The afternoon passed slowly. Ellie played with the kids, and then gave in and sat them down in front of a DVD so that she could make dinner. Her cell phone buzzed again. A text message from Jesse.

COUNTING THE MINUTES.

His words gave her heart wings. She floated through making supper, kept her sense of humor through Daniel's painting experiment with poop, hummed during bath time, then snuggled with the kids to read stories.

Claire and Cedar arrived just as she was putting the kids to bed, but that was probably for the best. That way Daisy and Daniel wouldn't be surprised to see them if they woke up in the middle of the night. While Claire gave the kids bedtime kisses, Ellie shut herself in her bedroom and tried to figure out what to wear.

What did a person wear to a ski lodge when they weren't going skiing and would probably spend most of the night naked?

She put on the bustier, thong, and stockings and slipped on a curve-hugging black sweater dress that reached her knees and knee-high boots. She hurried into the bathroom and put on makeup—eyeliner, eye shadow, mascara, blush, lip gloss. She studied her reflection in the mirror, a kind of excitement in her eyes she hadn't seen for so long.

She stepped out of her room, overnight bag in hand, and walked to the living room where Claire and Cedar were settling in with a DVD.

Claire squealed. "Oh, my God, Ellie, you look *hot*."

"Shh!" Ellie laughed. "You'll wake up the kids."

"You look good." Cedar pointed the remote at the TV. "Do you have any beer?"

"Get off your butt and go look," Claire teased. "The fridge is that way."

"I'll get one." Ellie had just pulled an Indian Peaks Pale Ale out of the fridge when a knock came at the front door. She hurried over to Cedar, handed him the beer, then answered the door. The sight of Jesse made her breath catch.

He stood there looking like a rock star in black jeans, a black crew-neck T-shirt, and a black blazer, his face clean shaven, his hair neat and combed, dark brown suede boots on his feet. His gaze traveled over her. "Damn."

"You remember Claire, my sister?"

Jesse nodded. "Hey, Claire. How's your knee healing?"

"It's better. Thanks. I hear you almost got blown up."

Jesse touched a finger to the stitches on his forehead. "Yeah. Stupid accident."

Cedar got to his feet, held out his hand. "I'm Cedar, Claire's partner."

Jesse shook hands with him. "Good to meet you."

"Let me just check the kids, and we can go." Ellie tiptoed into their bedrooms, kissed them, then tiptoed out to the living room. "I'm ready."

Jesse picked up her overnight bag, put his arm around her shoulder, and walked with her to the door. "Good night."

"Thanks so much, you two. See you at six a.m."

"Have fun," Claire called after them. "And use contraception!"

Ellie couldn't help but laugh.

J esse swiped the key card, pushed open the door, and held it for Ellie, anticipation warming his blood. He'd done a little recon earlier this evening. He'd wanted to check the suite out, make sure they had everything they needed—champagne in the fridge, condoms in each room, an antipasto plate and some fresh fruit in case they got hungry. He'd never done anything like this before. He wanted to get it right for her.

She walked inside, and her eyes went wide. "Wow."

He followed her, savoring the play of emotions on her face.

"Can you believe this place?"

It wasn't called the luxury suite for nothing. Floor-to-ceiling windows looked out onto the slopes, the vaulted ceilings crossed with polished wooden beams. Two contemporary chandeliers hung over the living room area, a blocky leather sofa and two matching armchairs arranged around a coffee table across from a large stone fireplace. Wood stood in a neat stack in an alcove beside the hearth, kindling in a basket. A door led to a small balcony outside, where chairs sat buried in snow.

"Where's the bed?"

He pointed. "It's through there."

She laughed at the sight of the king-sized bed with its thick, carved posts that had to be seven feet tall. There was another fireplace, a leather sofa sitting off to one side. A doorway to their right led to a bathroom with a large steam shower and a sunken hot tub.

He couldn't say what was running through her mind, but he was sizing up every room and every piece of furniture for its erotic possibilities. The fluffy sheepskin rug on the floor in front of the living room fireplace. The built-in bench in the shower. Those big bedposts.

"I've never been anywhere this posh."

"Yeah, me neither. Want some champagne?" He retrieved the bottle from the kitchen, popped the cork, and poured them each a glass. "*Salute.*"

"Cheers."

Their glasses clinked.

She sipped, wrinkled her nose. "The bubbles tickle."

"I'll build a fire in the bedroom, and you can settle in." He got to work and soon had a good blaze going, pine logs crackling. He stood and turned, about to ask her whether she was hungry, but the words never left his tongue.

"Where do you want me first?" She stood next to the bed, wearing a strapless, red lace bustier, tiny red panties just covering her triangle of dark blond curls, garters holding up red lace stockings. She turned, giving him the full three-sixty view, and he saw that the panties were actually a thong, her sweet ass bare.

His mouth watered, blood surging to his groin. "Damn."

He fought the urge to bend her over the bed and fuck her right there. A guy only had so many rounds he could fire in a single night, after all, and he didn't want their fun to end too soon.

He closed the distance between them, unbuckled his belt, and drew it slowly through the loops. "Give me your wrists."

Her pupils dilated, her gaze falling on the leather belt. "What are you going to do with me?"

"Everything."

He caught her by one hand, drew her over to one of the big bedposts, then turned her to face away from him and used his belt to bind her wrists to the carved wood. He made sure the belt was tight, but not painfully tight.

He moved around to the other side, kissed her lips, and unzipped his fly. He wasn't wearing underwear tonight, so his erection sprang free, the naked anticipation on her face making him even harder. While she watched, he gave himself a few lazy strokes. "I'm going to make you beg for every inch of this."

"You'll beg first."

"A challenge?" He was game.

He moved to stand behind her, shifted her hair to the side, and kissed her neck, nipping and licking that sensitive skin. She'd worn perfume—just a touch—its musk mingling with the clean scent of her skin, filling his head. "Ellie."

He let his hands have their way, running them over the swells of her breasts and down her belly, over the silky skin of her back and bare ass, beneath the garters on her thighs, savoring the feel of her. Then he reached inside her bustier, and cupped both breasts, his lips finding her pulse. Her nipples pebbled against his palms, inviting him to pluck them, flick them, rub them.

She gave a little gasp, her eyes drifting shut, her hips shifting, her body telling him everything he needed to know.

He kept up the onslaught, knowing how sensitive her nipples were. His mouth found her earlobe. He sucked, bit down gently.

She shivered, her hips moving from side to side.

He brushed his lips over the soft skin of her shoulder, bit her, soothed the pain with a kiss.

She moaned.

He let one hand drift down her belly to cup her. "You're already wet."

He pressed the heel of his hand against her just above her clit, made slow circles, increasing the pressure until her head fell back. "I can do this all day."

It was a lie, but she couldn't know that.

She wriggled her ass, pushing all that sexy back at him, brushing it against him. "I don't think so."

Okay, so maybe he wasn't fooling her.

Still, he kept it up, both hands busy, one between her legs, the other teasing an eager nipple. He could feel the tension inside her, could see the arousal on her face, but she wasn't ready to yield yet.

He caught her clit between two fingers, tugged on it, stroked it. "You are so swollen."

She didn't have a witty comeback this time, her fists clenched against the bedpost, her thighs parting to make room for him.

He found her entrance, teased it with slow circles, sliding just a fingertip inside her—enough to tantalize but not enough to satisfy.

She moaned in frustration.

He pushed his hips forward, rubbed his cock against her lower back, just to let her know what she was missing. The friction made him hornier, too. He ached to be inside her, ached to fill her and bring them both release.

And then she broke. "Fuck me, Jesse. *Please.*"

He reached into his pocket, pulled out a condom, and rolled it over his erection, then moved the red strap of her thong aside, forcing her legs wider apart with his knee. He gave a little nudge, buried just the head of his cock in her. "Like this?"

She whimpered. "More. *Please.*"

He pushed himself in another inch, then withdrew. "Was that what you wanted?"

She laughed, the sound more of a moan, her hips canting backward in invitation. "No! All of you inside me. Please. Please, Jesse."

He entered her again, slowly filling her inch by inch until he was buried to his balls. "God, Ellie."

"*Yes!*"

He'd meant to go slowly, but they were already past that point. He pounded himself into her, one hand busy with her clit, the other grasping her hip. His thrusts rocked her, lifted her onto her toes, desperate moans rolling from her throat.

She drew in a breath, held it, then cried out, ecstasy lighting up her face as she came, her muscles contracting around his cock. He rode out her climax, driving her pleasure home with deep thrusts, then shattered, ecstasy shaking him apart.

Ellie lay back against Jesse in the sunken hot tub, her body replete, jets sending up streams of little bubbles around them. A big arm encircled her waist, his hand playing lazily with one of her breasts. The empty bottle of champagne sat on the floor within arm's reach, two flutes beside it.

"Tell me your fantasies." His voice was deep and sleepy.

"My fantasies? You mean like sexual fantasies?"

"Yeah. Tell me every secret, dirty detail."

She found herself blushing—and she hadn't said anything yet. She'd never talked about her fantasies with a man before. "Well, I liked that tonight—being tied up. It might be nice to be tied to the bed spread eagle, you know?"

"Mmm. Tell me more."

"I've always wanted to be fucked up against the wall, but that would probably be hard work for you."

"I'm hard just thinking about it." He gave her a little nudge with his hips, revealing his erection. "Ever want to play doctor?"

"No. That would make me feel like I was at work, and, believe me, I think very differently about the human body when I'm at the hospital than I do when I'm with you. You don't want to go there."

He chuckled. "Got it."

"I like it when you're forceful."

"Really?"

"I've thought about having you shave me."

"You mean... here?" He reached down, cupped her.

"Yes."

"Jesus."

"And I like your bad-boy vibe."

"My ... what?"

"You know—the bad-boy vibe. Okay, so you've spent your life working as one of the good guys, but put you in black leather, and you'd look like a biker with those muscles and those tats."

He seemed to find this funny. "Good to know."

Chapter Seventeen

A call from the front desk woke them both at five. Ellie whimpered in protest and snuggled deeper into Jesse. "I don't want to."

He chuckled. "I don't think you have a choice."

She didn't. She dragged herself out of bed, her body pleasantly sore, and packed her things together, throwing on a pair of jeans and a sweater. By the time she was ready to go, he'd carried the leftover food to his SUV and had driven the vehicle around to the lodge's door for her.

The sun hadn't yet risen, tiny flakes drifting in a cold wind.

"More snow."

Jesse grinned, as if this were good news. "Yeah. They're saying we'll get another six inches tonight."

"That's not so much."

"That's not what you were telling me last night."

That made her laugh. "I bet you're bigger than six inches."

"I wasn't going to point that out myself, but since you mentioned it..."

They arrived at her house to find Cedar and Claire ready to go and the twins still asleep. Jesse helped Claire out to the car while Cedar carried their overnight bags.

"Thanks." Ellie gave her sister a kiss.

"You're welcome." Claire lowered her voice to a whisper. "Details."

Ellie changed the sheets on her bed—again—and then crawled under the covers, Jesse joining her, the two of them still dressed. And for a while, they slept.

It was just after seven when a little voice woke Ellie.

"Mama?"

"You can sleep," she said to Jesse. "I'll get them changed and make breakfast."

"You handle them. I'll make the grub."

It was almost like being a family—Ellie changing the twins' wet diapers and getting them dressed, Jesse in the kitchen, the two of them sharing the work of getting the day on its feet. It was just one of many things she'd never gotten to experience because of Dan's death.

She had no one with whom to share the day's chores and responsibilities or all the cute little things Daisy and Daniel did each day, the funny things they said. Yes, her parents and sister helped, and she took lots of photos and talked about her day with Claire and her parents. But this past week with Jesse had shown her that it was very different to have someone in the house to live those moments with her.

She combed Daisy's hair into pigtails, then followed the twins out to the kitchen. Full of energy, they chattered with each other and with Jesse, who probably couldn't understand a word of their toddler talk.

"What are you making?" She peered over his shoulder.

"Scrambled eggs, pancakes, and coffee." With his height and his broad shoulders, he dominated the small kitchen—and somehow managed to look sexy doing it.

In fifteen minutes, he had food on the table.

Ellie cut up the kids' pancakes and drizzled them with maple syrup, then sat, the mingled scents making her mouth water. "This is amazing."

He took a sip of coffee. "I guess I need to make breakfast for you more often."

The idea that there might be more mornings like this warmed her like sunshine, but she hadn't forgotten what he'd said about not being good with relationships or kids—or that he'd almost risked his life in a game of Russian roulette with a mountain.

Don't pin your hopes on this, on him.

"Have you told the kids where we're going today?" Jesse asked.

She shook her head. "Daisy and Daniel, we're going to see some horsies and some cows today. What does a cow say?"

"Mooooo," Daisy answered, then giggled.

Daniel echoed her. "Mooooo."

Jesse nodded. "Well, they've got that down."

"Are you sure you want to do this?"

"Do what?"

"Skijoring."

"Hell, yeah."

"Hell, yeah," said Daisy.

Jesse looked wide-eyed at her. "Whoa. Damn."

"Damn," said Daisy.

Ellie had just taken a sip of coffee and had to fight not to choke. "I warned you."

"What's wrong with skijoring?"

"Nothing—if you don't mind breaking bones or risking your life."

"I watched last year. No one died."

"Two guys got hauled to the hospital in ambulances, remember? I just don't want you to get hurt." There was no sense in arguing with him about it. The man climbed rocks for fun, played with explosives at work, and probably skied double-black diamonds without a single thought.

"You're worried about me?"

"Of course, I'm worried," she snapped, then noticed he was smiling. She reached over, took his hand. "I care about you."

He raised her hand to his lips and kissed it.

After breakfast, Jesse helped clean up, then headed home to get his gear.

Ellie called in to let the Wednesday playgroup know they weren't coming, then packed the diaper bag with an extra change of clothes and some snacks. She didn't want the kids to overheat in the car, so she zipped them into their coats and packed a second bag with their snowsuits, boots, hats and an extra pair of mittens each. She had all of it ready by the time Jesse pulled into her driveway.

"Is there anything else I should bring—food, a first-aid kit," she asked as they carried the kids' car seats to his SUV.

"We're going to a ranch, not the seventeenth century."

She climbed into the passenger seat, and they were off.

"Holy fucking shit." Jesse stared at the Wests' house. "That's their *house?*"

It was a mansion. Built of stone and logs, it was massive, with floor-to-ceiling windows that looked out onto the surrounding mountains. Stone chimneys jutted upward from the multi-pitch roof, smoke curling against the gray sky. The front door was set back from a portico driveway accented by a colonnade of polished logs. Off to one side stood several enormous outbuildings, including what looked like a large horse barn complete with several corrals.

Ellie stared, too. "I've heard about it, but I've never been here before."

"I was expecting a log house like in Bonanza or something."

She looked at him and laughed. "Bonanza?"

Jesse drove around to the back of the house and stared again, ogling the multiple-car garage that was attached at the rear. "I thought Jack West served as a Ranger. Rangers don't make this kind of money."

"His family has owned this piece of land for three or four generations. They've done really well for themselves with horse breeding."

"I can see that."

"Did you tell them the kids and I were coming, too?"

"Yeah. Nate said he was fine with that."

"Nate is a marine. He and Dan were friends. He was horribly burned in an IED explosion. It was in the paper every day for a while—updates on how he was doing. I didn't think he would survive, but he pulled through."

"He didn't mention that he was a marine. He must be a modest guy." Jesse climbed out, opened the rear passenger door and unbuckled Daniel, who reached for him with little arms, still clinging to his blanket. "Come here, big boy."

"Welcome to the Cimarron."

Jesse turned to see a man about his age and height walking toward him, a white cowboy hat on his head. "Hey. I'm Jesse Moretti."

The right side of the man's face was badly scarred from burns, as was the hand he held out. "Nate West." His gaze shifted to Ellie. "Hey, Ellie."

Jesse shook his hand. "You two know each other?"

Of course, they did.

"She was a few years behind me in school. I knew her husband, Dan. He was as good as they come. And these are your twins. Hey, guys." Nate took Daniel's hand, sadness flashing across his face. "Wow. You look just like your daddy. Come on inside and meet everyone."

Jesse followed him, carrying Daniel, while Ellie carried Daisy. They passed through the five-car garage—talk about a wet dream—and entered a mudroom.

"Don't worry about taking off your boots." Nate led them down a hallway to a kitchen, where an older man was stirring something on the stove. "Dad, this is Jesse Moretti and Ellie Meeks and her twins. Jesse, Ellie, this is my father, Jack."

"Always pleased to meet another Ranger." Jack shook Jesse's hand, his gaze fixing on Daniel. "He looks just like Dan."

"That's Daniel," Ellie said. "And this is Daisy."

"Hello, there, Daniel and Daisy." Jack's gaze moved to Ellie. "I was sorry to hear about your loss. I knew Dan from the time he was a little boy, watched him grow up."

"You came to the memorial service," Ellie said. "I remember. Thank you."

"Dad's making chili for lunch."

Jesse inhaled. "That smells incredible."

"Damn straight," said Jack.

"Damn," said Daisy.

"Uh-oh." Jack gave Ellie a sheepish grin. "I'd best watch my mouth around her. She's a smart little cookie."

"Like you watch your mouth around your grandkids, Dad?" Nate chuckled. "The rest of the family is in the playroom. Let me show you around."

In short order, they'd gotten a tour of a home that out-classed even the luxury suite at the Scarlet Mountain Resort and met Nate's wife, Megan, and their kids—Emily, who was eight, and Jackson, who was nineteen months old. Nate also introduced them to Jack's wife, Janet, and their little girl, Lily, who was eighteen months old.

Emily was fascinated with the twins. "Can they play with me?"

"I think they'd like that." Ellie set Daisy down.

Jesse did the same with Daniel.

"Why don't you and I go out and get started?" Nate said.

Jesse followed Nate outside. "Have you done this before?"

"I've done it on both sides of the horse." While Jesse loaded his gear into Nate's pickup truck, Nate went over the basics. "You'll want to keep your mouth shut and wear ski goggles. A couple dozen horses running down the same stretch of road means a lot of horse shit. Sooner or later, a clod is going to fly up and hit you in the face."

"I hadn't thought of that."

"You don't want to wrap the rope around your arm. That's how you end up with a broken wrist. Just hold onto it."

"Got it."

"And no slack. Make sure the rope stays tight, or you'll get jerked off your feet and maybe dislocate your shoulder."

"No slack."

"I'll ride straight down the middle. You'll use the edges of your skis to control your direction back and forth. Based on prior years, there will be three jumps, three gates to move through, and three rings at the end that you need to catch on your arm."

"I watched last year."

Nate grinned. "You're going to love it. One last thing. The road is hard-packed snow with asphalt beneath, so if you fall, the pain is real. Don't fall."

They climbed into the pickup and drove a short distance from the ranch house, past a small stone building that looked like a picnic shelter. In the distance, he could see a ranch hand holding the reins of a big palomino horse and...

Jesse stared. Nate had put together a full-sized skijoring course complete with two six-foot jumps, a four-foot jump, a couple of gates, and even rings. "Holy shit. You never do anything half-assed around here, do you?"

Nate chuckled. "Not if we can help it."

Ellie sat in the playroom talking with Megan and Janet while Emily played with the twins and the two littlest ones parallel played on the floor near their mothers. "She's really good with them."

Megan smiled, her gaze on her daughter. "She's had a lot of practice. She was so excited when she found out there were going to be two babies in the house."

"Does she understand that Lily is her aunt?"

Megan nodded. "She understood before Lily was born that the baby would be her daddy's little sister or brother. She's always just accepted that as normal, though she was a little jealous at first when Janet came into Jack's life. She adores Jack."

Janet laughed. "He adores her. You want to know who runs this ranch? She's eight and has big blue eyes and blond hair."

Emily ran up to them. "Have the twins ever seen horses?"

"No, they haven't. Would you like to show them?"

Emily's face lit up. "Can we, Mommy?"

Megan stood. "Let's bundle up. It's cold out there."

Ten minutes later, the small herd of children moved together through the house toward the back door, either in their mother's arms or on their own feet, Emily leading the way, Jack promising to join them in a few minutes.

"Buckwheat is my horse. He's a gelding. He's with my daddy today, but we have other horses," Emily told the twins.

"She's been riding since she was four," Megan explained. "That's when I met Nate. He adopted her after we got married."

A bittersweet longing washed through Ellie. "It must have meant so much to you—to give her a father, to have someone to raise her with you."

"Nate has been wonderful for her."

They stepped outside to find it snowing lightly, the sky overcast, the wind cold. Thankfully, it wasn't a long walk to the barn.

Inside it was much warmer, the mingled odors of straw and manure tickling Ellie's nose. They turned a corner and... "Oh! Look at them!"

The twins' faces lit up.

Daisy pointed and looked up at Ellie as if to ask, "What is that, Mama?"

"That's a horsie. Can you see the horsies, Daniel?"

A half-dozen palomino mares stood in their stalls, munching on hay. They whickered when they heard Emily's voice and walked toward their gates, clearly familiar with her and happy to see her.

Emily introduced them to the horses. "This is Baby Doe. She's my favorite mare. She's going to foal in March. I hope it's a filly because we might get to keep it."

They met Molly Brown, Chipeta, Isabella Bird, Julia Greeley, and Clara Brown—all beautiful palominos named after famous women from Colorado's history. All were in foal, which meant they were pregnant, Emily explained.

Ellie found herself laughing and in need of an extra pair of hands as the twins, curious and excited, stuck their hands in the stalls trying to touch the horses and ran every which way, chattering to one another. She finally picked Daisy up and did her best to hold onto the back of Daniel's coat.

Jack walked up to her. "You look like you've got your hands full."

He scooped up Daniel and helped him pet one of the mares. "Be gentle. There you go. See how soft her muzzle is? Can you say horsie?"

"Howsie."

"Good enough."

"Miss Emily, let's tack up Baby Doe." Jack took a lead rope from a nail on the wall and handed it to Emily, who entered Baby Doe's stall, clipped it to the mare's halter, and led the big animal out and down a walkway. "How old are your twins, Ellie?"

"They'll be three in April."

"Then it's high time they learned to ride." While Emily saddled the mare, Jack took a small riding helmet from a nearby shelf and put it on Daniel's head, fixing the strap under his chin. "Are you ready to ride this horsie, young man?"

Ellie shook her head. "Oh, I don't think—"

"This is what he does," Megan said. "The twins will be safe. He's ridden with kids with severe disabilities, kids who can't even talk. When he was two, he was riding by himself. So was Nate. Crazy, isn't it?"

It certainly seemed crazy to Ellie, who could imagine a dozen ways it could all go terribly wrong. Being a nurse meant having a vivid imagination where injury and catastrophe were concerned.

Emily rode the mare first under Jack's watchful eye, the child looking like she'd been born on a horse.

"My daughter loves to ride."

Ellie laughed. "I couldn't tell."

When Emily dismounted, Jack adjusted the stirrups, took her place in the saddle, and then reached for Daniel. "Are you ready, buddy?"

The moment Jack settled Daniel into the saddle in front of him, Ellie's fear melted away. Jack had absolute mastery of the animal. More than that, Daniel was in heaven. He smiled and laughed, petting the horse and squealing with delight when Jack brought the mare to a lope.

Then it was Daisy's turn. The sound of her laughter was precious to Ellie as Jack rode Baby Doe in circles through the soft sand. But when her turn was over, Daisy didn't want to come down. She started crying when Jack handed her to Ellie.

"You'll just have to come back and do it again sometime." Jack looked straight into Ellie's eyes. "You and the twins are welcome any time, Ellie. I mean that. After Dan's death, we didn't want to intrude. We knew Dan, but we didn't have a relationship with you. Now we do."

Ellie's throat grew tight, warmth blossoming in her chest. "Thank you, Jack. And thanks for this."

"You're welcome." He led the mare back the way they'd come. "Let me get Baby Doe back in her stall, and then we'll take a sleigh ride out to see what the idiot menfolk are doing. I had one of my hands hook a pair of geldings to the sleigh. Do you want to help me with the reins, Miss Emily?"

Jesse took the slack out of the rope, his body tensed and ready. "Go!"

His body was snapped forward as Nate brought the horse to a gallop, snow flying beneath his skis, wind in his face. He couldn't help but smile.

He turned to the right, made it through the first gate, then veered to the left, the horse pulling him up the six-foot jump and into the air. "Woohoo!"

He stuck the landing and swung to the right to catch the second gate, Nate urging the gelding to go faster.

The next jump was dead center.

He sailed up and over, catching air again.

Fuck, yeah.

He swung to the left and sailed through the last gate then veered hard to the right, rode up and over the third jump, another six-footer. He felt like he was flying.

He made the landing, then straightened himself up and let go of the rope with his right hand, aiming his arm like a spear to catch the three rings.

One. Two.

Damn it.

His fist punched the last ring off its hook, knocking it to the ground.

He skied to a stop and caught his breath, Nate riding back toward him.

"Hell." Nate shook his head, smiling ear to ear. "You almost had it."

"You know, even when you fuck it up, this is fun. It's a lot like wakeboarding."

"Yeah—except that you're not landing in water when you fall."

They took a break, drinking hot coffee from a thermos Nate had brought in the saddle bags. "So you and Ellie Meeks, huh?"

"Yeah. It wasn't anything I planned." He and Nate didn't know each other well, but Jesse had to ask. "What's it like being a dad?"

"It's great. I love it. Megan is the best thing that ever happened to me, and the kids are right there with her." He was quiet for a moment as if deciding whether to say more. "Megan had a rough life before I met her. Emily was four when we got together. I adopted Emily when Megan and I got married. I love that little girl like my own. She never knew a father before me. In every way that counts, I *am* her father."

"Wow. Yeah. That's great." It felt like a revelation to Jesse.

He'd always thought that his dad had beaten him because he wasn't truly his son. Some part of him had accepted it as natural that a man couldn't love children that weren't his blood. But now thinking of his feelings for Daniel and Daisy—and considering what Nate had just told him—it seemed to him that his father had beaten him because the man was an asshole.

"I'm going to go out on a limb here," Nate said. "I don't know you well, but I hear good things. You're on the Team. You're a patroller. You've saved lives. You've served your country. But don't hurt Ellie. Dan was a good friend of mine. I care about what happens to the woman he loved and the kids he never got to see."

Nate spoke the words in a friendly enough way, but the warning was clear.

"I don't want to hurt her. The last thing I want to do is hurt her. I knew Dan, too. We called him Crash, short for Crashhawk. He was the pilot on at least a dozen direct actions I was involved in, and there were a handful of times when he came in for a hot extract, guns blazing, and saved our asses."

Nate glared at him. "You were buddies, and you're with his wife?"

"I didn't know she was his wife." A sticky sense of guilt had Jesse defending himself. "She and I have been neighbors for two years. I helped her one night when her car broke down, and she and Daniel were sick. I knew she was a Gold Star wife, but it didn't click that she was Crash's wife. It's not like he and I were close buds. I only saw him a few times outside of his bird, and that was just in passing."

"Okay, well, that's different." The anger faded from Nate's face.

But now Jesse was pissed. "If you and Dan were so close and you care so much about Ellie, where have you been these past three years?"

"That's a fair question. We started a college fund for her kids. The whole town contributed. She knows it's there, but she doesn't know we started it. We didn't have a personal relationship, and we didn't want to impose on her grief." Nate's gaze shifted to something behind Jesse. "It looks like the old man brought lunch."

Jesse looked over his shoulder to see two horses pulling a sleigh, Jack and Emily at the reins, the women and kids piled into seats behind him and covered by blankets. "Wow."

Nate towed Jesse over to the picnic shelter, tying off the horse's reins while Jesse stepped out of his bindings. "Does Ellie know that you knew Dan?"

"No." At first, she'd been sick, and it hadn't seemed right to bring it up, and then... "I need to tell her."

Chapter Eighteen

Jesse was unusually quiet on the drive home from the Cimarron. Ellie didn't notice at first because all she could do was rave about how amazing their day had been. She didn't know what had been more fun—watching the kids ride for the first time, going for a sleigh ride, or getting up the courage to ask Jack if she could try riding. She'd also felt better after she'd watched Jesse fly through the skijoring course after lunch. It was only when he didn't seem to hear this comment that she realized something was wrong.

The kids had fallen asleep on the drive back to Scarlet Springs, worn out from all the excitement. Jesse carried in Daniel while she carried Daisy. They put them in their beds. On the way back down the hallway, she finally asked him about it.

"Are you okay? You're so quiet."

"We need to talk."

That didn't sound good. Had she said or done something to upset him? Had something happened at the Cimarron?

"Okay. Do you want a cup of coffee or something to drink?"

"No. Thanks. I'm fine."

They sat at the table, and she waited.

"There's something I should have told you when we first met. At first, it didn't seem important, and then I just let it go."

She reached for his hand. "What is it?"

"I knew Dan."

Blood rushed to her head. "Wh-what?"

"We all had nicknames over there, so at first I didn't make the connection. I knew him as Crashhawk. We all called him Crash. I should have told you, but at first it seemed irrelevant and after that .. I didn't want to stir up old memories for you. I should have told you before we got involved, and for that I'm sorry."

But Ellie's mind hadn't gotten past his revelation, rage making her face burn. "You knew Dan? You knew my husband, and now you're sleeping with me?"

"I didn't know him that well. We didn't hang together. He flew maybe fifteen actions for us, saved our asses a few times. We didn't hang out."

"So Dan flew you and your guys on some of your missions and maybe even saved your life. You came back, but Dan died in that helicopter."

Grief cut through her, sharp and dark.

Oh, Dan.

"If I could change that for you and take his place in Arlington, I'd do it."

"That's not what I meant. I don't want that." She'd said something pretty close to it, hadn't she? "I'm sorry. It came out wrong. I was just stating a fact."

She fought to keep herself together. "When did you figure it out?"

"The night you were sick. I saw the SOAR patch on my way out, and it finally clicked. Ellie Meeks. Dan Meeks. Crash."

"You didn't think it was important enough to tell me?"

"Not that night, no. You were sick, pale and dizzy. Daniel was sick and crying. You didn't need a stranger bringing up the past."

"Okay." That was fair. "What about later? What about the night we first kissed and I told you all about him? Or how about when you were in his bed and I asked you if the photos of him bothered you?"

Jesse's gaze went hard and cold, and he leaned in. "When I was in *your* bed, the only person I was thinking about was *you.*"

That made her mind go blank for a moment.

"I wasn't trying to withhold anything from you. With everything that's been happening, I just didn't think about it."

"You didn't think about it?"

"I should have told you before we got involved. I'm sorry. I care about you. I—"

"You should go now."

"Ellie, I—"

"I just need some time."

A muscle clenched in his jaw. He stood. "If that's what you want."

She stood and walked to her bedroom, fighting tears. There on the walls were photos of the man she'd loved—and lost. What would he say if he knew she'd been sleeping with a man he'd known?

She sank down on the bed, looked at the ring on her finger, and tried to straighten out the tangled mess of emotions inside her.

She needed to talk to Claire. She needed to tell her sister what had happened. She walked out to the kitchen in search of her cell phone, and that's when she saw it.

Her key.

He'd left it on the kitchen table.

Jesse held the bottle of rum, his resolve slipping.

Drinking won't make it better.

No, it wouldn't. He would just end up with a hangover to go with the sickness in his heart. Then again, didn't heartbreak and hangovers go together? Besides, it might make him numb for a while, and right now he desperately needed to stop feeling.

He poured himself a drink, tossed it back, poured another, then went to sit in the chair in front of his wood stove, taking the bottle with him.

He had fucked up, and he was paying for it. Why hadn't he told her? Why hadn't he come right out with it that first night? She'd been so hurt, so angry. But it wasn't as if he'd tried to deceive her. He'd just forgotten to tell her.

Jesus.

He'd been so close to having something special with her, to being more than he'd ever thought he could be. He might have married her. He might have done like Nate and been a father to her kids.

Regret, cold and sharp, cut into him.

Daniel and Daisy.

The thought of never seeing them again made him feel actual fucking pain in his chest, as if someone had just cut through his sternum.

You knew this wouldn't work out. You knew it was a bad idea.

He shouldn't have left the key. Then he would at least have a reason to see her again. He could have waited, then asked if she wanted the key back. But he hadn't been thinking tactically. He'd been hurt and angry, and so had she.

You came back, but Dan died in that helicopter.

She said she hadn't meant it the way it had sounded, but Jesse had meant every word he'd said. If he could change places with Dan, be the one who died, trade his life for Dan's life, he would do it. Dan had left behind two unborn children and a wife who loved him. No one would have missed Jesse.

Restlessness had him on his feet. He emptied his glass, set it down on the coffee table, and walked with the bottle to his front window. He took a drink, watched darkness cover the world outside, the last rays of sunlight fading away.

How was he supposed to go back to the life he'd had before Ellie?

Maybe he was overreacting. She'd said she needed time, not that she didn't want to see him again. Maybe she would call him or text him, and he could find some way to make it up to her. Maybe he could still make this right. Some part of him wanted to walk down the hill to her house, apologize again, and tell her exactly how he felt about her.

And how do you feel?

Did he love her?

No. Yes. Hell, he didn't know.

All he knew for certain was that he'd been a better man with Ellie than he could ever be without her.

O n Thursday morning, Ellie dragged herself out of bed, put her heartache over Jesse aside and got ready for heartache of another kind. Today was little Tyler Kirby's funeral service. She dressed in black, put the kids in their nicest clothes, and met her mother and father at St. Barbara's. It seemed that everyone in Scarlet Springs had turned out to stand by the Kirby family in their grief, the pews crowded, not even standing room available, the parking lot overflowing.

Eric Hawke passed by in his full fire chief dress uniform.

"You look snappy, young man," her father said.

"I broke out all the official jewelry today," Eric said, running his fingers over the golden badge and the pins and medals on his jacket. "Ellie, Mrs. Rouse."

He seemed to be there in an official capacity. He and his crew took their positions, standing at attention around the tiny casket, which was covered by a white pall and a spray of white roses.

She glanced around and saw Eric's wife Victoria sitting with Lexi and Lexi's dad and stepmom. Mrs. Beech was there. So was Joe from Knockers, together with much of his staff, including Rain and her daughter, Lark. Rose, always dramatic, was wearing a black lace veil over her silver hair. Frank from the gas station had come in his finest overalls. Megs sat in the back with most of the Team, no yellow T-shirts this time.

The service started, the guy with the bushy beard who ran the new marijuana dispensary playing hymns on the organ. Ellie wasn't Catholic, but she did her best to follow along in the program, which included the words they were supposed to say and when to kneel or stand.

The kids had a hard time being quiet, so she and her mom ended up taking turns with them in the nursery area, where they could talk and play without disturbing anyone and where they could hear the service piped in by some kind of microphone system. When communion was finished, Carrie Kirby stood and walked up to the microphone to eulogize her own son.

"All I have of my firstborn son are photographs and happy memories, so please indulge me while I tell you what a wonderful child he was."

Ellie, who was back in the pew with her father, could not hold back her tears while Carrie, who was remarkably composed, shared stories about Tyler. Ellie wasn't alone in her tears, audible sobs and sniffs coming from the audience.

"What he wanted most was to be a firefighter. He came home from school to tell me that the fire chief had come to his class and that he'd seen a fire engine. He wore a firefighter costume for that Halloween, and we had a hard time getting him to take it off."

Quiet laughter.

"Tyler, you are beyond us now. You are beyond pain. But we will always, always love you. God bless you and rest in peace, my sweet darling." With those words, her knees seemed to go weak, the priest and her husband helping her back to her seat.

Eric and his crew walked up to the little casket and saluted it. The pall was removed and replaced with a small American flag. Then Eric set a firefighter's helmet next to the flowers. And as the firefighters passed, carrying the casket out to the waiting hearse, Ellie saw tears streaming down Eric's face.

Ellie wept as she told Claire about the funeral and the graveside service that had followed and how Carrie had held onto her when she'd paid her respects. "She actually thanked me. I couldn't save Tyler. None of us could do anything for him, and still, she thanked us—all of us."

They talked until Ellie had cried herself out.

"So, do I get to ask how it went at the hotel?"

Okay, so maybe she wasn't quite finished with tears. "I think it's over between Jesse and me."

"What? How can it be over? What can possibly have gone wrong in thirty-six hours? You were practically fucking each other with your eyes Tuesday night."

Ellie told her about their night at the hotel and their day at the Cimarron—how perfect both had been and how horribly the day had ended. "He left the key on my table."

"Have you heard from him since?"

"No. Nothing. He left the key so that must mean he's done."

"Or maybe he thinks you're done."

"I told him I needed time, not that I never wanted to see him again."

"Can I ask you something without you getting mad at me?"

"I don't know."

"Okay, well, I'm going to do it anyway. So what if he knew Dan? What's the big deal with that?"

"It's a military thing." How could she explain this? "You don't fight beside your buddy, watch him die, then come home and use his wife's grief to get sex."

"That's not what Jesse did. It's not as if he moved into the cabin knowing who you were and spent the past two years waiting for your car to break down in a snowstorm so he could seduce you and babysit your kids."

"Well…" Ellie had nothing.

"Besides, you said he and Dan didn't know each other well, that they just did some missions or actions or whatever together. It sounds like you guys got caught up in something that neither of you expected and that his connection to Dan wasn't the first thing on his mind. That's kind of a compliment if you think about it."

Claire wasn't getting the point.

"He fucked me in the bed I shared with Dan with Dan's photos on the walls, and he didn't think, 'Maybe I should tell her that I knew her husband.'"

"Are you sure the real issue here isn't that you feel guilty? Maybe his bringing up Dan brought it all crashing in on you."

"No!" Ellie realized she'd shouted into the phone, rage mixing with a sinking feeling that her sister might be right. "Why should I feel guilty? Dan wanted me to be happy. He made me promise I would move on. How many times have you told me that?"

"You've spent almost four years saying you can't move on. Then you meet Jesse and you're magically cured—except that you're still wearing your wedding ring. Dan's photos are still all over the walls. Then, when he mentions Dan, you flip."

Ellie let out a breath, tried not to get upset. "It's not just that he mentioned Dan. It's that he knew him. They fought together. He said Dan even saved his life a few times. Dan saved his life. But it took him until yesterday to tell me any of this."

"Okay, so he ought to have told you. All I know, sis, is that a brave, sexy man cares about you and your kids enough to cook for the three of you, shovel your sidewalk, and fuck your brains out. You need to think hard before you end this."

"I didn't say I was ending it."

"Why would he leave the key unless he believed that's what you wanted?"

I t was after nine—and a lot of rum—when she knocked on Jesse's door.

"Jesse, I know you're in there. Please let me know you're okay. I've called. I've texted. I've left messages. But you're not answering."

She'd called? He hadn't gotten any damned phone calls or texts. Then he remembered he'd turned his cell phone off, the silence too hard to take.

"I can't leave the kids home alone for long. I shouldn't leave them alone at all, but I have to see you. I have to know you're all right."

So, this was a welfare check. She didn't really want to see him. She just wanted to make sure he hadn't done anything stupid. Well, he hadn't done anything stupid—if you didn't count getting drunk in his underwear.

"I'll call the police, and they'll break down your door. Please, open up. It's freezing out here."

Well, fuck.

He couldn't afford a new door.

"I'll call Megs."

Okay, now Ellie was just playing dirty. Megs would rake his ass over the coals.

He put the bottle down, got unsteadily to his feet, and walked to the front door, then realized she was standing at the side door. He turned, tripped over one of the legs to his sofa and almost fell on his face. He caught himself, straightened up, then walked to the door and opened it.

"Oh, thank God." She stood there in sub-zero temps in nothing more than a T-shirt and jeans, teeth chattering. "This is the second time you've opened the door in your underwear."

He looked down. "You're counting?"

"You've been drinking."

"Yeah. Seemed like the right thing to do. You've been crying."

"Today was Tyler Kirby's funeral."

Oh. Shit.

"Sorry. That must've been hard."

She nodded. "It was beautiful and horrible. They made him an honorary firefighter and buried him with full honors."

"That was a good thing to do."

Damn, it was cold.

"You got your stitches out."

"I took them out myself. It's not hard." He pointed toward his sofa and the wood stove. "You should come in before you become hypothermic."

She shook her head. "I can't leave the kids alone like this. I had to know you're okay. Also, you left something at my house. I want you to have it back."

She took his hand, pressed something into it.

The key to her house.

His gaze jerked to hers. "Why are you giving me this?"

"Because despite everything I said yesterday, I'm glad you're in my life. It might be my emotions getting in the way here as much as anything you did or didn't do. I care about you, Jesse. I said I needed time. I didn't tell you to get out of my life, did I?"

"It sure sounded like that to me."

"I'm sorry for that."

"I should've told you. I don't know why I didn't. I wasn't trying to trick you or pull the wool over those pretty green eyes of yours."

"I believe you."

He wanted to kiss her but realized his breath was probably a hundred proof. Instead, he reached out and cupped her cheek.

She turned her face into his hand, kissed his palm. "I missed you today."

"I missed you, too." He'd never spoken truer words in his life.

With that, she turned and hurried through his backyard, glancing over her shoulder at him. "Close your door, or you're going to freeze."

He didn't shut the door. Instead, he stepped into a pair of boots, grabbed his parka and stood there in his backyard in his underwear, looking like a total jackass and freezing his nuts off, watching to make sure she made it safely home.

When she locked the door behind her, he walked back into his cabin and dumped the rest of the rum down the drain.

Chapter Nineteen

O n Friday, Ellie was assigned to the recovery room to fill in for a fellow RN who was out sick. She spent eight long, slow hours taking vitals, administering pain meds, and reassuring groggy patients that they were okay. Compared to the ER, it was pretty quiet, giving her time to think—perhaps too much time.

Claire was right. Ellie had been so caught up in the emotions of being wanted and wanting someone again that she'd ignored her guilt about being sexually involved with another man. The intellectual side of her knew that Dan would want her to move on. Hadn't he made her promise she would?

But three weeks ago, she'd still thought of herself as Dan's wife. She'd still thought of him as her husband. It was a lot to set aside in such a short time.

Somehow, hearing that Jesse had known him had brought it all to the surface. He shouldn't have kept it from her, but she shouldn't have said the things she'd said to him.

You came back, but Dan died in that helicopter.

The memory of her own words made her wince. There'd been desolation in his eyes, as if he felt it was an injustice somehow that he had survived.

God, she hadn't meant that the way it sounded.

She texted him on her lunch break, wanting to know he was okay, wanting to know that the fragile bond between them was still intact.

SEE YOU TONIGHT?

How he was getting through the day with what must have been a killer hangover, she didn't know. Then again, he was a big man, and men metabolized alcohol faster than women. If she had polished off most of a bottle of rum, she'd have ended up in the ER getting her stomach pumped.

She was glad that he was seeing a therapist. She hoped he would mention the drinking. He was self-medicating, and it would hurt him in the end. Everything he loved—climbing, ski patrol, the Team—depended on him staying strong and healthy. Booze wouldn't fix anything.

He replied five minutes later.

I'D LIKE THAT.

Some of the tension she'd been carrying eased.

She finished her shift and was thrilled that her mother invited her and the kids to stay for supper. Walking through the front door of her parents' house always felt like slipping into a hot tub of water.

She stepped through the door, a heavenly scent in the air that made her mouth water. "What are you cooking? It smells incredible."

"Pork roast, potatoes, salad, and green beans," her mother called from the kitchen. "Pork roasts were on sale at Food Mart."

 Daniel and Daisy came around the corner and ran to her. "Mama!"

She slipped out of her coat and got down on her knees, hugging them to her, the feel of them precious in her arms. "I'm *so* happy to see you! What did you do today?"

They both spoke at once, the word "horsie" in there several times.

Soon, dinner was on the table.

"I've heard a lot about horses today—and a certain Jesse." Her mother was not one to bother with subtlety. "This is the gentleman who helped you and who needed your father to pay a house call, right?"

"Yes." Ellie looked over at her father, who seemed to be especially fascinated by the contents of his dinner plate.

"Just be careful—if you know what I mean," her mother said.

"Mom, I'm a mother, an RN, and I'm twenty-eight, not fifteen." Ellie knew how to make them change the subject. "Jesse is a former Army Ranger, a combat veteran. He knew Dan."

Her father's head snapped up. "He knew Dan?"

"I guess Dan flew him and his men on some of their missions. He said he thinks Dan saved his life a time or two."

Ellie's mother reached over, gave Ellie's arm a squeeze. "What a small and interconnected world it is."

"T he kid scared the bejesus out of himself." Matt stood across from Jesse and Kevin, arms crossed over his chest, Boomer at his feet, everyone else gone for the day. "He doesn't want to be on explosives, and I don't see how we can ask him to keep doing that. It's a huge liability issue if anything happens as a result."

Jesse had no argument there. "If he wants out, he should be out. We can't have someone handling live charges if they're spooked. His head would have to be in the game, and it's not."

"So, he's off explosives," Kevin said. "Do any of our patrollers want the job?"

"Amanda." Matt looked from Jesse to Kevin. "Amanda told me she wants to learn the skill. She has zero experience with avalanche work. I don't know how the two of you feel about that."

"What—you mean because she's a woman?" Kevin shrugged. "Who cares?"

A sense of uneasiness stirred in Jesse's chest, the idea of a woman working with explosives troubling for reasons he couldn't explain. It's not as if having a vagina or boobs made it harder to light a fuse or throw a charge accurately. He fought back his initial response. "It's fine with me. I can start training her right away, give her an overview, show her what not to do."

With that matter settled, Jesse changed out of his gear and headed down to the parking lot. Travis was there with a couple of young women, drinking beer out of a cooler stashed in the back of his pickup.

"I took a call about the guy with a broken nose." Travis waved to Jesse. "Man, I have never seen so much blood. It was gushing. I thought he was going to choke. The blood froze on the snow."

The women seemed impressed by this.

"Who's your friend?" one of the women asked, looking at Jesse.

"Hey, Jesse, come hang. I've got very attractive company—and beer."

"Nah. Thanks. I need to get home." Jesse had heard of patrollers taking advantage of the job to get laid but he hadn't thought much about it until now.

The woman who'd asked about him let out a disappointed moan.

"And, hey, Travis, if you're going to drink, don't drive." Jesse climbed into his Jeep and made the drive back to Scarlet, his mind taking the familiar path to the only woman who interested him—Ellie.

She wanted to see him tonight, and he didn't think it was to tell him to get lost. She'd had that chance already. She'd actually stood outside his door in a T-shirt and jeans in freezing weather to give him her key. No, she didn't want to end things.

But where was this relationship headed?

Hell, he had no idea.

He had fallen for her. He'd fallen hard. There was really no point in bullshitting himself any longer. He cared about her the way he'd cared about no other woman. He cared about Daisy and Daniel, too. If he was capable of feeling love, then he loved them—all three of them.

Who could have seen this coming?

Not Jesse. That's for damned sure.

The only way to find out where this would go was to keep moving forward. It was like climbing. You kept going up and up, not knowing where your next handhold would be until you got there, your ass hanging a thousand feet above the ground. The unknown excited him when it came to climbing. But when it came to relationships, it scared the shit out of him.

Well, that's just how it was. He'd never quit on a climbing route, and he wasn't about to quit on Ellie.

Ellie left a note on the back door telling Jesse just to let himself in. It's not that she didn't want to get the door. She wanted him to know he was still welcome. To pass the time, she curled up with a book on the sofa. She didn't realize she'd fallen asleep until warm lips pressed a kiss against her forehead. She opened her eyes, saw Jesse looking down at her, his blue eyes soft. He'd showered and shaved and was wearing a black cable knit sweater over faded blue jeans.

She sat up. "What time is it?"

"Nine-fifteen."

She'd sat down a half hour ago. "I guess I wore myself out today. Can I get you some tea or coffee or some water maybe? I'm going to make some tea for myself."

She didn't offer him scotch.

"No thanks. I'm good."

She walked to the kitchen, words she'd spoken last time he was here still weighing heavily on her. She had apologized, but only in a very hurried way, given that she'd been freezing outside his door.

"I'm glad you came." She deliberately kept her distance, not wanting to cross the bridge into physical contact again until they had sorted this out. She opened her mouth to go on, but he beat her to it.

"I'm sorry I didn't tell you, Ellie. You have every right to be angry. I wasn't trying to keep anything from you. I didn't want to tell you that first night, but there were other times, and plenty of them, where I could've said something and didn't. I don't understand why I didn't bring it up. I wasn't trying to deceive you."

"Apology accepted." Now it was her turn. "I am so sorry about what I said. Never in a million years would I wish that you had died instead of Dan. I never thought that. I never felt that. But I can see how it might sound like that's what I meant."

"I meant what I said. I would change places—"

"Please don't say that. Dan knew what he did might get him killed, but he chose to do it anyway for the good of others. I've had to accept that. He's gone. You're here."

The tea kettle whistled behind her.

She quickly made herself a cup of blueberry tea—something that wouldn't keep her awake—and they moved to the living room.

"I've been wondering…" She hesitated, afraid this might be hard for him to understand.

"Yeah?"

"Can you tell me anything about him? You knew him in a different way. I never saw that part of him—the pilot, the soldier on deployment."

He got a thoughtful frown on his face. "The man could fly a Black Hawk like no one else. I remember the first time my crew and I flew with him. He dropped us in the middle of nowhere, a few clicks from a village where AQ was stockpiling weapons. He gave us all a big grin and did a little flight attendant routine. 'We're going to be flying at ten thousand feet over some seriously fucked-up terrain tonight. If you look on the left side, you can see desert. On your right, yes, more desert.' That kind of thing."

Ellie found herself smiling, the person Jesse described definitely her Dan.

"He had a photo of you stuck to his dashboard, but I never got a look at it. He would point to it and call you his angel. 'I'm on leave next month. I'm going home to see my angel.'"

Ellie's throat went tight. "That's what he called me at home, too. His angel."

She listened while Jesse recounted everything he could remember about Dan—how he liked to poke fun at the other branches of the military, how he'd gotten a reputation for winning at poker, how he'd flown in under fire more than once to get Jesse and his men out.

"There was this time…" The color left Jesse's face. His eyes lost their focus and went wide. "*No. No!*"

A chill shivered down Ellie's spine. She got on her knees next to him, took his cheeks in her palms. "Jesse, talk to me."

*T**he IED explosion knocked him onto his ass, bits of rock, shrapnel, and sand spraying around him.*

Christine!

Ears ringing, he dragged himself to his feet. "Christine!"

And then he saw her.

She lay gasping for breath about twenty feet to his left, blood pouring from a shrapnel wound in her throat, both of her legs missing below the knee.

Jesse ran for her, sand blowing in his face, AK rounds whining past his head.

He dropped to his knees beside her, ripped his medic kit from his pack. "Stay with me, Christine. Stay with me."

"Don't … let … me … die."

Jesus. Not Christine.

"I'm not going to let you die. I'm right here."

The ambush had taken them all by surprise, and everyone was pinned down.

He tied a pressure bandage around her throat, holding it in place with one hand while he gave her an autoinjector of morphine with the other. Then he tied tourniquets around what was left of both legs.

Thudthudthud.

AK rounds hit the sand behind him in rapid succession.

Fuck.

He reached into his kit again, pulled out a twenty gauge IV needle. She'd already lost a lot of blood, and she would die if he couldn't get fluids into her. He turned her head to the side, searching for that external jugular, blood from her neck wound soaking through the bandage.

Son of a bitch.

"Hang on, Christine."

A Black Hawk passed overhead, guns opening up, raining death on the enemy. Crash was here with his crew to haul their asses out of this mess.

Jesse got the line going, hooked it up to a bag of lactated ringers, and let those fluids run. "Stay with me, Christine. We're going to take good care of you."

Out of it on morphine, she smiled up at him.

Holding the IV bag between his teeth, he scooped her into his arms and ran through the hail of weapons fire toward the extraction point, trying to shelter her small body with his. Sand churned beneath his boots, making it hard to build up speed, wind-driven sand biting his skin.

The Black Hawk began its descent, landing two hundred meters ahead of him.

Hang on, honey.

The rest of his element was heading toward the bird, too. He could hear their M-4s laying down suppressive fire behind him, keeping these motherfuckers off their backs.

Just a little farther.

Two men leaped out of the Black Hawk, ran toward him, taking Christine's weight from his arms, lifting her into the bird. Jesse jumped in right behind them.

But it was too late.

Christine was gone.

The memory washed over Jesse, shards of dread and pain piercing his chest, his stomach churning. "*No.*"

Someone squeezed his hand, arms sliding around him, holding him tight, a voice cutting through the waking nightmare.

"Jesse, I'm right here. Listen to me. I'm right here."

"Ellie?"

"Yes." She stood beside him now, her arms drawing him close, his head pillowed against her breasts. "I'm here. You're okay. You're okay."

He was trembling, his whole body shaking. "I think I'm going to be sick."

"Let's go to the bathroom." Ellie took his hand, led him down the hallway to the bathroom, her palm cradling his forehead while he threw up. "There you go. That's good. You're okay."

When he was done, Ellie gave him a glass of water to rinse out his mouth, then flushed the toilet.

He sank to the floor, his back against the tub. "It should have been me."

Ellie touched a cool washcloth to his forehead and cheeks. "You're okay, Jesse. Whatever happened—it's over. You're here with me now."

But Ellie didn't understand.

"It was my job to protect her. It should have been me."

"I'm sure you did the best you could." There was worry in her green eyes.

He buried his face in his hands. "Jesus."

"The floor can't be comfortable." She helped him to his feet, led him to her bed, and sat down beside him, her hand holding his, her touch an anchor.

Still shaking, he told her. "Her name was Christine Brown. She was a first lieutenant, part of a Cultural Support Team. CSTs we call them. Her job was to talk to the women in a community. We'd go out on a direct action, take one or two of the women with us. After we'd secured the place, they would go in, talk to the other females."

"I think I've heard about CSTs." Ellie still kept up with military news.

"She hated being called by her last name, said it was part of the army's stupid macho culture, so I called her by her first name. We hit it off. I was a staff sergeant, and she was an officer, so it was nothing like that. She was young—only twenty-three. She felt like a little sister to me."

He told her the rest of it. How Christine had gone in to do her job after he and his element had cleared the farm, not knowing that bad intel had set them up for an ambush. How the place had exploded with gunfire moments before an IED had knocked him on his ass. How Christine had been badly wounded. How he'd done everything he could to keep her alive. How she'd died in his arms while he'd run through the sand toward Crash's waiting bird.

"They pinned a medal on my chest, but I'm no hero. I left the army after that—resigned, went home, fell the fuck apart for a while. Then I came out here."

"Oh, Jesse."

Don't let me die.

"It should have been me."

Chapter Twenty

"I'm sorry, Ellie. I dumped my shit on you again."

It hurt Ellie to see him in so much pain. "Please don't apologize. I don't think of it that way at all."

She'd watched him slip away, watched one emotion chase the next across his face—shock, terror, desperation, anguish. She'd realized right away that he was having some kind of flashback. What he'd described would have been enough to leave anyone traumatized, the desolation he felt coming through in every word as he'd described Christine's death.

"I'm not a therapist, but I've had some psych training. It's not hard to connect the dots here. Three times you tried to save a woman—or girl—and three times you couldn't, despite doing everything in your power. You watched your mother take punches for you. It would be the most natural thing in the world for a child to believe that it was his fault. You tried to save Kayla Fisher, too, but the water was too strong. You tried your best to save Christine but couldn't. You're carrying a lot of guilt that doesn't belong to you, and I'm willing to be that most of it goes back to your parents."

It made Ellie want to cry, but she didn't. For his sake, she couldn't.

"It was my job to keep Christine safe."

"Was it your job to keep your mother safe? Or was it *her* job to keep you safe? She wasn't a child, Jesse. You were."

She watched his face and knew he was listening, his brow furrowed as if he were thinking over what she'd said. She gave him a moment to sit with that. "How old were you when that man started beating you?"

"I don't know—three or four."

"Daniel is going to be three soon. Would you expect him to be able to defend me if an adult man started beating me?"

Jesse stared at her as if she were crazy. "Of course not. He's too little."

"You were too little, too."

Something in his expression changed, and she knew she was reaching him.

"Think of Emily, Nate's little girl. She's eight. Would you expect her to protect Megan? No? Then how can you expect that of little Jesse?"

When he said nothing, she went on. "As for Kayla—you tried. You did everything you could do. You went above and beyond, risking your life. It's not your fault that you couldn't reach her. You shouldn't have gone into the water in the first place."

The furrow on his brow deepened.

"While it might have been your job to protect Christine, you were ambushed in a war zone. The fact that any of you got out alive..." Dan had been there. Dan had seen all of this happen. It had been part of the life he hadn't been able to share with her. "They wouldn't have given you a medal if they'd thought you'd failed in your duty. You hold yourself to an impossible standard."

"She died a terrible death."

"It would have been a lot worse without you. In an impossible situation, you gave her reassurance. She was suffering, and you dulled her pain. She was scared, and you held her. She drifted into unconsciousness knowing she wasn't alone."

"Yeah. I guess."

"Somehow, you buried her death in your mind, and the Fisher girl's drowning dug it up again." No, it wasn't only Kayla. He'd had the flashback when he'd been telling her about Dan. "Her death—and talking about Dan."

Because Dan was the pilot that day.

Regret cut at her, made her wish she'd waited or had never asked.

And then it struck her.

Maybe this was why he hadn't told her about Dan. Maybe some part of him had been guarding this terrible memory, doing all it could to keep it from rising to the surface again where it could tear him apart.

Now he sat beside her, silent, his eyes closed. He was no longer shaking, but he wasn't relaxed either, tension rolling off him in waves. Any minute now, he would explode, taking shelter in rage. He wouldn't take it out on her. He would do what he always did, what his parents had done—he would take his anger out on himself.

"You don't need this bullshit in your life, Ellie." He drew his hand away, got to his feet, rage simmering beneath his skin. "You didn't sign on for this shit show."

She stood, too. "I'm not afraid of what you're feeling. I'm not afraid of who you are or what you've seen or what you've had to do to survive."

He glared down at her as if she'd lost her mind.

"What scares me…" Tears. *Damn it!* "What scares me is what you're going to do in the next couple of hours, what you're going to do tomorrow."

A muscle flexed in his jaw, and then his gaze went soft. "I made you a promise, Ellie. I won't break it."

"Stay with me, Jesse. Please. Stay with me tonight." She touched a hand to his chest, felt his heart pounding beneath his sweater.

He rested his hand on hers, and for a moment she thought he meant to pry her hand away. "Why do you want me in your life?"

"Why don't you want me to care about you?" She raised herself onto her tiptoes and brushed her lips over his.

One strong arm slid around her rib cage, drawing her closer, his hand splayed against her back. "I didn't say that."

Then he bent down, his mouth claiming hers, all of the emotion he'd been holding back channeled into this kiss.

It was rough, almost violent. It was wonderful.

Her fingers slid into his hair, her tongue seeking his, answering his aggression with her own fierce demands, fear for him transforming into lust.

They fell together onto her bed, his hands reaching for her zipper, jerking her jeans down her thighs while she reached for a condom. She waited while he yanked open his fly then rolled the condom over his thick erection. And then he was inside her, driving hard, the friction making them both come hard and fast, giving them release.

They lay together afterward, holding each other, heartbeats slowing.

"I care about you, Ellie, more than I thought I could care about anyone. I care about Daniel and Daisy, too. But I don't have it in me to be the man you need, the man you and the twins deserve. For your sake, I don't think we should make this relationship out to be more than it is."

Ellie closed her eyes to keep back the tears.

It was a bright, sunny Saturday on the slopes. The parking lot was packed, the lift lines long, the lodge crowded. Every patroller was busy, one call after another coming in. A collision with injuries between a twelve-year-old skier and a snowboarder. An injury accident on Snow in Summer. A drunk man trying to grope women in the lift line. A broken wrist at the terrain park. A guy who got stuck in the lift chair when his backpack got wedged between the slats.

It felt surreal to Jesse to be skiing through a winter landscape of happy, smiling people when his mind was stuck in the hot sand of Iraq. All day, the memory replayed itself in his mind. The sudden onslaught of AK fire and the explosion. Fighting to save Christine's life. The headlong run toward Crash's Black Hawk.

But Ellie's words were there, too, and he held onto them with everything he had.

She was suffering, and you dulled her pain. She was scared, and you held her. She drifted into unconsciousness knowing she wasn't alone.

He'd tried to warn Ellie last night, done his best to define their relationship so that she would understand he had nothing more to give. Even so, she had kept in touch with him all day, sending text messages.

HOW ARE YOU?

He'd replied with a photo of himself drinking coffee.

PROOF OF LIFE.

She'd texted again.

HOW'S YOUR DAY?

He'd replied with a photo of Indian Peaks from the ski lift.

SUNNY SKIES.

Around noon, she'd forwarded a photo her mother had taken of the twins eating French fries with ketchup on their little faces.

MESS MONSTERS. SEE YOU LATER.

That made him smile.

Ellie was worried about him, and this was her way of checking on him. He ought to find it cloying or irritating, but he didn't. Knowing she was there when he got off work, knowing that she cared, made all the difference.

What had he done to deserve her?

You'd best hope she doesn't ask herself that question.

He'd made an appointment with Esri after work. She kept some Saturday hours for her clients who worked during the week, and although her schedule was full, she'd agreed to set aside fifty minutes for him when he told her what had happened.

He headed straight to her office from the slopes and found her waiting for him. He got settled in the seat across from her and found himself fighting for words, mind and body revolting against the memories in his head. "This isn't going to be easy."

"You're right. It won't be. But I think it will be worth it in the end."

He told her what had happened at Ellie's house, told her about Christine's death, then shared with her what Ellie had said, how she'd linked his mother, the little Fisher girl, and Christine together.

"Ellie's pretty smart. She's got some psychology training as a nurse, I'm sure. And you know what? I think she's right. This is why I wanted to talk about the impact that saving a life has on you. You seem to live for it, almost as if—"

"It makes up for the people I couldn't save." He understood now.

"Exactly." Esri leaned toward him. "Jesse, you are no longer that little boy who couldn't help his mom. You're no longer that helpless child. You're a grown man, and you've done more in your life to help people than most of us."

Her words made his throat tight, but fuck if he was going to cry in front of her. "Am I crazy?"

"First, no, you're not crazy. From where I'm sitting, you're completely normal for someone dealing with post-traumatic stress. In fact, you're in a better position than many. Do you know why?"

"No."

"You're motivated to deal with it, to face it. A lot of people spend their lives running away."

"But how could I have forgotten her? How could I have forgotten Christine? I cared about her. She died in my arms."

"The mind works overtime to shelter us from trauma. Think of it this way: Your mind locked that memory away until it felt you were safe, until it felt you could handle facing your feelings about what happened that day."

"It's Ellie, isn't it?" She'd come into his life, and everything had changed.

"What do you think?"

"I *hate* it when you do that." He took a breath, tried not to get pissed off. "I think I'm in love with her, and it scares the shit out of me. So how could I be feeling safe?"

This made Esri smile. "You're talking about two different things. For you to love her, I would think you trust her."

"Okay. Sure."

"Trust can make a person feel safe, especially if they come from a background of abuse, like you do. As for love—that can come with feelings of vulnerability. We're suddenly in a place where we can be hurt by another person."

But that's not what scared Jesse. "I'm not afraid for myself. I don't want to hurt her—or the kids."

Esri nodded. "Have you ever hit or shoved or threatened a woman?"

"No."

"How about a child or an animal?"

"God, no." He saw where she was going with this. "Some part of me is afraid that I'll be like my dad, that he's hiding inside me somewhere, that I'll settle down with someone I love—and then destroy everything."

"The fact that you haven't demonstrated abusive behavior is a good indicator that you won't head down that path in the future. We can talk about that more at our next session."

He glanced at the clock, surprised to see that fifty minutes had gone by already.

"Jesse, I'm going to suggest something. Why don't we schedule a regular, weekly appointment rather than doing this ad hoc crisis-management thing? That way, you'll know you're going to see me, and we can focus on treating your PTSD."

"Okay."

PAMELA CLARE

"Read through these when you get a chance." She gave him a couple of flyers about PTSD, then made an appointment with him for Wednesday morning.

"I can't believe you're still not charging me."

"Karma." She turned out her office light. "You save people, remember?"

The next two weeks passed quickly, Ellie busy with the twins, work, and the final details for the first-aid tent. One of her volunteers—a firefighter—came down with mono, so she'd had to replace her. She'd also tracked down phone numbers—the names and numbers of the staff members in charge of delivering the supplies, as well as the contact information for the person with the Town of Scarlet who oversaw hooking up the tent with electricity. She didn't want to get stuck at seven in the morning in the freezing cold with a problem she couldn't solve and no idea whom to contact.

But although her days were busy, she couldn't stop worrying about Jesse. He seemed to be okay. He wasn't drinking as far as she could tell—and she had a pretty good nose for that sort of thing. He came over almost every evening, sometimes early enough to play with the kids before bedtime. One night, he'd brought his lasagna, which had been every bit as delicious as he'd said it would be.

Their sex life had gotten even better—if such a thing were possible. He knew how to make her scream, how to make her come fast and hard, or how to draw it out until she thought the pleasure would kill her. But he never slept with her. When it was over, he would hold her for a while, then kiss her goodbye, and leave her to sleep alone. There was a barrier between them now, and Ellie couldn't seem to breach it.

I don't think we should make this relationship out to be more than it is.

He'd said it that terrible night when he'd had the flashback. For whatever reason, he still seemed to believe that keeping his distance was better for her. She hadn't brought it up—not yet. She wanted to give him time, give him a chance to sort through all of this himself. He was seeing Esri, which was good.

Still, she couldn't let this go on forever. She loved him. Somehow, she'd fallen in love with Jesse Moretti, and there was nothing he could do about that.

T he Friday morning of SnowFest, Ellie got up at five just like she would on any regular work day. She showered and dressed in layers—polypro long underwear and turtleneck under her blue scrub pants and snowflake scrub shirt. Then she bundled the kids up and dropped them off at her parents' house and drove the short distance to the SnowFest grounds.

The sun hadn't yet risen, but Ellie could see that Scarlet Springs had been transformed. First and Second streets were lined with booths and stalls. Merchants, artists, and restaurateurs from Scarlet Springs, Boulder, and the surrounding mountain towns bustled about, getting ready to sell their wares to the thousands of people who flocked to Scarlet for the festival. Stalls and tents adorned with white fairy lights stretched all the way to the reservoir, electric lanterns that looked like old-fashioned miners' lights hanging above the walkways. Crews had plowed the snow away and laid wooden walkways to keep people dry and minimize the mud. Trucks stood on the periphery of the event like circled wagons, people pushing dollies up and down their ramps, working in the darkness and frigid cold to be ready for the public by eight.

Ellie parked and walked through the cold in search of the first-aid tent. Thank goodness she'd dressed warmly because it was freaking *cold*. She found the tent standing close to the reservoir where the polar bear plunge would take place. That made sense, given that some of her first patients would inevitably come from that event. The fire department had already cut a hole in the ice, marking it with tape and orange cones so that no one would fall in.

Larger than the other tents, the first-aid tent was made of heavy, insulated green fabric, a white cross on both sides, a banner running across the top that said "FIRST AID" in big white letters. Ellie opened the flap to find the tent cold and dark. A row of light bulbs hung from the ceiling. She reached up and tugged on a pull chain, and light filled the space. She might not have heat yet, but at least she could see.

There were two rooms—the larger front room and a smaller back room that would serve as the warm-up room. The supplies that Megs and the other Team members had helped her inventory sat on their pallets still wrapped in plastic. The oxygen equipment, blankets, and AEDs were there, too, along with cots, two folding tables, and an aluminum shelving unit.

She was supposed to have all of this set up in an hour and a half.

The only way to get it done was to start, so Ellie got busy and was soon joined by Lolly, who had brought her a latte. "Oh, God, you are an angel."

Lolly fluttered her lashes. "I know."

Gus, one of the hospital's pharmacists, showed up ten minutes later. "Sorry. I slept through my alarm."

They worked together in the cold to set up tables and the shelving unit, where most of the supplies would go. Then they set up two cots, covering the canvas with cotton sheets and placing folded blankets at the bottom. The back room—the warm-up room—was smaller. They managed to fit the oxygen equipment, IV poles and two cots back there, too, as well as the blanket warmer. They were unpacking supplies when a woman walked in wearing a hard hat, a tool belt around her waist.

"I'm with the Town of Scarlet. I'm here to make sure all your equipment is hooked up to electricity and running."

Ellie, Lolly, and Gus waited outside while the woman went to work, taping electrical cords out of the way and running them beneath the wood floor out the back. In ten minutes everything was operational, from the infrared space heaters that sat in the corners to the blanket warmer in the back.

Ellie bent over one of the space heaters to warm her hands. "Ahhh."

Now it was just a matter of getting all the supplies on the pallets opened and set out in a functional way. They were almost done when they got their first patient.

"You got a minute?" A man in a hardhat stood near the entrance holding his hand in a blood-soaked handkerchief. "I ran a drill bit through my own damned hand."

Chapter Twenty-One

Jesse got off early to take his volunteer shift at the first-aid tent. He dropped by his cabin and grabbed a quick bite to eat then drove into town. Scarlet Springs had doubled in population, SUVs and pickup trucks parked every which way along the roads, every parking lot downtown full.

He ditched his vehicle and made his way toward the first-aid tent in the center, the wooden walkways crowded with people who shopped and ate and listened to music despite the cold temperatures. He knew from the schedule that Ellie had worked seven to three-thirty p.m. today. He wished their shifts had overlapped. Even though they'd be working, it would have been nice to spend some time with her. Maybe he could stop by her place tonight and …

She stood just outside the tent, bundled in a parka and scarf and sipping something hot from a paper cup, steam rising into the air from between her hands. She smiled and waved when she saw him, then walked back inside.

He stepped into the tent and was surprised by how warm it was—and how complete and well organized. "Wow. It's like a mini-ER."

She sat on a metal counter stool, still sipping her drink. "It's warm enough to take off your parka—most of the time. When we get a lot of traffic, the heat escapes. They've got coffee and hot cocoa across the way if you need something warm."

"Thanks. How about water?" He'd had enough caffeine today to kill an elephant.

She pointed to the bottom shelf. "There."

He grabbed a bottle, ripped off the cap, and drank. "How has the day gone?"

He knew she was troubled by the fact that he wouldn't stay with her at night, but how could he explain it? He needed to know that he was right in the head, that he was worthy of her, that he wouldn't hurt her or the kids, before he let this relationship get any more serious. Not that it wasn't already serious…

The horses are out of the barn on that one.

"It started bright and early with one of the workmen running a drill bit through the pad of his thumb. We've had four cases of hypothermia—three from the polar bear plunge. A woman tripped over one of the wooden walkways and twisted her ankle. We transported a man who was having shortness of breath. All in all, a pretty quiet day."

Jesse found another stool and sat. "I thought you were off at three thirty."

"I knew you were on this evening, so I traded shifts with someone else. I took a break in the middle of the day, spent some time with my mom and the kids. That's the kind of thing you get to do when you're in charge."

So, she had wanted to see him. "I like the way you think."

Her gaze narrowed. "Are you growing a beard?"

So, she'd noticed. *Damn.*

He lied. "I just haven't had time to shave."

Bear stepped into the tent, and Jesse could see he was unwell. "Jesse Moretti of the Team. Ellie Rouse Meeks."

How he knew their names, Jesse didn't know, but Hawke had told him once that Bear remembered the name of every person he'd ever met or heard about.

"Hey, big guy. Why don't you come over here and sit down?"

Wearing his bearskin coat, Bear walked to one of the cots and sat. He took a furry mitten off his left hand to reveal large gash that was badly infected. When he finally spoke, his words and manner of speaking were like that of a child. "I hit myself with my ax. Stupid, stupid, stupid."

Jesse patted him on the shoulder. "Accidents happen. Let's see what we can do to help you feel better. How long ago did this happen?"

"Seven days," Bear answered. "Stupid."

Jesse met Ellie's gaze, both of them thinking the same thing. It was too late for a tetanus shot.

With Ellie's help, Jesse coaxed him out of his coat and the buckskin beneath it so they could take his vitals.

"You've got a fever, Bear," Ellie told him. "That means your body is fighting hard to stop this infection. We need to clean your wound and stitch it. I think you're going to need intravenous antibiotics, too. Do you know what that means?"

Bear shook his head.

Jesse got out an IV kit and showed him, explaining what everything was for. "We can't give you the stitches or the antibiotics you need here, but we can get the IV going and get you to the hospital."

Bear's eyes went wide with fear. "The hospital?"

Ellie rested a hand on his shoulder. "We care for everyone there. That is our job. 'For I will restore health to you, and your wounds I will heal, declares the Lord.'"

This seemed to make the big guy relax.

Jesse called for the ambulance, leaving the IV to Ellie, who had more experience than he did and would probably cause Bear less pain. But when the two EMTs walked in with the gurney, the fear returned to Bear's face.

Ellie took his hand. "Do you know Lolly?"

"Lolly Cortez," Bear answered.

"Yes. She's there at the hospital. I called her to tell her what has happened, and she's going to take good care of you."

Bear got up onto the gurney, hugging his big bearskin coat against him, clearly going on faith that this trip into the unknown wasn't going to harm him. "Thank you."

"You'll be feeling much better soon. I promise."

Jesse waited until Bear had gone. "Damn, you're good. I didn't know you were religious."

"I'm not, but Bear is."

A man with blisters and an ice climber with hypothermia rounded out the next hour. And then it was time for Ellie's shift to end, one of the fire department's paramedics taking over for her.

"Are you coming over tonight?"

He wanted to draw her against him, to answer the question with a kiss, but they had an audience. "I'll see you around nine."

And he was bringing trouble.

Ellie heard the back door open and finished shimmying into the lavender silk chemise she'd bought to surprise him. She walked out of her bedroom, excited to see his response, and froze.

He stood in the living room in a pair of heavy black work boots, faded, tattered jeans, and a black leather jacket, his chest bare, his jaw dark with stubble. His gaze moved over her, his expression inscrutable.

Oh, God.

He was acting out one of her fantasies.

She was wet in a heartbeat.

He took a slow step toward her—and she ran.

Back down the hall toward her bedroom she ran, his heavy footfalls right behind her, adding excitement to his pursuit. She tried to shut the door, but the toe of his boot stopped her.

"Oh, no, you don't. You're not getting away from me." He shoved the door open, then shut it behind him—and locked it. "There's nowhere left to run, babe."

A shiver ran down her spine.

She backed away from him, no idea what he had planned, but so turned on by this little game that she would have said yes to almost anything. "Don't hurt me."

He reached out, caught her wrist. "Don't fight me."

He dragged her against him, caught her jaw with one big hand, and bent his mouth to hers, claiming her with a brutal, crushing, delicious kiss.

She struggled to get away—but not really. Her lips yielded to his onslaught, her mouth opening readily, her body turning to liquid, especially between her thighs. But she couldn't give in so easily. She wriggled, twisted, tried to pull away.

He broke the kiss, crushed her tighter against him then forced a hand between her thighs, delving into her wetness. "Oh, yeah. No reason to waste time, not when your pussy is ready for me."

Her heart gave a hard knock, lust making her inner muscles clench around his finger, betraying her desire.

His lips curved in a dark grin, and he slid a hand into her hair, fisting it just enough to take control. "Unzip my fly. I want you to see what you're getting."

"No! I won't help you." She had to fight not to laugh.

He grasped one of her hands, pressed it against his jeans on top of his erection. "I'm going to bury every inch of my cock inside you and fuck you until you scream. Now, unzip my fly—unless you want my seed inside you."

Her knees almost gave out.

She did what he'd told her to do. Meanwhile, he reached into his pocket, pulled out a condom, then tore the packet open with his teeth and handed it to her.

"Stroke me first. Yeah, just like that. Now with your mouth." Fist still in her hair, he forced her to her knees, a hiss of breath escaping him as she gave him what he wanted. "Look at me."

She looked up the length of his muscular torso to the fierce expression on his face, her tongue circling the head of his cock, her heart almost bursting with desire for him.

"Now put the condom on."

When she had finished, he drew her to her feet, released her hair, and grasped both buttocks, lifting her off her feet and wrapping her legs around him. Then he turned her against the wall, his gaze meeting hers as he buried himself inside her.

They moaned in unison.

His cock felt so freaking good inside her, the hard length of him filling her, stretching her, driving deep. Her arms went around him, all pretext gone, her fingers digging into the leather of his jacket, her legs tightening around his waist. She wanted him. God, she wanted him just ... like ... *this*.

His hips were a piston, driving his cock in and out of her now, each thrust making her cry out, bringing her closer to the edge.

"Come, babe. *Now*."

Climax washed through, a scorching wave of bliss. He prolonged her pleasure with deep thrusts and then joined her, burying his face against her throat, moaning her name as he came.

Breathless, her eyes closed, she held onto him, blown away by what he'd just done for her. When she opened her eyes, he was watching her, the gentleness in his gaze making her heart melt. Still inside her, he carried her to the bed, where he held her as if she were the most precious thing in his world.

Jesse got off work early again and headed down to SnowFest for his two-hour shift. Ellie had changed her shift again and was there when he arrived. She was in the warm-up room starting an IV on a white-haired older woman, the soothing tone of her voice carrying through the tent.

"The IV fluids are warmed, and so is the oxygen. They'll help raise your core temp."

The woman saw Jesse and pointed. "Can he warm me up?"

Ellie glanced over her shoulder at him, clearly fighting not to laugh, then finished the IV. "Mr. Moretti, I believe Donna here would like you to take over. She still needs a warm blanket, and you'll need to turn on the heating pad. I've already called for an ambo. Donna used to be the town librarian."

"I got to reserve all those sexy romance novels for myself—a perk of the job."

Ellie walked out of the back room, a little smile on her face. She lowered her voice to a whisper. "You certainly know how to bring the heat."

Jesse couldn't help but smile, memories of last night on both of their minds. He took off his parka and walked into the warm-up room. "So, your name is Donna?"

She nodded, looking like she was about to fall asleep.

"We're going to have you feeling better soon." He reached into the blanket warmer, took out a heated, thermal blanket, and tucked it around her, then flipped on the heating pad that lay beneath her.

She smiled at him from behind the green oxygen mask, then gave him a wink. "I feel better already. I like men, you know."

Ellie spoke from behind him. "Jesse is a ski patroller. He's also a member of the Rocky Mountain Search and Rescue Team, an EMT, and a former Army Ranger."

Donna's smile got brighter. "Be still my heart."

Jesse looked over at Ellie, wondering what the hell she was doing.

She gave him an innocent look, those green eyes wide. "I just want Donna to understand that she is in *very* good hands."

Just then Ellie's father walked in carrying Daniel. A woman who looked so much like Ellie that she could only be her mother walked behind him holding Daisy.

The children's faces lit up, Daisy reaching for Ellie. "Mama!"

"We thought they might like to see all the pretty lights and the snow sculptures," Ellie's mother said.

"Great idea." Ellie took Daisy, gave her a little bounce, the pink tassel on top of her hat bobbing. "Are you ready to see some snowmen?"

"They've been talking about horses nonstop—and they've mentioned you a lot too," Ellie's father said, looking Jesse squarely in the eyes.

Uh-oh.

Yeah, the old man knew.

"Are those your kids?" Donna asked Jesse.

Some part of him wished he could say they were.

"Those are Ellie's twins."

"They're cute."

He couldn't disagree with that.

Ellie's parents stayed for a few minutes, leaving with Daisy and Daniel just as two of Hawke's crew— Brandon Silver and Jenny Miller—pushed through the door with a gurney, playing EMTs today instead of fighting fires.

"Who have we got here?" Brandon asked.

"Ooh, he's handsome, too," Donna said. "You mountain boys grow up big and strong, don't you?"

Silver blinked, looked at Jesse.

Jesse couldn't help but laugh. "This is Donna. She likes men."

While Ellie went over Donna's chart with Jenny, Jesse and Brandon lifted Donna onto the gurney. Jesse moved the bag of IV fluids, then bent down and gave Donna a peck on the cheek because, well, why the hell not?

She giggled.

Jesse and Silver maneuvered the gurney through the tent and outside, and then Jenny stepped in. "We've got it from here, Moretti. Thanks."

"Have you seen Daisy?"

The words had Jesse's head turning.

Ellie's mother stood about twenty feet away, glancing around her. "I set her down for just a second to zip Daniel's coat."

Jesse stopped where he was, looked around.

His heart gave a hard knock.

Jesus Christ!

A pink tassel. Blond hair.

He started running. "She's by the water!"

Ellie's parents turned and saw her, but it was too late.

Daisy slid on the ice and slipped over the edge and into the frigid reservoir.

Ellie heard Jesse's shout, heard her mother scream.

"Daisy!"

She ran outside to see Jesse sprinting toward the polar bear plunge area, her parents running behind him. Her father had Daniel. But where was Daisy?

Oh, God! No!

"Daisy!" She ran, slipping on snow, her heart slamming in her chest. "Daisy!"

Jesse reached the water and without a moment's hesitation jumped in. He looked around for a moment, then dove under the water.

A crowd had begun to converge, people drawing closer to see what had happened.

Ellie fought her way through them. "That's my little girl! Move! My little girl's in the water!"

She broke through, saw Jesse come up, take a breath and go under again. "Daisy!"

Dear God, not Daisy!

"Daisy!" She sank on her knees next to the hole in the ice, oblivious to the cold, every catastrophic scenario she'd ever seen as a nurse flashing through her mind. Daisy drowning. Daisy's heart stopping from cold shock. Daisy severely hypothermic.

And Jesse.

The human body could only last so long in 34-degree water.

His head came up again, teeth chattering. "The current took her."

His words made her panic crest. "Not Daisy. Not my baby, too."

He looked into her eyes, took a deep breath, and dove under again.

"The fire chief's on his way!" someone shouted.

A thousand prayers raced through Ellie's mind.

God, no. Please don't let me lose her. Don't take Jesse either.

She couldn't take that. She couldn't lose her baby girl. Not Daisy, too.

But where was Jesse? He'd been down there a long time now. He had to breathe. Daisy had to breathe, too.

"He's been down there a long time. Maybe he drowned, too."

Dear God, she was going to lose *both* of them.

No. No. No no no no!

Then Jesse broke the surface, gasped for breath, Daisy in his arms.

He held her up to Ellie, who grabbed her and pulled her onto the ice.

Daisy was blue. She wasn't breathing.

Ellie tried to rein in her panic. She needed to start CPR.

And then Eric was beside her with Brandon Silver. "We've got this, Ellie."

They took Daisy from her, forced her to scoot aside.

"Start chest compressions and don't stop," Eric told Brandon, then he turned to the crowd. "Is anyone from the Team here? Moretti's still in the water."

Ellie glanced over, saw Jesse struggle to climb out and then slide back in, his strength gone, his muscles no longer cooperating. "Help me! Someone, please!"

She reached for him, took hold of one wrist, and pulled, but Jesse's weight dragged her toward the edge of the ice. If only she'd had a rope or something.

Eric caught Jesse's other wrist. "Don't you fucking dare go into shock and drown on me, Moretti!"

"We got the page, Hawke. What the hell…"

Megs?

Megs and Mitch Ahearn were there—and Creed Herrera.

"Ellie, let go before he pulls you in, too!" Megs barked, a rope in her hands.

Ellie did as she asked and backed out of the way, crawling over to where Brandon was still doing chest compressions and rescue breaths for Daisy.

It was all a blur after that.

Her father wrapping his coat around her shoulders. The sound of her mother crying. Two paramedics lifting Daisy onto a gurney, wrapping her in a warm blanket while continuing CPR. Someone wrapping a heated blanket around Ellie's shoulders, helping her to her feet, telling her she was probably hypothermic.

"You've been out here for a while with no coat, lying down on the ice. Your scrubs are wet, and in this wind…"

Mind and body numb from shock and cold, she followed Daisy to the ambulance. "Jesse? Where's Jesse?"

She looked back over her shoulder to see him lying motionless on the ice.

E very bone in Jesse's body hurt. His muscles ached. He struggled to speak, to open his eyes, fear snaking through him. "D-daisy? Where…?"

"You got her out, buddy. She's in the ER by now. Ellie is with her."

"S-she's a-a-live?"

They didn't answer.

"Body temp is ninety degrees."

Hypothermia.

"Let's get a line going, get some warm fluids in him."

They'd already put him on oxygen, and they'd wrapped him in a heated blanket, one of fancy ones that blew warm air against the skin. Jesse was so cold, so numb, that he could barely feel it.

"Hey, Moretti, how do you feel, buddy?"

But Jesse was drifting again.

It was dark, so dark, the cold sucking the breath from his lungs. Where was she? He couldn't see her. The current pulled at him, carrying him away from the open water and beneath the ice. He reached but felt nothing.

Come on, little girl!

God, please!

"Jesse! Hey, Moretti, you got her. You found her."

Hawke?

Jesse opened his eyes, found himself being wheeled into the emergency room. He was shivering now, his teeth chattering, his body shaking. "Is Daisy... Is she...?"

"You did everything you could for her, buddy. Now let us take care of you."

You did everything you could.

Was she...? Jesus, was Daisy ... dead?

His heart seemed to crack, pain lancing through him.

Jesus, no!

And then he was out again.

"We've got a pulse."

Ellie could hardly breathe, her gaze shifting from the cardiac monitor to Daisy. She lay still and pale, her little body resting on a heating pad inside a forced-air warming blanket, warm oxygen going into her lungs through a ventilator, IVs in both of her arms and electrodes on her chest.

Ellie held her little hand, still so cold. "Daisy, sweetie, can you hear me? It's mommy. I'm right here, honey."

They'd flown the two of them via Life Flight to Children's Hospital in case it became necessary to perform a cardiopulmonary bypass on Daisy, using a heart-and-lung machine to warm her blood and restore her body temperature. But Daisy's little heart was beating again, her body temperature slowly rising.

"You're a fighter, Daisy Mae." Ellie kissed her forehead.

"Your parents are here," said one of the nurses. "They're out in the hallway."

"Thank you." Ellie didn't ask for them to be brought back. She didn't want to talk to them right now. They'd somehow let Daisy wander off, and she'd almost died. She might still die—or have brain or cardiac damage.

If it hadn't been for Jesse…

He had rushed forward when everyone else had stood by, frozen by fear or shock or indecision. He'd jumped into the water without a moment's hesitation, risking his life for her precious girl.

She'd asked how he was doing, but no one here knew. She would have called or texted him, but her cell phone was in the first-aid tent back in Scarlet. He'd been so weak when they'd taken him out. Hypothermia could kill. She'd seen it happen. She couldn't bear to lose him, either.

Her father came up beside her, his gaze on the monitor and Daisy's vitals. "Thank God. Is there anything we can get you, Ellie?"

Ellie struggled with her anger. "How could this have happened?"

"Your mother and I feel terrible about it, just awful."

You should.

Ellie bit back the hurtful words. "Could you please call Mountain Memorial and find out how Jesse is? I have to know."

"Yes, I can do that." Her father nodded and walked out of the treatment room.

Chapter Twenty-Two

as Daisy alive? Was she okay?

__ _No one would answer Jesse's question. They said they didn't know.

"They were still doing CPR when Life Flight flew her to Children's Hospital," one of the nurses had told him.

"She's in the best place possible," said another.

"We've all worked with Ellie. We're praying for her."

That was great—but it didn't answer his question.

His cell phone was shot—it had been in his pocket when he'd jumped into the water—and there was no phone in his little treatment room. He'd asked the nurse and the doctor and the guy who'd drawn his blood to call Children's Hospital to find out how Daisy was doing, but no one had come back to him with news.

Jesus.

He'd tried. God, he'd tried.

Ellie.

He couldn't imagine what she was going through. He'd seen the terror on her pretty face when he'd come up for breath, and he'd vowed to himself he wouldn't come up again, not without her baby girl. And when his right hand had finally touched that pink tassel on Daisy's hat...

Jesse wanted to rip the fucking IV out of his arm, get out of this damned bed, and drive to Denver. The only thing that stopped him was his core temp. He was still hypothermic—drowsy and chilled to the bone. He didn't want to get into an accident and hurt someone in the hour-and-a-half drive to the city.

What the hell was everybody doing? Could no one help him?

Fuck this.

He climbed out of bed and walked out of his treatment room, dragging the IV pole with him. He was going to find a goddamned phone and call Ellie. He walked over to the nurse's station. "I need to use the phone."

A nurse in green scrubs looked up at him, a startled expression on her face, phone pressed to her ear. She held out the receiver. "This is for you."

Jesse grabbed the phone. "Ellie? How is Daisy?"

"This is Troy Rouse, Ellie's father. Daisy looks like she's going to pull through, thanks to you. I don't know how we'll ever repay you." The man's voice cracked. "Her little heart is beating—normal sinus rhythm—and she just started breathing on her own. She's still very hypothermic, but her core temp is rising."

Jesse sagged against the counter, relief making him boneless, tears blurring his vision. "That's good. That's such good news."

"Ellie wanted me to call and find out how you're doing. She's with Daisy and doesn't have her cell phone."

"I'm fine. My core temp is still a little low. I jumped in the water with my cell phone in my pocket, so I don't have a phone at all."

"You did an incredible thing today. You saved my granddaughter—and my daughter. Ellie…" His voice cracked again. "Ellie wouldn't have made it through losing Daisy. Let me give you my number. You can let us know if there's anything you need."

"I appreciate that. Thanks." Jesse grabbed a piece of note paper off the desk, along with a pen, and took down the doc's number. "Tell Ellie…" *I love her.* "Tell her I'll be there as soon as I can be."

Jesse handed the receiver back to the nurse. "Daisy's breathing on her own. She's going to make it."

The nurses cheered.

"You belong in bed." An older nurse named Lolly came around the desk, guided him back toward his room. "You're going to need your strength. There are newspaper reporters and camera crews out there in the waiting room hoping to interview you."

"What?"

"You're a media star. A Denver TV station was there doing a piece about SnowFest. They got it all on camera. The reporter from the Scarlet

Gazette is here. Lots of bystanders filmed you with their cell phones, so you're trending right now. I can see how thrilled you are by all of this."

"Jesus." Jesse didn't understand people. Why hadn't they put their phones and cameras down to help?

"I can bring you some paper and a pencil if you want to write a statement. It might be best to give the reporters something. Maybe they'll go away."

"What should I say?"

"Hell if I know. I'm an LPN, not a public-relations consultant."

That gave Jesse an idea. "I need to make a phone call."

An hour later, Jesse's body temperature was back to normal, and Victoria and Hawke sat next to his bed, proofreading the statement Victoria had helped him write.

"It looks good," she said. "If only I had a printer..."

"I'm sorry," Lolly said loudly as if she wished to be overheard. "We can't let you use the hospital's printers." Then she whispered. "Give it to me. I'll type it in at my station and print it from there."

Jesse opened his mouth to ask when they were discharging him.

Lolly pointed at him. "*You* stay put. I'll get back to you as soon as I'm done breaking the rules."

She and Victoria left the room together.

Jesse sat back in the bed, impatient to be out of here. He wanted to get to Denver, to see Daisy for himself, to see Ellie. He had so much he wanted to say to her.

"You did a hell of a thing today, man," Hawke said.

"Thanks for being there, for getting me out."

"You saved that baby girl's life, Moretti."

"Hey, you and Silver did your part, too."

Hawke shrugged. "We did our job, but you risked your life. You seem to have a habit of doing that."

"I couldn't let her die. I love that little girl." He loved her mother, too, but that was harder to talk about with another guy than his feelings for Daisy.

Hawke changed the subject. "Once we get this printed out, we'll wait till you're discharged. Vickie will go out to the waiting room and read the statement while you take the hallway and head out the loading dock door. I'll meet you there and drive you to your vehicle. How does that sound?"

It sounded good to him. "Thanks so much for your help. I just don't have it in me to deal with reporters right now."

"Happy to do my part."

It was dark outside and bitter cold, the chill bothering Jesse in a way it hadn't before. "Can you crank the heat?"

"Sure."

The escape plot went off without a hitch—until Hawke pulled up to Jesse's Jeep. A woman stood next to it, camera bag over her shoulder.

"That's Wendy from the Scarlet Gazette. She had us figured out."

When he stepped out of Hawke's vehicle, Wendy hurried over to him, a copy of the statement Victoria had helped him write in her hand. "Please just answer a few questions for the hometown paper. Let us tell the story before the TV stations and the big papers get it. And, chief, I want to talk to you, too."

Something in that touched Jesse, broke through his aggravation. "Okay, but can we sit in my vehicle? I'm freezing."

They sat in the Jeep with the heat running, Jesse telling Wendy what had happened, answering her questions. She'd done her homework. She knew he was a member of the Team and a ski patroller. She also knew about his military service.

"So, you know the little girl and her mother?"

"We're neighbors." He left it at that.

"How long have you lived in Scarlet Springs?"

"It's been almost three years. Still a newcomer, I guess."

"You're not a newcomer now, Mr. Moretti. You're a hometown hero."

Her words slid over him, strangely soothing.

They spoke for maybe twenty minutes, and then she let him go. "Thanks for what you did—and thanks for giving us a chance to tell the whole story first."

She climbed out and went to pester Hawke, who waved to Jesse as he backed out of his parking spot and drove toward home and a hot shower.

Ellie went with her parents to the hospital cafeteria, more because they needed to talk than because she was hungry. They sat together at an open table, all of this feeling surreal to Ellie.

"I am so sorry. I let go of her hand to pay for cocoa and then zipped Daniel's coat, and she was gone."

Ellie saw the regret and anguish in her mother's eyes and fought not to lash out at her. "I know it was an accident. I know you love her. You've done so much to help me with the twins. But, Mom, I've never been more afraid in my life. My baby girl... almost died today. Her heart quit beating. She wasn't breathing. My Daisy Mae..."

Ellie dissolved into tears. They were tears of release now, washing the horror of the past few hours away.

Her mother wrapped an arm around her, while her father got to his feet, his arms encircling them both.

"She's going to be okay," he said.

Yes, she was going to be okay. She was breathing again. She'd woken up for a few minutes, reached for Ellie, and said, "Mama."

It was the most beautiful sound Ellie had ever heard.

Thanks to Jesse.

They ended the embrace.

Ellie's mother handed her a tissue. "I'll understand if you want to find someone else to watch them when you work."

"Mom, stop torturing yourself. It was an accident. Daisy is a handful. We all know that." She told her parents how Daisy had stuck her hand on the waffle iron simply because Ellie had warned her not to. "No one I could pay to babysit her could love her more than you do."

Ellie wiped her tears away, stood. "I want to get back upstairs."

"We're going to pick up Daniel from your sister's house and take him home." Her mother put her cell phone in Ellie's hand. "You keep this so you can stay in touch."

"Okay. Thanks."

Jesse was sitting outside the Pediatric ICU, waiting for her, the sight of him putting a lump in her throat and making her heart soar. He stood when he saw her, and she ran to him, sinking into his embrace, tears streaming down her cheeks again.

"Thank you." She said the words again and again. "Thank God for you. Thank you for saving Daisy. I was so afraid."

He kissed her hair, held her tight. "I know. Me, too."

Holding hands, they walked together into the PICU and back to Daisy's bed.

"I'm so glad you're here." Ellie squeezed his hand. "She's alive because of you."

Of course, a lot of people deserved credit—Hawke, Silver, the ER staff, the paramedics and nurses on the Life Flight helicopter, the doctors and nurses here at Children's Hospital. But none of them would have been able to do a thing for Daisy if Jesse hadn't gotten her out of the water so quickly.

Jesse reached out, smoothed the hair off Daisy's forehead. "I was so afraid I wouldn't find her. I went under, and it was so dark. I couldn't see her. I couldn't see anything. The cold was unreal. I knew she would drown, go into cardiac arrest. I heard you scream, saw you there. And the look on your face… Jesus, Ellie."

His voice was tight now. "I swore to myself that I wouldn't come up again unless I found her."

"God, Jesse." What a terrible vow to make.

He went on. "She had drifted with the current. I let it pull me, too, reaching for her. If it hadn't been for her little hat … I felt that tassel, pulled her hat off. But I knew where she was then. I swam to her, pulled her to me and doubled back, trying to find the hole in the ice before I blacked out. Everything after that is a blur."

Ellie's stomach churned to hear what he'd gone through, to know how very close she'd come to losing Daisy—and Jesse, too. "I've never been so scared in my life. I was so afraid I was going to lose you both."

Daisy stirred, opened her eyes, reaching with one hand for Ellie. "Mama."

Then her gaze shifted to Jesse, her little lips curving in a smile. "Jesse."

He bent down, kissed her cheek. "I'm right here, Daisy. We're both right here."

Ellie sang to her little girl, rubbing her back, stroking her hair, until she was sleeping again. Then Ellie brought Jesse up to date. "They need to make sure she's suffered no organ damage before we go home. Her heart and kidneys seem to be doing okay, but they're worried about pneumonia. They're giving her antibiotics and watching her for any signs of organ failure."

A nurse walked in behind them. "I'm sorry, but only family members are allowed. Your friend is going to have to go."

Ellie turned to face her. "He *is* family. He's the one who saved her life. He's her stepfather."

"Okay, well, I'm going to need him to sign in, and we'll get him a wristband."

"Thanks." Ellie looked up to see what Jesse thought of her little lie.

A dark eyebrow arched, his lips curving in a smile. "Stepfather?"

E llie managed to find an extra sleeper chair and, with Jesse's help, dragged it into Daisy's room so that he could stay overnight, too.

"I'm not leaving her, and I'm not leaving you," he'd said. "Matt called and told me he doesn't want me coming in tomorrow anyway."

Ellie fell into an exhausted sleep somewhere close to midnight but woke a short time later to the sound of Daisy's voice. She sat up, found Jesse standing next to Daisy's bed, holding her little hand.

"Cold," she whimpered.

"Are you cold? Well, old Jesse here will get you a warmer blanket."

"Water cold."

Ellie got a knot in her chest. She had wondered what Daisy would remember about what had happened, if anything.

"The water was cold and dark, wasn't it? Was it scary? Yeah? Well, we got you out, and now we're taking good care of you."

Daisy sat up, reaching for him, wanting him to hold her.

Jesse scooped her into his arms, and, careful of her IV and EKG lines, held her against his chest, the blanket wrapped tightly around her. He hummed to her, rocking back and forth, sometimes kissing her hair.

If Ellie hadn't already been in love with him, she would have just fallen head over heels. She needed to tell him how she felt, but she didn't want to freak him out. He'd told her not to expect more from him, and he'd kept his distance from her these past two weeks. The fact that he'd been there in a moment of crisis and had saved Daisy's life didn't change anything. He'd have done the same for anyone's child.

He was just that kind of man.

Still, she wanted him to know how much he meant to her, even if he didn't feel the same way. It was obvious that he cared for her. He wouldn't be here otherwise, spending the night on a tiny folding bed that was about six inches too short for him.

If only he could see himself as she saw him. Or maybe it was better that he didn't. It might have turned him into a pompous ass. His humbleness was one of the things she loved about him. Just now he hadn't said, "*I* got you out of the water." He'd used the word *we*, though he'd been the only one to go into the water after her.

He carefully lowered Daisy into her hospital bed, straightened out the tubes, and covered her with the blanket again. "Sleep, little angel. I'm not going anywhere."

He walked back to his bed and stretched out beneath the blanket, seemingly unaware that Ellie was watching him.

J esse didn't sleep well, some part of him listening for Daisy all night long. He did manage to fall asleep early in the morning, only to be woken at the change of shift by a bright and cheery nurse named Aisha, who wanted to give him a hug.

She squeezed him tight. "I saw on TV what you did to save this precious angel. God put you in the right place at the right time, yes, sir, He did."

Daisy woke up hungry and very cranky. Jesse couldn't blame her, as she endured exams by a series of doctors and therapists—and a nasty blood test that made her cry.

"Her kidney, pulmonary, liver, and pancreatic tests are all normal," said the last doctor, the one in charge. "We've detected no neurological deficits. I say we discharge her. Keep her on the antibiotics, and watch for coughing or fever or any other indication of infection. She is one lucky little girl."

Ellie reached over and squeezed Jesse's arm. "Yes, she is."

Ellie's parents arrived soon after that with Daniel, as well as a change of clothes for Ellie and Daisy.

Daniel's face lit up when he saw his sister. He threw both arms in the air. "Day!"

Okay, *that* was cute as shit.

Ellie's mother held her hands to her face, clearly choked up. "Daniel has asked about Daisy from the moment he woke up. They've never been apart like this before."

Daisy was still upset about the blood test but seemed to draw comfort from Daniel, who hugged her and patted her and even offered her his blanket. Soon the two of them were chattering in a language Jesse didn't understand, while Ellie and her parents worked out the logistics of how to get everyone home.

"We can put the child seats in Jesse's Jeep, and he can drive us back. That way you don't have to wait around."

"What are you going to do about the reporters?" Ellie's mother asked.

"Reporters?"

Shit.

Jesse had hoped it would've blown over by now.

"There are dozens of them outside," her father said. "Turn on the television."

The story was on almost every channel, complete with cell phone footage:

"Coming up next," said one news announcer. "A Scarlet Springs toddler is rescued from freezing water by a former Army Ranger and brought back to life by doctors."

Damn it.

The hospital administrator, an apple-shaped man in a suit, came down to invite Ellie, Daisy, and Jesse to be part of their press conference in an hour, a request that seemed to leave Ellie feeling torn.

"I guess I'll do it," she said. "It gives me a chance to thank publicly everyone who played a role in saving Daisy's life."

Jesse could understand her reasoning, but the idea of going in front of cameras, of all that attention, didn't sit easy with him.

With the help of some of the nurses and one of the TV reporters, Ellie got a quick makeover—Jesse didn't think she needed it, but she did. By the time she was ready, Daisy's discharge papers were finished. They headed down the elevator together—the administrator, Ellie carrying, Daniel and Jesse carrying Daisy.

The moment they stepped into the room, cameras began clicking, so many of them going at once that it sounded like insects. Daisy and Daniel glanced around, taking it all in, the two of them more focused on each other than the sea of adults around them. The hospital had set up a long table with a white tablecloth, the administrator and Daisy's primary physician taking their places and motioning for Ellie and Jesse to do the same.

The administrator spoke first, then Daisy's doctor answered medical questions. Then the administrator introduced Ellie, Jesse, and the twins, who drew laughter by completely ignoring what was going on around them.

Ellie made a statement. "I would like to thank all of the first responders who helped keep Daisy and Jesse alive yesterday—Eric Hawke and Brandon Silver from the Scarlet Springs Fire Department, Megs Hill and the Rocky Mountain Search and Rescue Team, Life Flight, and the doctors and nurses here at Children's Hospital and at Mountain Memorial in Scarlet Springs."

"Do you have any questions for Ms. Meeks?" the administrator asked.

"Where were you when your daughter fell into the water?"

"How did it feel to see Daisy fall into the water?"

"Daisy's father died serving his country, isn't that right?"

Ellie did her best to answer them. "I was at work. I'm an RN and was working at the first-aid tent. I didn't see her fall in. I heard my mother scream and heard her shout Daisy's name. When I stepped out of the tent, I saw Jesse jump into the water, and I knew what must have happened. I was terrified—for both of them. Yes, Daisy and Daniel's father died in Iraq about three and a half years ago."

"How old are the twins?"

"They'll be three in April."

Jesse didn't have a statement, but the reporters seemed to have saved most of their questions for him.

"What went through your mind when you were in the water?"

"How cold was that water?"

"Did you worry that you might die, too?"

"Did your combat experience as an Army Ranger prepare you to act yesterday?"

"You're Ms. Meeks' neighbor, correct? Housing records show you bought the house near hers a couple of years ago. What is your relationship with Ms. Meeks? Are you two friends, or is there something more?"

"Do you think of yourself as a hero?"

Jesse gave short answers, wanting to get this bullshit over with as fast as possible. "What was going through my mind? I just wanted to find Daisy. The water was about thirty-four degrees—just above freezing. No, I didn't think about that. I was focused on finding Daisy. As a Ranger, I've been trained to act. I'm Ms. Meeks' neighbor and friend. I've watched her twins before. I was volunteering in the first-aid tent, too, on behalf of Rocky Mountain Search and Rescue Team when the incident occurred. My relationship with Ms. Meeks is none of anyone's business. No, ma'am, I was in the right place at the right time and did what anyone would have done."

Then one of the reporters asked the twins a question. "Are you happy to be going home, Daisy? Are you glad to have your sister back, Daniel?"

Daniel looked at the reporter, then hugged his sister. "Day!"

The room dissolved into a chorus of "Awwww."

Chapter Twenty-Three

"I'm sorry about how the press conference went." Ellie knew Jesse hadn't wanted to be a part of it. "I had no idea their questions would get personal."

"Hey, don't worry about it. It's not your fault."

It was a long drive home, so she used the time to call Pauline. She apologized for missing work today—and for not calling sooner.

"We managed. Your friends on the Team stepped up to help out with the first-aid tent today, so it's covered." There was a hint of disapproval in her voice. "You were right about it being a bad idea to bring your children. You should have stuck with your first instinct."

It took Ellie a moment. "I didn't bring them. My parents were watching them all day and brought them to SnowFest to see the snowmen. I wasn't with them when Daisy... when Daisy fell in."

"Oh! I thought... Okay, well, that changes things. I'm just glad it all turned out well for your little girl. I marked you out as sick today. You'll need to check with HR, but I think you've got only one paid sick day left, and it's still January."

"Pauline, my daughter almost *died*. She went into cardiac arrest. She was blue and lifeless when she came out of that water. A dozen people fought for an hour to bring her back to me. Do you think I care about how many sick days I have? I will make do. I always have. I am a widow, the only parent my children have. *They* are my priority."

Pauline was silent for a moment. "Of course they are. I'm sorry. Sometimes I get too focused on the business element of this job. Let us know if you need anything."

"Thank you. I appreciate that."

Jesse looked over at her when she ended the call. "Your boss is an A-S-S."

"Yeah, sometimes she is."

"Damn." Jesse muttered the word under his breath. "I need to reach Nate. The skijoring race starts in about three hours. I don't know if he's heard what happened or whether he's tried to call me. I don't want him to show up with Buckwheat if I'm not there. That would be a lot of work for nothing."

"You're not thinking of backing out, are you?" Then she realized he might not physically feel up to it. "Are you feeling bad or—"

"No, it's nothing like that. You've been through a lot in the past twenty-four hours. I don't feel like adding to that by breaking my neck."

Ellie reached over, gave this thigh a squeeze. "I appreciate your thinking of me, but if you want to race, you should race. I felt better about the whole thing after watching you run the course with Nate a few times."

Okay, she'd barely been able to breathe each time, but she'd felt better afterward. Jesse was such a natural athlete that he'd made it look easy. Yes, she would feel relieved if he withdrew from the race, but it had to be his decision. Asking Jesse to stop participating in dangerous mountain sports would be like asking Dan to give up flying. She hadn't had the heart to take the sky away from Dan, and she couldn't take this away from Jesse, even if it scared the hell out of her.

"I'll call him when we get to your place and see what's up."

Ellie found her car in her driveway, her handbag and cell phone on the front seat, courtesy of Megs. A stack of newspapers sat on her front steps—copies of the Scarlet Gazette with a banner headline that read "Hometown hero" and a photo of Jesse handing Daisy to Ellie. She showed them to Jesse, then brought them inside and set them on the coffee table. She would read the article later when she could face it all again.

"Did nothing else happen in the world yesterday?" Jesse grumbled.

"Not in my world." Ellie made black bean quesadillas with corn for lunch, while Jesse stepped outside with her mother's cell phone to call Nate.

When he came back in, he seemed lighter, excited, and she knew he'd made his decision. "God, that smells good."

"I made enough for you, too, if you're hungry."

"Nate says he's good to go if I am." Jesse watched her, as if trying to gauge her reaction. "The Wests are all coming into town to watch."

She tried not to let her worry show. "I'd love to see them again. If the kids are up from their nap and Daisy is doing well, we'll join you all."

J esse took a quick nap, curling up with Ellie after the kids were asleep. He felt refreshed when his watch beeped an hour later. Careful not to wake Ellie, he got up, checked on the kids, then went out the back and hiked up the mountain to his cabin. He changed into ski pants, grabbed his gear, and was on his way.

Parking downtown was almost impossible, and traffic was bumper to bumper, pedestrians filling the crosswalks, standing on the roundabout where Bear was preaching, and darting across the roads wherever they felt like it. Jesse decided to park his Jeep at The Cave and walk the couple of blocks to the starting area, where Nate would be waiting with Buckwheat.

Sasha ran out when he stepped out of his vehicle and gave him a hug. "God, I just love you so much right now. I'm so glad you were able to save that little girl."

He didn't know what to say. "Thanks."

Belcourt stepped outside, too, walked over to him, and also gave him a hug, slapping him on the back. "It's good to see you safe and sound, brother. You were a warrior yesterday."

Again, Jesse was at a loss for words. "I did what anyone would have done."

"Really?" Belcourt raised a dark brow. "I didn't see anyone else go in that water. You doing the skijoring race?"

Happy that the subject had changed, Jesse told Sasha and Belcourt how he'd done some practice runs earlier in the week. "I'm hoping to get through it without making a fool of myself or breaking something."

Sasha jumped up, planted a kiss on his cheek. "You're going to rock it. I'll be cheering you on. See you there!"

Jesse made his way to the starting area, people he knew waving as he passed—Frank from the gas station, Rose, Jenny Miller, the guy with the big beard who ran the marijuana dispensary on First Street.

Bear, now hale and hearty again, called out to him from the center of the roundabout. "Whoever saves one life, it is as if he saved an entire world!"

Shit.

Bear, too?

Jesse made his way along the busy sidewalk to the west end of the street where dozens of horses stood with their riders, waiting for the race to start. He found Nate and Buckwheat standing beside a trailer with "Cimarron Ranch" painted on the side.

Nate gave him a brother handshake and a clap on the shoulder. "Good to see you. I didn't get a chance to tell you how damned grateful I am for what you did yesterday. Dan's little girl wouldn't be alive today if not for you."

For some reason, it wasn't as awkward to hear this coming from Nate, perhaps because he'd known Dan, or perhaps because they'd already talked about some pretty serious shit. "It was one of the scariest damned moments of my life."

"I bet it was."

A door on the side of the trailer opened, and Megan stepped out, holding little Jackson, Emily darting out behind her. Jack and Janet followed with their baby.

"Good to see you, Jesse." Jack wore a cowboy hat on his head and a big sheepskin barn coat, his face a wide grin. "You've been busy. Thank God for you, son."

"Where are the twins?" Emily asked.

"They're home with Ellie taking a nap right now."

"How is Daisy?" Megan asked.

"You'd never know that she went for an hour without a pulse yesterday."

"Thank God," Megan said. "I watched the footage. I felt sick for Ellie. I'm so glad you were there."

"So am I."

"Do you have time to come in and warm up?" Janet set Lily on the ground and zipped her coat.

Come in? Into where?

Then Jesse realized that they had all stepped out of the trailer. It wasn't just a horse trailer. There was living space inside.

Nate glanced at his watch. "We need to get a look at the course. The race starts in about fifteen minutes."

Jesse thanked Jack, Megan, and Janet and walked with Nate along the length of the course, getting a feel for it.

Nate pointed. "It's different than what I set out."

There were three jumps and three gates as there'd been on his practice course at the Cimarron, but there were also *three* sets of rings to catch rather than one.

"This is going to be a little tougher." The rings hadn't been Jesse's strength.

"Just remember what we practiced. Keep your mouth shut. No slack. Land the jumps. Don't miss the gates. And get all the rings. You ready?"

"As ready as I'll ever be." He glanced around hoping to see Ellie with the kids, but she wasn't there.

Ellie made her way down the crowded sidewalk, the twins tucked beneath blankets in their stroller. There were a lot of people from out of town who'd come for the race, and some of them weren't kind enough to step aside for her. But there were lots of locals, too, people she'd known all of her life. They said hello when they saw her, told her how happy they were that Daisy was okay.

When a couple of young men almost knocked her over, Harrison Conrad from the Team grabbed them both by their collars and jerked them to a stop. "Apologize to the woman here. Do you see she has two small children?"

They looked sheepishly at Ellie. "Sorry."

Harrison let them go, shook his head. "Flatlanders. Good to see you, Ellie."

When Ellie finally reached the skijoring course, there was almost nowhere to stand, especially not with such a wide stroller. She'd just found a spot where she could *almost* see the street when she heard someone call her name.

Megan waved. "Ellie! We saved a spot for you over here."

Ellie made her way through the crowd to find the West clan except for Nate sitting together on folding chairs with one chair left for her. "Thanks so much. It took me so long to find parking, I was afraid I was going to miss it."

"They're just about to start." Megan helped her move the stroller to a good spot. "Hi, there, Daniel. Hi, Daisy. She looks so healthy and happy."

"We are very lucky."

Megan gave Ellie a hug. "We saw the news coverage. I can't imagine what you've been through."

Then a man's voice boomed over the speakers welcoming everyone and telling the first competitor to come to the starting line. Then he gave the crowd the rundown on the rules. Each skier got one chance to complete the course with added time penalties for anyone who missed a gate or a jump or dropped or missed a ring. The skier-rider team that finished the course with the fastest time got to split a prize of five thousand dollars.

Ellie willed herself to stay calm. "After Dan, I made a promise to myself not to get together with any man who enjoyed taking risks, and look at me now."

Janet leaned closer. "That recklessness is probably why you're attracted to Jesse in the first place."

Ellie thought about that for a moment. "You're right. I'm drawn to the part of him that rushes in when other men are afraid."

That's why Daisy was alive today.

The announcer's voice ended their conversation. "First up are Carina Johnson and Billy Springer riding Thor. Is the team ready? They are ready."

A pistol shot sent the horse galloping forward, hooves churning up clods of snow. The skier was promptly jerked off her skis and dragged a short distance down the street.

It was hard to watch, and Ellie had to remember that she wasn't here as a first responder or an RN today.

God, she hoped Jesse wouldn't be hurt.

The next pair had trouble when the horse, spooked by the pistol shot, reared rather than ran, and then stomped in nervous circles. The next finished the course, but missed one of the gates and failed to catch most of the rings.

"They're racing in the order they signed up, so Jesse and Nate are going to be one of the last teams," Megan told her, shouting to be heard above the cheers. She patted Ellie's arm. "He's going to be okay. Nate said he was a natural."

Ellie drew a deep breath and did her best to get into the spirit and enjoy the show.

J esse stood near the starting line, heart pumping with anticipation.

Nate was talking to a skier who'd wiped out on the last jump, leaving blood on the snow. He came back, shared what he'd learned. "He says the course is running fast. He says he caught an edge on ice on the way up the ramp and lost his balance. I guess you'll need to watch those edges."

"Right."

They were the second-to-last team to compete, with three more teams ahead of them. The first of those three finished the course with the fastest time so far—one minute and nine seconds. The second finished, as well, but was penalized for missing a gate by having four seconds added to her time of one minute fifteen seconds. The third wiped out coming off the first jump, injured his ankle, and was taken away by EMTs.

"You ready?" Nate took Buckwheat's reins.

"Hell, yeah. Let's do this."

The announcer's voice boomed through the air. "Next up, Jesse Moretti and Nate West riding Buckwheat."

Cheers.

Jesse glanced around. "I guess everyone in Scarlet knows you and your horses."

"You think they're cheering for me? They're cheering for *you*, buddy. Everyone in this town knows your name now."

Jesse didn't believe that for a moment.

Nate mounted Buckwheat, rode over to the starting line, while race volunteers, Sasha among them, straightened the tow rope.

"Good luck!" she called to him.

Jesse drew the slack out of the rope, adjusted his grip, flexed his knees a few times, then waited for the announcer.

"Is the team ready? The team is ready."

A moment went by and then …

Pop.

The gelding responded to Nate as if the two were one, doing what quarter horses had been bred to do, exploding into a gallop, its hooves kicking up clods of icy snow.

Jesse was ready for the sudden acceleration, sailing over the snow, through the first gate and toward that first jump—a four-footer. The ramp was icy, but he'd been warned. Careful not to catch an edge, he flew up and over, nothing but air beneath him for a good fifteen feet, adrenaline making his blood sing.

But now for the hard part—the rings.

He swerved to the right, bunched up his fist, held out his arm.

One, two, three.

He had them.

The crowd cheered.

He held up his arm so the judges could see the rings, then dumped them onto the snow, his gaze focused on the next gate, which came up hard and fast. He made it then swung to his left, his skis scraping over ice as he flew up the six-foot ramp and into the air. "Woohoo!"

The crowd cheered when he stuck the landing.

Three more rings.

One, two...

He bumped the third with his fist, knocked it to the ground.

Shit.

A two-second penalty.

He didn't have time to think about it as the third gate was ahead of him and to the right. He swung over, just made it through, then turned hard for the final jump. Up and over he went, soaring, his skis landing on blood-stained snow, only three rings between him and the finish line.

He raised his arm, clenched his fist.

One, two, three.

Fuck yeah!

He sailed across the finish line, fist in the air.

"Fifty-six seconds, folks! That's Jesse Moretti and Nate West on Buckwheat, ladies and gentlemen, and we have a new SnowFest skijoring record! Fifty-six seconds with a two-second penalty!"

The crowd roared.

Jesse skied to a stop, stepped out of his bindings, and met Nate, who leaped from Buckwheat's back, for a full-on man hug.

Nate slapped him on the back. "I told you we could do it. No one's going to beat that. We've won."

And then Ellie was there.

She jumped into his arms, laughing and crying at the same time. "You're a lunatic! I am so crazy proud of you."

He held her tight, inhaled her scent, his heart filled with her.

I t was the first time Jesse had gone to Knockers and hadn't sat with the rest of the Team. Jack had invited him and Ellie to join them at the restaurant, which had set aside a table for ten with four high chairs in a quiet corner. But that didn't keep his fellow Team members from finding him. They came over in ones and twos to rib him, congratulate him, and generally be pains in his ass.

Sasha hugged him. "I knew you would kick butt."

"What are you going to do with all that money?" Conrad asked. "I mean, besides buy me a drink."

Jesse pointed toward the donation jar. "You're out of luck man. I donated it."

Nate had done the same thing, the jar now almost full.

"You learned to climb and became a primary Team member in less than a year, so forgive me if I'm not amazed by your win today," Megs said.

But she gave him a kiss on the cheek.

"You looked good on the winner's podium, Moretti," said Taylor, who was there with Lexi, Hawke, and Victoria. "I might have to race next year to give you some competition."

Jesse chuckled. "You can try."

"Taylor here was the state's high school ski champion, but he forgets that high school was a long time ago," Hawke said. "Good job today."

Ellie pointed toward Lexi's swollen belly. "How much longer?"

"Five weeks," Lexi answered. "I can't wait till she gets here."

"I get to be there," Victoria said. "I've never seen a birth. I'm so excited."

"It's a special experience," Ellie said.

Jack ordered a round for everyone at the table and made a toast to Jesse, Nate, and Buckwheat in honor of their victory, then went off to shoot the shit with Joe, who stood behind the bar, long hair in a man bun. He was back by the time the food arrived.

Jesse helped with the kids, who again showed their love of French fries by tossing as many as they ate. He'd finished his bison burger and had lifted Daisy into his lap so that he could clean her up when Liz Pascoe, the organizer of SnowFest, stepped onto the stage and took the mic.

"Hey, everyone. I just wanted to thank you for making this another great year for SnowFest. We broke attendance records this year, which is a reason to celebrate. Without the support of the Town of Scarlet Springs and all the volunteers from the community—the Team, the hospital, the fire department—this wouldn't be possible. Let's give a round of applause to our volunteers."

When the cheers had died down, she went on. "We weren't able to award the prize to the winning shotski team last night due to a town ordinance that prohibits giving alcohol to visibly intoxicated persons."

People burst into laughter and cheers at this.

"So, to give out that prize, here's Caribou Joe."

Joe got on stage. "Thanks for being here tonight, folks. It's great to have a full house. I've got a bottle of Glenmorangie 1981, with a retail value of twelve hundred fifty-five dollars, to give to last night's winning shotski team, Bottoms Up."

"Damn!" Nate said. "Next year, Moretti, we enter the shotski competition."

"Fine by me."

"Damn!" said Daisy.

The members of Bottoms Up went up to the stage to collect their prize, and Jesse recognized Kenny, one of the lift operators, among them.

Jesse laughed. "Way to go, Kenny!"

Joe waited for the cheers to die down before going on. "Before I step down, I wanted to take a moment to thank a member of our community who went above and beyond yesterday and risked his life to save another."

Ah, shit.

"Jesse Moretti moved here from out of state after serving as an Army Ranger. He took our town and us Springers to his heart and became one of us. He learned to climb and ski, and spends his days saving lives with the Team and working as a ski patroller. And today, he and Nate West set a new skijoring record. You've all heard the story and seen the images of him diving into the reservoir yesterday to save Ellie Meeks' two-year-old daughter, Daisy. I ask you to join me in showing your gratitude by raising your glasses for Jesse Moretti, a true Scarlet Springs hero."

There was a scraping and rustling as chairs were pushed back and people got to their feet. Everyone at Jesse's table stood, too, including Ellie, who had tears streaming down her cheeks.

Joe held up his glass. "To Jesse Moretti."

"To Jesse Moretti!"

It was the first time that being called a hero didn't make Jesse feel guilty or unworthy. "Thanks, Joe. Thanks, everyone."

Daisy put her arms around his neck and hugged him. "Jesse."

And that *right there* was all the thanks he'd ever needed.

Chapter Twenty-Four

Ellie drove to her house with the kids, while Jesse went home to shower and stash his gear, promising he'd come by later. She gave the kids their baths, bundled them into pajamas, and read them bedtime stories, getting about halfway through *The Blub Blub Fish* before she heard the back door open.

He was here.

"Jesse home," chirped Daisy.

Oh, Ellie could get used to that—if Jesse would give her a chance.

He came into the playroom and sat beside her, taking over so she could slip into the shower. The hot water felt heavenly, washing away the stress of the past two days. She shaved her legs, then got out and slipped into her nightgown and bathrobe, not bothering with makeup.

She found Jesse sitting next to Daisy's little bed and patting her back. She watched while he soothed her daughter to sleep, her heart overflowing for him. She'd hoped to get the chance tonight to tell him how she felt about him, but maybe it was too soon. Maybe he needed time to deal with all that had happened before she put any additional emotional weight on his shoulders.

A few minutes later, they tiptoed out of Daisy's room together.

Jesse took Ellie's hand. "She said she was scared."

Ellie twined her fingers with his. "My poor baby girl. She doesn't have the words to tell us what she's been through. Some part of her must know that something terrible happened."

Did she know Jesse had saved her?

"Come." Ellie led Jesse into her bedroom and began to undress him.

"Is there something you want?" he teased.

"You."

He helped her, pulling his T-shirt over his head, pushing down the jeans she'd unbuttoned and tossing them aside, shedding his boxer briefs.

She pulled off her nightgown, and for a moment they stood there, his gaze moving over her and hers over him. She planted her palm in the center of his chest and gave him a push. "Lie down, and let me take care of *everything*."

His cock was hard before his head hit the pillow.

She straddled his hips, splaying her hands across his chest, taking in the feel of his torso. "You're so beautiful."

She bent down, kissed a flat brown nipple, then explored him with her hands and mouth. Every inch of him was precious to her, everything about him a miracle, from the softness of his skin to the hardness of his muscles to the springy curls on his chest. His warmth enfolded her, his heartbeat matching the thrum behind her breast, his scent like a drug to her.

She took his cock in hand, licked him, swirled her tongue around the engorged head, then began to devour him.

His hands slid into her hair. "Ellie, you're too good at this. You shouldn't..."

Whatever she shouldn't do was lost in a gasp as she sheathed him with her mouth and hand, moving them in tandem along his length. She kept up the rhythm until his balls started to draw tight, then stopped and reached for a condom.

His gaze was hard now, erotic tension making his jaw clench.

"Seeing all those horses today made me want to ride, too." She straddled him once more, rolled the condom onto his erection, and guided him into her.

She savored the feel of him—so hard and thick. Then she began to move, riding him, taking him into her again and again.

"God, yeah." He held his hips still, let her determine the pace.

But he wasn't passive—not Jesse. He reached up, took her breasts in his hands, and had his way with them, his fingers teasing and torturing her nipples, his touch making them pucker and sending frissons of pleasure straight to her belly.

"You ... feel ... *so* ... fucking ... good." Needing release, she reached down to stroke her clit.

He moaned. "Mmm, yes, honey, make yourself come."

He was thrusting now, beyond the point of holding still, his cock driving into her, carrying her toward that bright edge.

"Jesse!" Climax washed through her in a surge of bliss, his thrusts drawing out her pleasure until she lay weak and panting against his chest.

He kissed her hair, his fingers stroking her spine, his cock still inside her—and still rock hard.

Without warning, he moved out from beneath her and pinned her on her belly, his thighs straddling her hips, his cock penetrating her from behind. He supported his weight with one arm, reaching around her with the other to cradle her throat in one big hand. He forced her head back, compelling her to arch her back until she was supporting herself on her elbows, her hips still flat on the bed. It was a position of strength, of complete dominance—and it made her horny all over again.

He kissed her cheek, her temple, nibbled her ear. "I didn't start this, honey, but I'm sure as hell going to finish it."

He moved in and out of her with slow, smooth strokes, the angle of penetration making his cock glide over that sensitive spot inside her.

She closed her eyes, savored every deep thrust, arousal building in her again until she was moaning every time he drove into her. "Fuck me, Jesse. Fuck me!"

She came with a cry, the sweet shock of it singing through her, his body trembling as he claimed his own climax inside her.

Jesse held Ellie in his arms, her head resting against his chest. She was as limp as a rag doll, her breathing deep and even. He'd never been in a

sexual relationship that had lasted this long, and what amazed him about it—
what blew his mind—was that the sex kept getting better. As impossible as it
seemed, it was true.

Maybe that's because the sex had stopped being about fucking. It was
about her, how he felt about her. It was about showing her he loved her.

Because you sure aren't good at telling her with words.

He wasn't. He didn't know how to say what he needed to say. He'd
never been in love before. He'd never opened himself like that before to
anyone. Hell, he was less afraid of running through enfilading AK fire than
throwing his heart on the ground at someone's feet. But Ellie wasn't just
someone.

Her fingers toyed with his chest hair. "Please stay with me tonight."

"If that's what you want."

She propped herself up on an elbow. "What do *you* want?"

It's now or never, buddy.

"I saw you with the twins the day I came to view the cabin. You were
out back on a blanket. The kids were tiny then—they couldn't even sit up. My
realtor told me you were a Gold Star wife, that your husband had died in Iraq.
It wasn't a coincidence that we didn't meet until that night at Food Mart. I
avoided you. I didn't want to hear what had happened to your husband. I
didn't want to witness your grief. I had my own emotional shit to deal with. I
kept my distance."

Was that really what you wanted to tell her, man?

Rather than the look of disgust Jesse had expected, she smiled. "You
might have closed yourself off to knowing me personally, but you were still a
good neighbor. You shoveled my walk. You put my trash on the curb when I
forgot. You even mowed my lawn on weekends when I was at work."

He stared at her. "You knew I was the one?"

She shook her head. "I had no idea—until I saw you shoveling my walk
the night Daniel and I were sick. It didn't take long for me to put the pieces
together."

He reached up, tucked a strand of blond hair behind her ear. "The point
I'm trying to make is that I could have reached out, but I didn't."

"That was self-preservation. You'd come to Colorado to get the war out
of your head. Why would you want to connect with a woman whose husband
had been killed in that same war?"

Jesse sat up, cupped her face in his hand, steeled himself. "I love you, Ellie."

There. He'd done it. He'd said it. The world hadn't imploded, but now he lay, naked and shivering, at her feet.

"What?" She stared at him through startled green eyes. "You ... you love me?"

"God, yes, I love you. I've been fighting it, trying to ignore it. But I can't stay away from you. I've tried."

She ran a hand down the length of his arm. "You're trembling."

Shit.

"Feeling this way—it scares the hell out of me."

"What scares you?"

Wasn't it obvious?

"I'm afraid I'll do something stupid and hurt you or one of the kids. I don't want to be the man you trusted who disappointed you."

"You're not like the man who raised you, Jesse. Sorry, but I can't call him your father—not after how he treated you and your mom."

"How can you be sure that I—?"

She pressed her fingers to his lips. "I'm sure."

"It's not just that. I'm a mess. You know that. Since you've known me, I've had recurring nightmares, a meltdown, and a full-on flashback. How can you be sure that there isn't more shit hiding in my head?"

"How can you be sure I won't get hit by a car tomorrow?" She took his hand, squeezed. "The only thing we can depend on is each other. We'll deal with whatever happens. I'm not afraid of what's inside your head."

He took comfort from her confidence. "There was a moment yesterday when I couldn't find my way back to the hole in the ice and I was sure neither Daisy nor I would make it. My lungs were ready to burst. I was seconds away from blacking out or going into cardiac arrest. I thought of you, of how much I wanted to get both of us back to you. I swear that's the only thing that kept me conscious and moving at the end."

"Oh, Jesse." She kissed him. "I can't imagine how it must have been for you down there. Hearing that, just thinking about it..."

She shuddered.

"I didn't say that to upset you. I wanted you to know what you do to me. You are a miracle, Ellie. You've pulled me back from the brink in more ways than you know. I've never been happier in my life. I love you, Ellie. I love Daniel and Daisy, too. If you'll give me another chance, I'll try to do right by you and the kids."

"I thought you didn't want a complicated relationship—especially not one involving children. What changed your mind?"

He looked into her eyes, tried to explain. "When I'm with you, all the bullshit falls away, and the answers to all the questions become simple."

She smiled, but there were tears in her eyes now. "I never thought I could love anyone the way I loved Dan. When he died, a part of me died, too."

"I don't expect you to stop loving him. I don't expect you to forget him. He's the father of your children."

She sniffed, laughed. "God, you're sweet, but can you let me finish?"

He wiped a tear from her cheek with his thumb. "Okay."

"I was angry when I found out you knew Dan. It seemed strange that I should end up having sex with a soldier whose life Dan had saved when Dan had been killed."

Yeah, there was that.

"But now I think Dan saved your life so that you could save Daisy—and me. You brought me back to life, Jesse. I love you."

*T*wo *months later*

Ellie stood in the doorway to her bedroom, a cup of coffee in her hand. She had asked her mother to keep the kids this morning so that she could get ready for their birthday party tonight—and because she wanted to sort through everything in her closet. It was time to say goodbye to the past.

"Is Jesse moving in with you?" her mother had asked.

"Mom, he's been living with me for two months, but everything he owns is still at his house." Ellie was tired of Jesse having to trudge uphill just to grab a clean T-shirt or his gear. "I need to move forward."

"Do you need me to bring anything to the birthday party tonight?"

Today, Daniel and Daisy were three years old.

"Nope. I've got the cake and the drinks. Claire is picking up decorations. Just bring yourselves."

Ellie started with her bedroom closet, taking down the boxes that held Dan's clothes and personal things. She'd kept them in plastic bags, so Dan's scent was still there. She inhaled, the familiar smell stirring memories and grief.

"I miss you, Dan. But I'm keeping my promise. I'm moving on."

In tears, she sorted through one box after the other, separating the handful of things she wanted to save for the kids, like his dress uniform and dog tags, from the things she would take to the thrift store. But the tears soon passed, and she found herself smiling and even laughing at the good memories.

There was the shark T-shirt he'd bought on their honeymoon in Hawaii. Here was that ugly sweater he'd gotten from an old aunt that Ellie had always teased him about. A dozen pairs of jeans. She would donate those.

Other things she decided to keep. His high school yearbook. A certificate for making Honor Roll his senior year. A box of seashells he'd collected as a child.

She went through her things, too, culling clothes she hadn't worn for a while. When she finished with her closet, she moved on to her dresser, hoping to make room in a couple of drawers for Jesse. The lingerie she'd worn for Dan went in the thrift store pile, along with old T-shirts and the skinny jeans from high school that she'd always dreamed she'd one day wear again.

"Not going to happen," she told herself, holding them up to her waist.

She packed the keepsakes carefully away in a single box, which she stuck on a shelf in Daniel's closet, then carried everything else out to her car. Fifteen minutes later, she was home again, that weight off her shoulders.

She walked back into her bedroom, looked around at the walls. She couldn't just take the photos of Dan down and shove them in a box. She wasn't trying to erase him from her life. She was just trying to put things in perspective.

On a sudden inspiration, she went to the garage, found her hammer and some hooks for hanging pictures. Then she rounded up all of the photos of Dan that sat around the house and divided them up. She went to work first in Daniel's room and then in Daisy's, creating an arrangement of photos on their walls.

Dan was their father. It was right that they should grow up knowing what he looked like, seeing his face every day.

She left the portrait of him on her dresser, setting the flag from his funeral and the shadow box with his medals and patches next to it. He was gone, but she would always honor him. He'd been her first love, her husband. He was the father of her children. And he'd been an incredible pilot.

There was one more thing.

She took off her wedding ring, kissed it, and tucked it into her jewelry box, her throat growing tight. "I love you, Dan, but I have to let you go."

And that was it.

She stepped back, looked at her bare bedroom walls. They wouldn't be bare for long. She and Jesse would cover them with new memories.

But for now, she had a birthday cake to bake.

Jesse had an important errand to run and got home from work a little later than usual. He parked in the driveway and walked through the front door to find Daniel in full meltdown because no one could find his blankie.

Daisy sat beside him, in tears over her brother's distress.

Ellie was on her hands and knees, looking under the sofa. "I can't find it anywhere. I know I brought it back from my parents' house."

"Could it be in the car?"

Her eyes went wide. "I bet that's where it is."

She started toward the coat closet, but Jesse held up a hand. He was still in his parka and boots. "I'll go check."

He found it half in and half out of the vehicle. It had probably gotten caught when Ellie had shut the door, and no one had noticed. He went back inside, blue blanket in hand. "Here you go, little man."

Daniel's eyes went wide, anguish disappearing from his face. He reached with both hands, hugging his blanket to his chest.

Daisy smiled, too. "You founded it."

The twins were learning more words every day.

"Yep. I founded it." He took off his parka and hung it in the coat closet, then stepped out of his boots.

Ellie walked over to him, wrapped her arms around him. "The past half hour here has been nothing but wailing over that blanket."

"Maybe we should search for a duplicate somewhere to keep on hand in case of emergencies."

Ellie looked up at him. "What a great idea."

"What smells good?"

"It's a recipe for chicken parmesan I found online. It should be ready in about ten minutes." Ellie walked toward the kitchen. "How was your day?"

He told her about the calls he'd taken on the slopes, some part of him marveling at how much he loved his new life. It didn't matter what happened out there in the world because, at the end of the day, he came home to Ellie and the kids.

They ate dinner together, then Jesse did dishes while Ellie got the kids cleaned up and dressed in their birthday doodads—a pink party dress for Daisy and a little shirt, vest, and bowtie for Daniel.

When the dishes were done, Jesse hiked up the hill, took a hot shower and shaved. He dressed in an actual shirt—not a T-shirt—and a pair of jeans without holes. It was a special night after all.

By the time he got back to Ellie's place almost an hour later, Claire and Cedar were hanging puffy decorations and streamers from the ceiling and tying helium balloons in every color to the chairs.

"Hey, Jesse." Claire gave him a hug. "What do you think?"

He glanced around. "It looks like a party."

Ellie had set the table with photos of the twins as newborns in the center.

Jesse picked them up one at a time. "I can't believe they were ever this small."

But Ellie was busy. "Can you reach the crystal cake dish? It's too high for me. Watch out. It's heavy."

"Sure." He reached over her head and lifted it down with one hand.

"Show-off," she said.

But it earned him a kiss.

He checked his watch, starting to feel impatient.

What was keeping them?

The doorbell rang, and Ellie's parents stepped inside, arms full of brightly wrapped gifts. Daisy and Daniel ran to greet them.

"It's my birfday," Daisy told them.

"It my birfday, too," Daniel said.

The doorbell rang again.

Finally.

Claire answered the door, then walked back to the kitchen carrying the bouquet. "Oh, Ellie. Look at this. These are for you."

It looked as beautiful as he'd hoped it would—three dozen perfect, long-stemmed roses in a crystal vase.

"Oh, my God. They're beautiful." Ellie looked up at Jesse through wide green eyes. "Are these from you?"

"You'd better read the card and find out."

She set the flowers down in the center of the table behind the photos of the twins, then took out the card, opened it, and read it silently.

Jesse had worked long and hard on that card and had the words memorized.

My dearest Ellie,

Three years ago today, you gave birth to two beautiful babies. You were alone then, facing motherhood by yourself. Here are three dozen roses, a dozen for each year you raised Daniel and Daisy on your own.

I wasn't there then, but I'm here now. You will never be alone again.

Love,

Jesse

Tears filled her eyes, and she pressed the fingertips of her right hand to her lips. Her head bowed for a moment, her eyes squeezed shut. Then she looked up at him, tears on her cheeks, a quavering smile on her lips. She set the card down and slid into his embrace. "I love you."

Ellie made a trip out to the recycling bin with cardboard and wrapping paper, a warm glow in her chest. She wasn't sure she'd ever gotten a gift that had touched her more than the roses Jesse had given her today. Somehow, he understood how difficult it had been to become a mother when her husband had just died. Everyone else had told her how lucky she was to have the twins, ignoring her grief and loneliness. But with just a few words, Jesse had acknowledged the hardship of these past three years. Instantly, it had all seemed easier.

Well, she had a surprise for him, too.

She waited until everyone had gone home and the kids were in bed, then snuggled up beside him on the couch with a glass of wine, the house filled with the scent of roses. "The roses, the card—that's the sweetest thing anyone has ever done for me."

He kissed her temple. "I'm glad you liked them."

They talked about the party—and the ridiculous number of toys her sister had gotten for the kids.

Then Ellie changed the subject. "I've got something for you."

"You do?"

She let a sultry tone slide into her voice. "It's in the bedroom."

He nuzzled her ear. "I like surprises that happen in the bedroom."

She stood, set her wine down, and drew him after her. "I have something that needs to be filled. Can you fill it for me?"

"I'm happy to die trying."

Fighting not to laugh, she led him to her bedroom and flicked on the light, then drew him over to the closet and opened the door. "Jesse, I want you to fill … my closet."

He took in the sight of the empty shelves on the left—and the open rack. Then he stepped back, his head turning as he glanced around her bedroom. "The photos of Dan—they're gone."

He took her left hand, his brow furrowed. "Your wedding ring. You took it off."

"I've had it off all evening. You didn't notice the things missing from the mantel either." She pointed to the flag and shadow box on her dresser, then told him how she'd spent the day sorting through all of Dan's things. "I put off dealing with this for so long. When I dropped his clothes off at the thrift store, I felt so much lighter, like a weight had been lifted off my chest."

Jesse's eyes narrowed. "Why did you do this now?"

Was she moving too fast for him?

"I want you to move in with us. I'm tired of you having to run up the mountain every time you need to change clothes. I hate that you have to get up earlier in the morning just to get all your gear. I made room for you, Jesse."

"I'm touched. I really am. But what will I do with my cabin?"

She'd thought about that. "You could rent it. You could keep it as a man cave."

He chuckled. "That would be one hell of a man cave."

She unbuttoned the top button of his shirt. "We could use it for secret trysts."

"Now you're talking." He bent down and kissed her, the two of them still standing in her closet doorway. "So, you want to live in sin, is that it?"

She didn't want to rush him. "Only if you're ready."

He nudged her with his erection. "With you, I'm always ready."

Epilogue

"I think this is as close as we're going to get." Jesse pulled into a parking place and turned off their rental car, then glanced at the app on his smartphone, his tan beret tucked into the front pocket of his dress blues.

Ellie slipped her handbag over her shoulder, picked up roses she'd brought, then stepped out of the car and smoothed the wrinkles out of her black linen dress. She glanced around. Nothing seemed familiar. Then again, it had been four years since she'd been here, and she'd been numb with grief.

She got Daniel out of his car seat and straightened his little suit. Jesse joined her with Daisy in his arms. They sat both kids down on the nearest bench, and she knelt in front of them, looking them straight in the eyes. "Do you remember what I told you? We're in a very special place. You can't run or play here, and you can only use your inside voices, okay? No yelling or being noisy."

"Okay," said Daniel.

Daisy squirmed.

Ellie stood again. "I'm not sure where to go from here."

Jesse pulled his beret out of his pocket and put it on. "Section sixty is over there."

He picked up Daisy and started down the sidewalk.

Ellie took Daniel's hand and followed.

She'd come to Washington, D.C., for a nursing conference, and they'd decided to make a family vacation of it. She had attended only the workshops she'd needed to attend to keep her certifications current, giving them time to visit the sights.

But today, they weren't tourists. They had come to Arlington National Cemetery to pay their respects. It had been Jesse's idea, but as soon as he'd mentioned it, she'd been on board. Dan had never seen his kids, and they had never known him.

Today, she would take them to his grave.

The June sunshine was warm, the air much more humid than she was used to, living in Colorado.

"Over here." Jesse pointed, waiting for Ellie and Daniel to catch up.

Section 60 had more graves than she remembered, but then soldiers were still fighting and dying in Iraq.

Jesse turned down a row and stopped, setting Daisy down. "Hey, Christine. So, this is where they put you."

Ellie walked up, watching as Jesse paid his respects to the woman who had died in his arms. He knelt down, touched the white marble headstone, then pulled the chocolate bar out of his pocket.

"I brought you chocolate. It's Godiva—the dark stuff you like so much." He was quiet for a moment, and Ellie knew this was hard for him. "You begged me not to let you die, and I did my best. It just wasn't enough. I'm so sorry, Christine. If I could have taken that blast for you, if I could have caught that shrapnel, I would have. If I could have worked miracles… I was supposed to protect you, but… There was just no way."

Ellie blinked away tears. She had promised herself she would not cry today. She wanted this to be a positive experience for the kids, something they remembered not with fear, but with reverence and happiness. Still, she knew how hard Jesse had worked to put aside the sense of guilt he'd carried with him since the day of Christine's death, and it was impossible not to get choked up.

He unpinned a medal from his uniform. "They gave me this for that day. Bunch of idiots. I want you to have it."

He placed the medal on the chocolate bar and bowed his head, his eyes squeezed shut. When he got to his feet, there were tears on his face.

Ellie handed him a red rose.

He took the flower and stood it up against the headstone. "Rest easy, Christine."

He stepped back, stood at attention, and saluted.

They started toward Dan's grave, stopping along the way so Jesse could pay his respects to some of the men he'd fought with, fellow Rangers, men he'd known well. They left roses on each of their graves, too, each visit ending with Jesse giving a salute.

Another row down and one over.

The breath left Ellie's lungs.

Oh, my God.

Daniel Thomas Meeks

Captain

US Army

Iraq

Dec 15 1985

Oct 5 2013

Silver Star

Loving husband and son

Operation Enduring Freedom

Ellie knelt in front of his grave marker, the grass cool and damp against her bare knees. She ran her hand over the smooth marble and traced his name with her finger, tears blurring her vision. The headstone hadn't been there on the day of his funeral service. She had never seen it in person.

How strange it was to think that his body had been here every day since then, under sun, stars, rain, and snow, while the world had moved on without him.

"Daniel and Daisy, look," she said when she could talk. "This is your daddy's grave. When his spirit went up to become an angel, his body was buried here. Can you tell your daddy hello so he knows you're here?"

Daisy reached out and patted the marble as if to comfort it. "Hello."

Daniel followed his sister's lead, doing the same. "Hello."

"Dan, here they are—your twins. They're three now. You wouldn't believe how sweet and smart they are. Daniel looks just like you. Everyone says so. I named him Daniel Otis. I just couldn't name him Otis Henry. Sorry. Daisy has the name you picked for her—Daisy Mae."

"I'm Daisy Mae," Daisy said.

"Yes, sweetie, you are." Ellie reached into her handbag and took out the bag of things that people in Scarlet Springs had put together for Dan. "I brought some things—a little care package from home."

And for a moment it was too much, tears spilling down her cheeks.

A big hand came to rest on her shoulder, gave her a gentle squeeze, Jesse standing behind her now, giving her his support.

She wiped the tears off her face, reached into the bag, and pulled out a photo of Denver's football team. "Austin and Eric wanted you to have this photo from our last Super Bowl win. They're both married now. Austin married Lexi like we always thought he would. They have an adorable baby girl. She has Lexi's red hair."

Ellie reached into the bag again, pulled out a tiny bottle of scotch. "Caribou Joe from Knockers sent a shot. Remember him? Joe Moffat? He tells me I have to pour it out like they did in the old days, so get ready."

She opened the little bottle and poured the amber liquid onto the grass where it met the marble, a libation for a fallen warrior.

"Rose sent a sage candle." She pulled it together with matches out of the bag and lit it, the breeze making the flame flutter, the faint scent of sage rising in the air. "She said something about it purifying this space and freeing your soul."

Ellie laughed at that, then took out her gift to him. "I brought pictures of Daisy and Daniel. I wanted you to be able to keep these."

She put double-sided tape on the back of the photos, which were laminated to protect them from the weather. Then she let the kids stick their pictures on the back of the headstone one at a time. "Good job. Now your daddy can keep pictures of you with him."

"Can my daddy see me?" Daisy asked.

Ellie didn't know for certain, but what could she say? "Yes, sweetie."

Daniel stepped up. "Can he see me, too?"

"Yes, honey, he sees you, too. He loves you both very much."

But Ellie had more to say to Dan. "Dan, you made me promise I would move on if anything happened to you. I wanted you to know that I'm engaged. I'm marrying Jesse Moretti. He was an Army Ranger. You flew him and his men in your Black Hawk a bunch of times. He says you even saved his life. I love him, Dan. He's so good to me. He's good to the kids, too. He made me feel alive again, and we're happy together. We haven't set a date yet, but I wanted you to know."

Talking to Dan like this was harder than Ellie had imagined, tears filling her eyes again, happiness and grief tangled inside her. "We've started the adoption process so that Jesse can adopt the kids. It makes a lot of things easier and helps protect them. But Daniel and Daisy will always know that you are their father. We've decided that they'll keep your last name. I don't want to take that from you."

She lay the rest of the flowers on his grave. "We will never forget you."

She stood, smoothed her dress. "Kids, can you say goodbye?"

Daniel waved. "Bye, Daddy."

Daisy hugged the marble stone, an angelic smile on her face. "Bye-bye, Daddy."

Ellie turned to Jesse.

He wiped the tears from her face with his thumbs, kissed her. "Can I have a moment alone with him?"

"Sure." Ellie took the kids by the hand and went to sit on a nearby bench, emotionally drained.

She watched while Jesse knelt down. He looked so handsome in his dress blues with all of his medals and that tan beret, though it had cost him emotionally to put on the uniform again. She tried to make out what he was saying but caught only bits of it.

"Thanks for keeping my men and me alive... I love her with everything I am... really does look *just* like you... sweetest little girl in the world... promise to take care of them... all I can to make her happy."

He got to his feet, stepped back, and saluted, holding the salute for a solid few minutes. Then he reached down. "Rest in peace, Crash. I'll take it from here."

Ellie's throat went tight, a bittersweet ache in her chest.

Somewhere in the distance, rifles fired a salute.

Jesse threaded his way over to her, his gaze meeting hers, the love she saw there making her heart swell.

She stood, slipped into the sanctuary of his embrace, the feel of his arms around her smoothing away her jagged edges.

"Are you okay?" he asked.

She smiled, nodded. "Yeah. How about you?"

"I'm good. I thought that since these monkeys were so good, we should go get some ice cream." He scooped the kids up, one in each arm. "You want ice cream?"

The kids nodded, big smiles on their faces.

In the distance, a bugler was playing "Taps."

A life ended. A new life beginning.

Ellie sent a silent farewell to Dan, then fell in beside Jesse, the path ahead of them bright with sunshine.

Also by Pamela Clare

Romantic Suspense

I-Team Series

Extreme Exposure (Book 1)

Heaven Can't Wait (Book 1.5)

Hard Evidence (Book 2)

Unlawful Contact (Book 3)

Naked Edge (Book 4)

Breaking Point (Book 5)

Skin Deep: An I-Team After Hours Novella (Book 5.5)

First Strike: The Prequel to Striking Distance (Book 5.9)

Striking Distance (Book 6)

Soul Deep: An I-Team After Hours Novella (Book 6.5)

Seduction Game (Book 7)

Dead by Midnight: An I-Team Christmas (Book 7.5)

Contemporary Romance

Colorado High Country Series

Barely Breathing (Book 1)

Slow Burn (Book 2)

Falling Hard (Book 3)

Historical Romance

Kenleigh-Blakewell Family Saga

Sweet Release (Book 1)

Carnal Gift (Book 2)

Ride the Fire (Book 3)

MacKinnon's Rangers series

Surrender (Book I)

Untamed (Book 2)

Defiant (Book 3)

Upon A Winter's Night: A MacKinnon's Rangers Christmas (Book 3.5)

About The Author

USA Today best-selling author Pamela Clare began her writing career as a columnist and investigative reporter and eventually became the first woman editor-in-chief of two different newspapers. Along the way, she and her team won numerous state and national honors, including the National Journalism Award for Public Service. In 2011, Clare was awarded the Keeper of the Flame Lifetime Achievement Award. A single mother with two sons, she writes historical romance and contemporary romantic suspense at the foot of the beautiful Rocky Mountains. To learn more about her or her books, visit her website at www.pamelaclare.com. You can keep up with her on Goodreads, on Facebook, or search for @Pamela_Clare on Twitter to follow her there.